Thankyou for buying this e-book. It is the second in the 'Margot' series by Karen Eaketts, and as with it's predecessor, Karen is donating all the profits from sales to support the FIMBA (Federation of International Masters Basketball Association) GB Over 55s Womens' team, of which she is a member. Karen, together with the rest of the team, represented FIMBA GB at the FIMBA European Championships in Pesaro, Italy, in June 2024 where they finished in a creditable fifth position. Money raised from current fundraising efforts, including from the sales of **Margot – Missing Pieces**, will help the team to prepare and compete in the FIMBA World Championships in Switzerland in summer 2025.

All characters in this publication are fictitious and any resemblance to real persons living or dead s purely coincidental.

Margot - Missing pieces

Margot

Margot was sitting at her desk looking despondently at her phone. She had gone viral. Not once but twice. She stared at the image of her rather-larger-than-she-had-thought backside whilst two particularly handsome firemen were cutting her out of the fence she was stuck in. The rest of the squad had gone home having left her a tin of grease on her desk and a fake crime report – "The murder of Whitney Houston at The Three Stars" (The Three Stars would actually only get one star if the stars were really a rating system). And this was only her first day back after suspension.

The day had started well enough. She had arrived at work feeling very nervous. It was like her first day all over again. Only this time was far worse. Not a small rural station with only four people to welcome her, but a huge multi-storey shiny new-build. The Force's flagship new police station. Full of police officers. She had been worried that because she was now out of uniform, people might think she wasn't supposed to be there. She had bought a new black top yesterday to make sure her ID really popped against the dark of the blouse. She now worried that with the black trousers she'd paired it with, people might think she'd rushed to work straight from a funeral.

She'd been warmly welcomed back by Luke, who was still her DS, and then her immediate boss DI John Hall; and also by Detective Superintendent Jasmine Walker, which made her feel better. She had then been hurriedly introduced to the rest of the squad who were all busy with an ongoing murder enquiry. Margot had been dispatched to get the bacon sandwiches. She'd witnessed a purse snatch and had given chase, rather hopefully, running wasn't her forte. Neither, she soon discovered, was squeezing through railings. She was stuck fast on the busiest high street imaginable.

A drunken crowd of last night's revellers, still making their way home at nine o'clock in the morning, had put it on TikTok to the soundtrack of their very unoriginal shouts...

'Is it a bird, is it a plane?'
'Here's the bus. Oh no wait, it's a person stuck in the railings.'
'How much do you charge pet? Where should I put the money?'
'In the slot.'

She sighed. She thought black was supposed to be slimming. She had made it back three hours later with the bacon sandwiches, by which time everyone had given up and gone for lunch. She had been so excited later when she'd been given her first case on MIT*. A missing child. She'd soon put the railings metaphorically and physically behind her. He'd run off from his new foster parents. Everyone assumed he'd turn up somewhere or other. He usually did. He had a long list of convictions and had run away forty-eight times before. He usually came back to light when he was caught for his latest crime. Margot had been pleased to see in the file that Mo had taken the missing-from-home report. It meant she could have a good catch up with him.

Together they had tracked down a few of the missing child's associates. All of whom, with more grunts than words, denied seeing him or knowing where he was. One had quietly suggested Margot try the Three Stars later. Despite the missing-from-home being fourteen, the local beat officer confirmed that he could often be found in the pub dealing drugs.

The Three Stars had a reputation. Unfortunately Margot didn't know this. Although hearing that a fourteen-year old was dealing drugs in it should have been a big clue. She'd gone on her own. Everyone else was hurrying around trying to get enough evidence to charge the guy in the cells who'd stabbed his best friend to death for sleeping with his girlfriend. Margot could see they were too busy to go with her. Besides she needed to prove herself. She'd heard the whisperings from some of the squad. She wasn't ready she was too young in service. She was odd. Mo was off duty by the time the pub was busy enough to warrant a visit. She had no choice but to go on her own.

She'd walked in to find chairs and beer glasses flying. She'd called for assistance straight away, showed her warrant card and shouted

'STOP' to no effect. She walked over to the Karaoke machine and picked up the mike. She tapped it. It was live.
'Stop, police,' she said, holding up her warrant card.
Everyone did stop and look at her.
'Or what? What you going to do about it pet?'
Everyone was staring at her.
'If you don't stop I'll sing!'
The fighting recommenced.
'Whitney Houston, I will always love you,' shouted Margot to the terrified man who was trying to hide behind his Karaoke machine. Margot started to sing.

'Christ, woman!' said a man with blood pouring down his face. At that moment back-up arrived, accompanied by the new Chief Constable, who was on a meet-and-greet-the-troops PR exercise, with the press in tow.

Margot kept singing. She had since tried to work out what the hell had been in her head at the time.

Why didn't she stop singing? Oh no, she had to sing the whole bloody song. I Will Always Love You. The clientele all turned on the cops and were dragged out one at a time. Helped by the teeth of a snarling Belgian Malinois, filmed by the news crew - and someone else who'd also put it on TikTok and captioned it "The singing detective".

Her music teacher at school had warned her about singing. 'You are completely tone-deaf Margot, let's find an instrument for you to play. Here, have the triangle - just hit it when I nod at you.' Invariably Margot was looking elsewhere. she never did get to hit the triangle.

She may as well go home. She was out of ideas. It was getting late now anyway. She headed out the police station and headed off to find her car, which was parked on a dodgy back street between two industrial sized wheelie bins. She'd been too late to grab one of the prized limited spaces in the safety of the police compound. She hoped her beloved pink Beetle had been alright all day.

Margot hurried down the street. There were no streetlights and she felt uneasy for some reason. She thought she saw rising cigarette smoke coming from behind one of the wheelie bins against the thin glow of the city sky. It will just be one of the guys from the takeaway on a break out the back, she told herself. Nevertheless, she hurried to her car. As she put the key in the car door a figure emerged from behind the wheelie bin. Margot jumped.

'I'm not going to hurt you. You were at the Three Stars looking for Rory Elliot weren't you?'

'I was,' said Margot nervously; all she could see was a dark figure.

'Look, I ain't no grass and I ain't giving no statement. He was supposed to stay at mine. He didn't show. Nay one has seen him. That's three days he ain't been seen. Just saying he really is missing this time. Word of advice pet. If you go in the Three Stars again you are going get yourself hurt.'

'Was my singing that bad?'

'You're a police. I just hope you're better at your job than you are at singing. What the fuck were you thinking?'

Margot couldn't answer that. The figure took off, running down the back lane. By the time Margot had got in her car and driven off he was nowhere to be seen. Whoever it was had probably taken the time to come across town and wait for her to finish work. How did he know that was her car and to wait behind that wheelie bin? Margot knew one thing; Rory Elliot was probably in trouble. She turned round and drove back to work. Parking in the compound this time.

Rory Elliot was a little shite, she concluded. He was also fourteen and had a terrible start in life. His mother had been a heroin addict, he was born with a heroin addiction. Taken into care the minute he was born. And bumped around a string of foster parents and homes, none of which could cope with his behavioural difficulties. Margot wanted to be the one that saved him. She cared.

Margot figured one of two things had happened. Either the foster parents were responsible, or he'd run off as he always did and got into trouble. She preferred the later explanation. Mo had said the foster parents were lovely and that was good enough for her, for now. They told Mo Roy had walked out the house at six o'clock on Sunday evening, saying he was going for a short walk to clear his head. She pulled up the crime reports and incident logs for the area the foster parents lived in. She rang Patrick.

She drove to the location Patrick had given her. A dark lane outside of Stamfordham. For the third time that night she felt nervous. She

had not seen Patrick since the night he'd killed Mark. She had intended to leave a message at the pub where Caroline had met him and had been surprised when he came to the phone. And now here she was waiting for him. There was a knock on her window, she jumped out of her skin. He opened the passenger door and sat beside her.
'I need your help,' she said.
'Sure. What with?'
'Three days ago a fourteen-year-old boy went missing, on Sunday evening. I know he likes to break into places. He favours open windows or doors. He was living with foster parents here in Stamfordham. The night he went missing three burglaries were reported. All the same MO, he slipped in through a small window, cash and jewellery taken. I'm wondering if there was a fourth property and something happened at that fourth property.'
'Or something happened with his fence.'
'Was that a joke?'
Patrick smiled.
'It looked like a bigger gap than it was. No, I think I've just met the fence - he was waiting for me outside the police station. If I show you the three properties could you find the fourth?'
'I'm not psychic Margot.'
'No, but you think like a burglar don't you?'
'Not all burglars think the same. I'm here now and I do owe you so let's give it a go. You're weird Margot, you do know that?.'
'I sang 'I Will Always Love You' at the Three Stars.'
'Christ.'

Margot liked Patrick. Considering she didn't really know him and she had seen him slit someone's throat, she shouldn't like him as much as she did. Margot pointed out the houses. Three detached houses on the edge of the village, all with gardens backing onto fields.
'Okay, I'm guessing he probably watches for a bit, makes sure no one is moving around. Then tries doors and windows. I'm guessing this is a low-crime area normally so people may be a little slack. The trouble is Margot, pretty much every house in this village can be watched from the seclusion of somewhere. He may also just be brazenly walking around trying doors and windows.'
'Where would you break in next?'
'I'm not him. Does he have form for TWOC* or burgling houses for cars?'

'He's mostly anything he can carry. He does have a few TWOCs. What are you thinking?'
'That it's a long walk back to town. If I was fourteen I'd have taken some car keys too.'

Margot looked at her watch. It was one in the morning. It was so quiet; the only sound apart from their footsteps was a hooting owl. The night air had a chill and dampness to it. Not a sole seemed to be awake in the whole village. She was surprised at the ease she and Patrick were walking round the village into peoples' gardens with. Burgling was easier than she thought it would be. No doubt after the little spate people's doors and windows would be all locked tonight. Patrick had made a very good point however. Car keys were usually really easy to find, they were never far from the front door. Had Rory arranged a lift? Surely you'd take the first set of car keys you'd found? Come back for the car - or if you found a better option just toss them. No cars, or car keys for that matter, had been reported stolen. She came back round to her first thought - Rory Elliot hadn't left this village. She should double-check if car keys were taken.

She had to be in work early tomorrow. She called time.
'Can I drop you anywhere Patrick?'
'No I'm good. Look I'll keep my ear to the ground. Give me a list of the stuff missing.'
Margot did. She wondered what Patrick was going to get up to after she left. Patrick was after all a bloody good burglar, according to Caroline. This was like dropping a hormonal teenager in a sex shop, locking them in, leaving them there alone for a few hours and saying don't touch anything. She looked at all the lovely houses as she drove home.

Margot

Margot was in work before anyone, even Luke. Despite her late night. She hurriedly checked the overnight logs for burglaries in Stamfordham and was relieved to find none. She grabbed some car keys and headed off to visit the three previous burglary victims.

She pulled up to the first one. A lady and her teenage sons were just having breakfast. Margot was starving, but after seeing her backside yesterday she was on a diet. She had sacrificed breakfast. Her stomach was now rumbling away so loudly the lady offered her toast. Margot reluctantly declined.
'I don't think there's much mystery. I'm on the Neighbourhood Watch committee. Apparently the Ward's latest foster child has a criminal record,' said the lady, smearing butter and marmalade all over a slice of delicious smelling toast.
'Quite possibly, but that lad is missing.'
'Good riddance, I say. This is a lovely village. It shouldn't be allowed.'
What shouldn't be allowed, wondered Margot? Giving a child a home?
'You aren't missing any car keys are you?'
'No, but my mother's ring is beyond value to me. I suppose you are doing your best.'

Margot excused herself and drove the short distance to the next house. An old lady who lived by herself. Margot accepted a cup of tea. And a biscuit. The lady didn't own a car, on account of surrendering her licence when she mistook her neighbour's fish pond for her driveway.

Margot headed to the next house. A GP and his wife. They had three cars and no keys were missing. Margot looked at the cars on the drive. A Range Rover. Nissan Juke. And a sporty little thing. She wasn't sure what it was.
'Where do you keep the car keys?'
'In a bowl on the hall table.'

Margot headed back into work. It's the first time since TikTok-gate that she would have been in the office with everyone else there. She was dreading it. She couldn't stay out of everyone's way forever. She could feel the heat rising as she headed up the stairs to the office. She opened the door.

'Morning Margot, you're with me. Another missing schoolboy,' said Luke. Margot was swept back out. 'I'll fill you in as we drive.'

Luke ran down the stairs. Margot did her best to keep up.
'Kyle Morgan, 9 years old. Left home to walk the half mile to primary school this morning. Never got there. We are off to see the mother. Father is out of the picture, but he's being tracked down. It's on our old patch. Daisy is with the mother now.'
'I think I should have adopted. When I couldn't have children I should have adopted or fostered instead of feeling sorry for myself.'
'Where's this coming from Margot?'
'Rory Elliot. I think he has actually disappeared.'
'He always comes back Margot. He'll be caught burgling someone's house in a few days. It's not the first time his file has landed in MIT. It's only because of his age we keep getting it, he's an habitual MISPER*.'
'I think this time is different. I'll tell you about it later.'
'Boss wants you back with me. Apparently you're not safe to be let out on your own.' Luke smiled.

They pulled into the estate where Kyle lived, an estate of generic ex-council houses with overgrown small gardens. Margot remembered the estate well. She had always thought the overgrown gardens odd, and had decided they were two small to warrant the investment of a lawn mower. She'd eventually found out all the garden sheds had been burgled and all the gardening implements including lawn mowers stolen. There wasn't much mystery as to who was responsible. Fifty percent of her jobs had revolved around one road in this estate. King street. Margot often wondered which came first, the residents or the name. One family accounted for what seemed to be half of the street's residents. In Newcastle they would be just sprats something you threw back. Here in this otherwise nice town, they thought they were big fish – the Kings. They had a reputation, so if they dealt drugs or had a fight or broke your windows or borrowed anything, you said nothing. They strutted rather than walked. Margot had grown up on a very rough estate, but at least there had been a community, people looked out for each other. This family were anti-community. The Nolans. Margot always thought about the singing sisters. She needed to stop thinking about singing.

The house they were going to backed onto King street. They knocked on the door. Daisy answered.
'Hi Margot, Luke. I didn't know it would be you coming. She's in the living room with her mother. I'll introduce you. Helicopter has been up. PolSA* are running the search. She's in a state as you can imagine. Seems genuine.'
'Thanks Daisy,' said Luke.
'Catch up later Margot,' whispered Daisy.

'Shelly, this is DS Luke Jones and DC Margot Jacks. They need to ask you a few questions.'
Shelly was sobbing on the sofa, looking out the window into the distance. Margot wondered if this is where she sat after every school day, watching for him coming home. Shelly blew her nose and wiped the tears from her eyes. Margot wanted to give Shelly a big hug.
'Are you okay to answer some questions now Shelly?' asked Luke softly. Shelly tried to stop sobbing. She nodded. Silent cries caused sudden snorts on her intakes of breath. Mascara was darkening the skin around her eyes. Her hands were shaking and her right leg bounced up and down.
'I understand Kyle left here at eight thirty. Can you take me through what happened this morning please?' asked Luke. Margot tried to focus on Luke's questions.
'It was just normal. We both got up at half seven. I made his breakfast, checked his school bag. I had a quick shower, got ready for work. I saw him off at half eight, waved him off down the road. I was about to leave for work when the school called to ask where Kyle was.'
'He always walks to school on his own?'
'Since the beginning of this term. I used to walk him, he insisted he wanted to walk by himself because all his friends did. Nothing like this has ever happened before. I gave in but only because he walks with Nathan from the next street, but Nathan had his wisdom teeth out yesterday so is off school today. It's the first place I checked in case he was shirking school. I should have walked him this morning with Nathan not going.'
'He doesn't have a mobile?'
'No. I thought he was too young. I know all his friends do. I was holding out till secondary school. Do you think it would have

stopped the person taking him? If he'd had a mobile?'
'Why do you think that someone took him?'
'Because there's no other explanation.'
'He wasn't having problems at school?'
'No.'
'What about his father?'
'We are separated. It won't be Dan. Dan can see him whenever he wants. He's a good father. We were just not compatible, he wasn't a bad husband or anything. Kyle adores his Dad.'
'Would Kyle go off to his Dad's on his own?'
'That must be what's happened. He's gone to his Dad's but got lost. I should've let him have a phone. His Dad wanted to buy him a phone for his birthday. I said no. We argued about it. Mum, can you drive me to Dan's, see if we can spot him?'
'It's better if you stay here in case he comes back. I'll make sure someone does that. I need to ask you if Kyle had become friendly with anyone else you know about besides Nathan.'
'Oh God, is there a paedo on the estate?'
'No, not that we are aware off. And any sex offender must be registered.'

Margot couldn't think of anything to ask. Then Shelly was no longer able to hold back the tears and burst out crying again. Margot had to think of muffins and cakes to stop herself crying too. She headed out with Luke.

'Let's head to Nathan's and then the school,' said Luke 'I'm going to call the boss and suggest we get family liaison officers in. I have a bad feeling about this Margot.'
'I think Rory Elliot might be missing too, could it be connected?'
'I doubt it very much, but we have nowhere near enough information on either boy to be thinking anything yet. I think Division have made a start on the CCTV and house-to-house. I don't think from memory there is any CCTV in the estate though.'
'That's because the Nolans insisted on people taking it down, if they put any up.'

They knocked on Nathan's door. His mother answered.
'Are you the police?' She didn't wait for a reply. 'I've spoken to Nathan, I'm pretty sure he doesn't know anything. Nathan is pretty sensible.'

'I'd like to talk to him myself if that's okay,' said Luke.
'Of course.'
She led them upstairs. Poor Nathan's cheeks were puffed out. He looked a sorry sight, playing on his phone. Luke bent down beside the bed. At first Margot thought Nathan was lying in a coffin, which she thought was a bit creepy and a definite red flag. She looked around for signs of the occult, wondering if Kyle had been sacrificed. She saw only planets, stars and astronauts. Margot realised the bed was supposed to be a rocket.
'Nathan you're not in trouble but no one can find Kyle. Did Kyle say anything about running away?'
Nathan shook his head.
'I know Kyle wasn't allowed a mobile phone. Did he ever borrow yours?'
Again Nathan shook his head.
'When you walked to school did you or Kyle ever see anyone strange hanging around?'
Again he shook his head.

Margot and Luke saw themselves out.
'Did you think Nathan was telling the truth?' asked Luke.
'It was hard to tell given he didn't speak. I'm not sure it was the truth about the phone.'
'I don't think so either. Let's check in and see if the Dad has been traced. What did you make of Shelly, Margot?'
'I don't think she has done anything to him.'
'She has a new man. I wonder why she didn't mention it.'
'How do you know that?'
'There was some men's clothing in the washing. Boxers to be precise.'
'Perhaps the mother doesn't know. The mother didn't say anything but she made sure she was in earshot the whole time,' said Margot, annoyed with herself for not noticing the washing. She'd let her emotions take over. If there had been a dead body in the kitchen she probably wouldn't have noticed that either.

They headed to the school. Margot looked at the neat yard. The perfectly manicured lawn. The freshly painted doors and windows. Margot thought it looked very different from how she remembered her primary school. She didn't think there would be a need for needle patrol before school every day here. It even smelled nice. They were quickly ushered in to see the Head and Kyle's year teacher - Miss Broadbent with the emphasis on 'Miss', and Mr Graham respectfully.

'I've already spoken to a police officer,' said Miss Broadbent a little too testily for Margot. Margot thought 'no wonder you are still Miss'. Then thought she might be being a little bitchy.

'We need to make sure we've not missed anything, with the life of a child potentially at stake. If it's okay with yourselves I'd like to ask you some questions. Better to ask them twice than to assume they have already been asked,' said Luke.

That shut you up, thought Margot. Mr Graham on the other hand was looking upset. Luke had noticed too.

'Mr Graham, has Kyle said anything to you that could throw any light on this?'

'No. Kyle is quite quiet in class. He is polite and considerate.'

'Have you noticed any changes in his behaviour lately?'

'No.'

'Who are his best friends?'

'Probably Nathan and George.'

'Has their behaviour changed lately?'

'No. George is a Nolan so he has some behavioural issues. We have been working on boundaries. I'm sure you know the family.'

'Is George in school today?'

'Yes.'

'Have you had any reports of people hanging around that shouldn't be?'

'No, absolutely nothing,' said the head.

'He was reported as missing very quickly. Is there a reason you jumped to that conclusion so quickly?'

'School procedure is to call a parent if a child is not in registration that we are expecting. This is a good school. Pupils don't skip school here detective. We spoke to his mother and she said he'd left for school. As is school policy we called you straight away,' said Miss Broadbent defensively.

Margot and Luke walked out to the noisy chatter of children on a break. A sound that always sounded the same, despite the fact it was made by totally different children and totally different words each time. Margot had always found the sound difficult to cope with. She couldn't help but notice that feeling had almost gone. Was that just her diminishing hormones? Or had this job completely changed her? she wondered.

'So Margot, what do you think?'

Margot almost answered that she thought it was the hormones, but remembered just in time that Luke hadn't been party to her inner thoughts.

'I thought when he said Kyle is polite and considerate that was odd. Out of context I don't know if it means anything. He was also very upset, for a man.'

Luke looked at Margot.

'We need to check the CCTV on the high street. According to what he told Division he was already in school at eight thirty - he stated he arrived at eight fifteen. Let's check see if his car is on CCTV, at least verify that.'

'Is he a suspect then?'

'Everyone is, until they aren't. The boss is checking the sex offenders' register, and checking on any anywhere near but quite often Margot it's someone they know. Come on, let's work out who the Mum's new man is too.'

It felt so good to be back working with Luke. She was seeing his Dad Mervin tonight, although she was probably going to have to cancel, she wouldn't be going home at five with a child missing.

The river was being searched. The helicopter was back buzzing over it, whilst the marine unit and fire brigade searched on the ground. The sound of the helicopter stabbed home the gravity of the situation to Margot. It was on her and her colleagues to find Kyle, in that instant the responsibility really hit home. The words of the fence came back to her 'I hope you're better at your job than singing.' Was she? She couldn't help but think she'd fumbled her way to this point. More fluke than ability. More luck than judgement.

They headed to the small newsagents on the high street, where Mo was checking CCTV. Mo had been Margot's replacement, which she thought had a nice sense of karma. No, that wasn't the word she was looking for. Balance? That probably wasn't the word either. Ying and Yang maybe. Mo was still in his probation and still being supervised by Daisy. She guessed resources were tight; he had been dispatched to do the CCTV on his own. Or more probably because Mo was far more competent than she'd ever been.

'Hi Margot, did you have any joy with Rory Elliot?'

'Not so far. How far have you got with this?' Margot noticed he had a large school photo of Kyle upright against the CCTV screen. He was wedged in the cramped back office of the newsagents, eyes glued to a screen. He was surrounded by boxes, Margot could see Walkers crisps written on the side of one. She imagined some of the other boxes must have chocolate in. Margot stoped trying to think of food and looked instead at Kyle. He was smiling, he looked like he didn't have a care in the world. A mop of ginger hair flamed on top of his head, his face was covered in freckles which had joined up in places especially across his nose, it was as if his face was slowly freezing over with freckles. Margot couldn't bear the thought of him being scared somewhere right now.

'I've gone 8.30 to 9.27. So far the time is accurate. He didn't get as far as the High Street, not yet anyway. According to his Mum and Nathan's Mum this is the way they go. It doesn't make any sense to go any other way either, you'd be adding quite a detour. So there's a good chance he disappeared in the estate before he got to the High Street. Look, you can see right down the street to just before the entrance to the estate.'

Luke tried to squeeze in behind Mo so he could get a better look. 'Sorry Mo, I need you to check again for the teacher's Mini. I've written down the details for you. Can you download everything they have please?'

'Already done. I'm just using their system to save some time.' Mo handed Luke three memory sticks. All sealed in evidence bags, together with a statement from the owner of the newsagents.

Margot noticed how much like a policeman Mo was already. She still didn't always feel like a policewoman. Although Luke was joking when he said she wasn't safe by herself, she suspected that's exactly what everyone thought. Probably what Luke thought too. What she thought too if she was being honest. It didn't help Margot's confidence to use Mo as the yardstick either.

'I'll start again and look for the Mini this time,' he said smiling.
'He said he got to the school at 8.15, see if that's correct, might save you some time,' said Luke.
'Okay. I'll start just before then. He definitely comes past this camera?'
'We didn't ask but if he came from home he would,' said Luke.
'I'll call you if I find anything. Or even don't find anything.'
'Thanks. Catch up later when it's a bit less hectic.'
'Definitely.'

'So are we on the new man next?' asked Margot.
'Yes.'
'Why don't we just ask her?'
'We will. I just want to see how much we can find out first. We need the estate gossip. Let's go and see Donna, she likes you.'
Margot had first met Donna when she'd complained about a mattress being dumped in her garden. Margot had attended. Donna gave her occupation as a retired topless pole dancer and Margot had written that down without batting an eyelid. Margot had been warned about Donna and she knew damn well she had worked in the butchers. Margot had soon worked out who the mattress belonged to - Colleen Nolan. Most people on the estate would have backed down at that point but not Donna. She and Margot dragged it down the road and into King Street and threw it back over Colleen's fence.

Colleen had crashed through her front door and into her garden, a torrent of abuse flying off her tongue. Margot had said 'Colleen, someone stole your mattress. We've brought it back for you.'
Donna had said 'if that ends up back in my garden the next time then your husband calls round pissed trying to get his leg over I'll say yes and charge him double for the pleasure.'
Colleen had retreated into the house. If Donna ever needed the police after that she always asked for Margot.

Margot soon realised what her colleagues had said about Donna was true. She wasn't living on this planet. She inhabited a world of her choosing. A world where she had dated Ross Kemp, Prince Andrew (although not anymore) and Gino D'Acampo. A world where she had holidayed not in Blackpool, as the plastic tower on the mantelpiece suggested, but in Monaco and on the French Riviera rubbing shoulders with Hollywood stars.

They knocked on her door.
'Margot, what a lovely surprise,' she said.
Despite the time of day - now nearly lunchtime - Donna was still in a dressing gown, although her make-up was done. Margot liked pink, but Donna *really* liked pink.
'Sit down,' said Donna, removing a fluorescent sparkly pink dildo off the even pinker sofa. Luke and Margot sat down; they sank right down into the sofa. They were both now significantly lower than Donna. It was the kind of sofa that prevented a quick getaway, it

held you captive like an elderly relative that didn't stop talking.
'Donna are you aware Kyle Morgan is missing?' asked Luke.
'Everyone is, there's been police buzzing around all morning so I checked the local Facebook page. It's all over there,' she said, whilst conducting Luke and Margot with the dildo.
'How well do you know his Mum Shelly?' asked Margot.
'You want to know who the man was that stayed last night don't you?'
'Yes,' said Margot trying to hide her excitement at the unexpected breakthrough.
'Tall, nice arse, drives a blue Ford Focus.'
'Anything else?'
'I only saw the back of him, it was dark. Got there just after midnight and left about seven thirty. Could have parked right outside the house was space but didn't, parked further up the street and walked down.'
'You didn't get the registration number did you?' asked Luke.
'Too far away.'
'Has he been before?' asked Margot.
'First time I've seen him, but then again I've been busy lately. Business is booming as they say Margot.' She winked at Margot. 'I'll keep an eye out, I'll call you if I see him again. She's from the Toon you know. Moved out here to get away from the husband, be nearer her mother. The mother walks round with a stick up her arse, thinks she's too good for the likes of us. Posh cow.'

Luke and Margot left. Margot had noticed that Luke looked pink in the house but with all the pink she had just put it down to reflections. Luke was still pink. His ears were red, they looked sunburned.
'Are you okay?'
'Fine thanks Margot.'
'So shall we confront the wife?'
'I think we should.'

Just then Luke's phone rang.
'Hi Luke it's Mo. I don't see the Mini. I've checked 7.30 to 8.30 for you.'
'Okay thanks Mo.'
'Sergeant Linn wants me to help with the house-to-house. Anything else before he picks me up?'
'No thanks, Mo.'

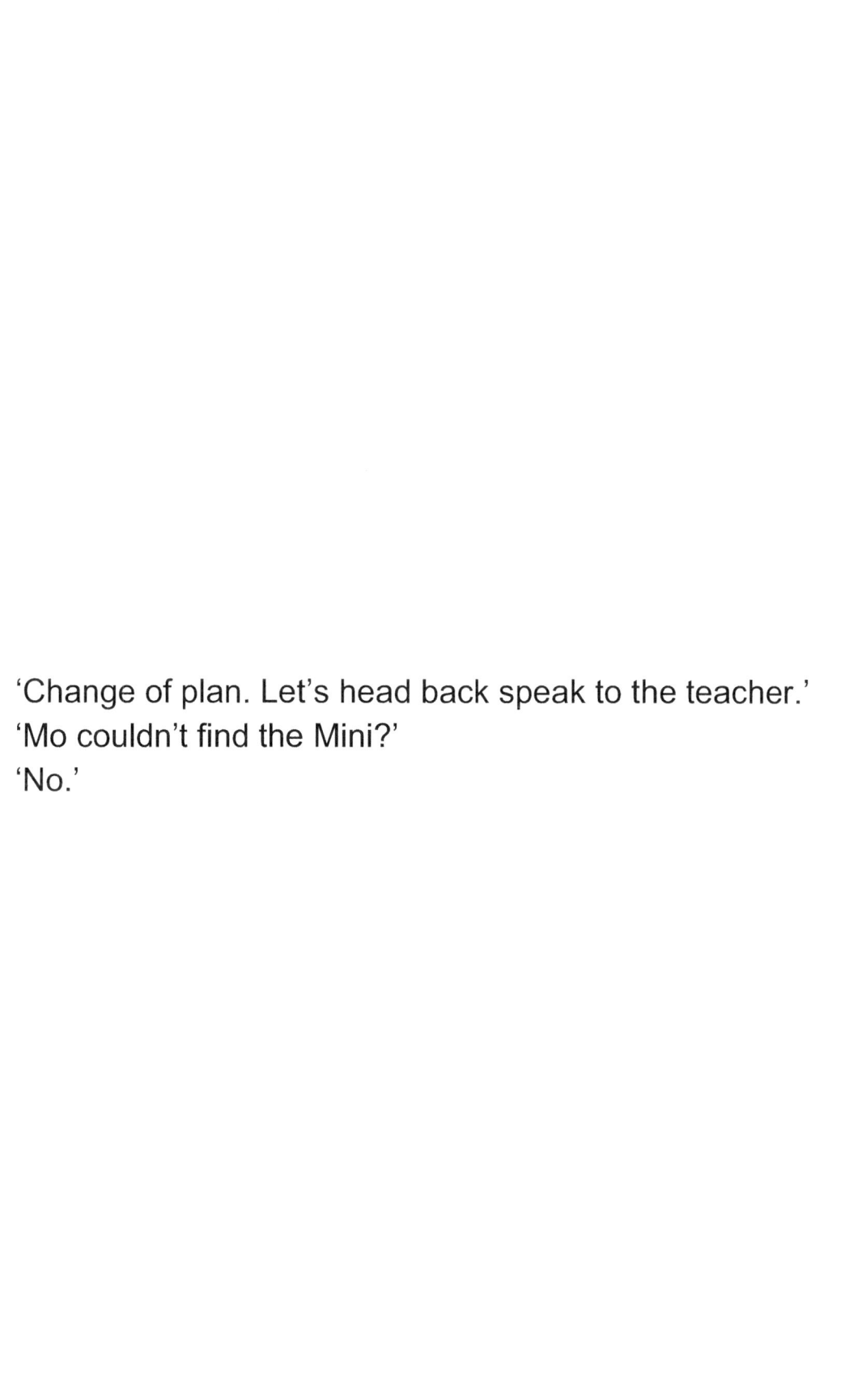

'Change of plan. Let's head back speak to the teacher.'
'Mo couldn't find the Mini?'
'No.'

Margot

The teacher Mr Graham was in class. Miss Broadbent took over his class. Margot noticed how the children's body language immediately changed - they sat upright, arms flat against their sides.
'Have you spoken to the class about Kyle?' asked Luke as they walked down the corridor to the small staff room.
'Yes and no one seems to know anything.'
'Can anyone verify you were in school from 8.15?'
'The head was already in.'
'Which way did you drive into school?'
'I didn't. I left the car here overnight. I stayed at my girlfriend's; the parking is a nightmare so I just walked. It's only ten minutes.'
'I'll need her address. The quicker we can eliminate you the quicker we can move on.'
'No I understand. Do you think Kyle will be okay?'
'I can't answer that but I know time is of the essence,' said Luke.

Mr Graham gave them his girlfriend's address. Miss Broadbent confirmed Mr Graham had indeed got there at 8.15.
'Is that his usual ti me?' asked Margot.
'I run a very tight ship. Staff must be in by 8.20, pupils may arrive from 8.30.'
Margot wondered if that answered the question or not. By the time she considered it Miss Broadbent had ushered them into her office where a worried young woman stood.
'Sara, tell the officers what you have done.'
'Hello…Obviously with what has happened we sent out a text to say all pupils must be collected from school this afternoon. To text back to let us know if that wasn't possible. I put on the text that Kyle had gone missing on his way to school. It's an automated list. I didn't think. It's gone out to his Mum and Dad.'
'Don't worry. I'll explain the mistake to them,' said Luke.
She looked relieved. Margot felt sorry for her. She was close to tears.

Luke and Margot walked back to their car.
'Let's check with the teacher's girlfriend while we are here. I need to let the boss know about that text. The father is self-employed, a painter and decorator. He hasn't been found yet, he's not at home.

Odd don't you think, if he had received that text you would have thought he'd drop everything and come running,' said Luke. Margot hadn't even thought of that. She was cross with herself for not picking up on it.

Luke made his phone call and Margot thought about what it could mean. Had the father found out Shelly had a new man and taken Kyle? She hoped that was the case and that he was safe with his Dad.
'Boss says to verify the teacher's alibi. He'll get the FLOs* to ask about the man that stayed the night. Then he wants us to talk to George Nolan in the presence of his mother.'
'Oh God, Colleen absolutely hates me.'
'She hates everyone Margot.'
'Do you think that headmistress is a little cold? She's just like my headmistress was at primary school but that was thirty years ago. We thought our headmistress was old-fashioned way back then.'
'Maybe. It can't be her. The teacher and her are each other's alibis. I'm sure they aren't in it together.'

Mr Graham's girlfriend confirmed he'd stayed the night. And confirmed he'd left for work at the same time as her at 8.05. It was about a ten-minute walk to school. Luke looked at his watch. Two o'clock. Margot knew why he was looking. Seven and a half hours.

Her phone rang. She didn't recognise the mobile. She answered.
'Margot, it's Patrick. I found the guy you spoke to outside the police station. You were right, he does handle the stolen goods normally. Kyle rang him just before six on Sunday from the foster parents saying he was going to run away. Told him he'd be at his later. He never showed. He didn't say he was going to do any jobs but that part was implied. The guy was fully expecting him to arrive with jewellery. He'd swap that for drugs. Then go out and get cash for the drugs.'
'Why not get cash for the jewellery?'
'The guy needs his gear shifting. That was just the arrangement they had.'
'Okay. Thanks.'
'Do you want me to break into everyone's houses in the village, find the dodgy bastard?'
'No. So is this your number?'

'This phone is for you. I had an arrangement with Frank. I'd help him, he'd help me.'
'Thanks.'

'Who on earth was that Margot?'
'Patrick. I asked him to do some digging around Rory Elliot. He moves in that world.'
'Careful with Patrick Margot. I know he saved your life but he's not to be trusted. If you invite him in, it will bite you. If he tells you anything register him as an informant. Make sure it's recorded. Did he find out anything?'
'Not really, only what I already knew. Can I run it by you Luke? I really do think something has happened to him.' Margot brought Luke up to date with her enquiries.
'Tell the boss. It needs ramping up. Who was the guy in the back alley?'
'I don't actually know, it was really dark, male about five ten, thin.'

It was Luke's phone that rang next. Luke just listened. He said 'Thanks' and pressed end call.
'Shelly said no one stayed last night. They believe her.'
'So either Donna is lying, which is very possible, or Shelly is. What about the boxers?'
'She said they were her husbands, and she uses them as dusters.'
'So she's an accomplished liar if she's lying.'
'Exactly Margot.'
'What next?'
'Boss wants us to help with the house-to-house on the estate. Someone must have seen something. It's our best shot.'

A few hours into the house-to-house and Margot's feet and back were starting to hurt. She looked at her watch - half past seven. Eleven hours. And not one single sighting of Kyle from anyone they had spoken to. Luke agreed with Margot that that was unexpected. At half eight in the morning someone should have seen something. Plenty of people had said they we're heading to work, dropping kids at school, or just up and about.

Margot

Everyone had convened at the nearby station for a briefing, which was nearly over now. Despite everything that had been done there wasn't a single lead, Kyle had literally disappeared.
'Okay let's take a really good look at the mother and father,' said John. 'I'm not sure Kyle ever left that house. The father has just got home. He's agreed to come to the station voluntarily, at this point in time. I'm going to head back see what he has to say for himself. Luke, Margot, go and see this George Nolan then go home, I need you fresh for tomorrow.'
Margot's heart sank. Her last real hope for Kyle being okay had just been snatched away.
'What about Rory Elliot Sir?' asked Margot.
'I'll put a rush on the forensic from the burglaries. I don't doubt they were him but I need to be sure. Then when we can, we will go house-to-house, see if anyone looks nervous. Right now Margot we are stretched on this. Your theory of a burglary gone wrong is a good one though, which is why I'd rather we do the house-to-house ourselves but that's a big undertaking on top of this.'
Margot didn't disagree with any of that, but she felt she was letting Rory down. Kyle was getting all the attention.

She walked out to their car with Luke, feeling that despite never having stopped all day they had wasted too much time. And to add to her low mood they were now en route to speak to George, which meant trying to get past Colleen. Luke drove to King Street and hammered on Colleen's door. It was flung open.
'If you haven't got a warrant piss off. That fat pig isn't coming in my fucking house even if you have got a warrant,' said Colleen, spitting her words.
Margot could hear a young girl screaming the house down.
'Colleen we just want to talk to George see if he can help us with finding Kyle,' said Luke.
'He doesn't know anything. Fuck off.' She slammed the door in their faces.
'She's not going to let us in,' said Margot.
'You're right. Let's go home. I'm knackered. It's going be another long day tomorrow.'

They drove back to the station. By the time they got back it was half past ten. Fourteen hours. They bumped into their boss on their way back down the stairs.
'How did it go with the father, boss?' asked Luke.
'Not sure. He said he's mislaid his phone so he reckons the first he heard of his son being missing was from us when he got home. No alibi as such, he was allegedly decorating a house in Jesmond. Occupants were out at work. Neighbour confirms his van was there all day from about nine, doesn't mean he was. His house was clear. He seemed genuinely worried. Jury is out. I've seized his van. I'm letting him walk for now.'

Luke and Margot said their good-nights in the car park. It had been a really long day, Margot started to drive home. She wouldn't sleep. The searches had been called off for the night. Perhaps she'd just have one last look. Everyone said he liked the park. It had been searched with dogs but perhaps he'd go there at night. It was worth one more shot. Margot turned the car about and drove to the park. She parked her car in the street and walked through the dark narrow alleyway that led into the park. Her heart rate increased. Someone was searching the bushes by the burn that ran through the middle of the park. She could see torchlight sweeping back and forth. She wondered if it could be one of her colleagues then she heard a tiny voice 'Kyle, it's George.'

She made her way over.
'George is that you?' she said.
George spun round, shining the torch in her eyes dazzling her. She squinted.
'Oh it's you, you came to my house earlier. Mum told you to fuck off.'
'Yeah, your Mum doesn't like me.'
'That's cos you're a police. I know you, you're the one that got stuck in the fence.'
'Is my arse that memorable?'
George laughed. 'You're funny, I like you. Why are you here?'
'Same as you I guess, looking for Kyle.'
'I done the whole park. Mum reckons some nonce has taken him.'
'What do you think?'
'I know he wasn't happy cos he said his Mum was seeing a man. She was trying to keep it secret from him. He wanted his Mum and Dad to get back together. If I tells you something don't tell my Mum

I told you?'
'Promise.'
'He said he was going to run away back to his Dad.'
'Do you think that's what happened?'
'Dunno.'
'Why don't you walk to school with Kyle, you're just round the corner?'
'I got to walk with me sister, she's six. Kyle has to walk with Nathan and Nathan's Mum doesn't want him to be friends with me so I can't walk with Kyle because of Nathan anyways. Kyle is still my best friend though. Kyle is really nice to me.'

Margot's job phone rang.
'DC Jacks it's the control room. Sorry to bother you off duty. I have a Donna on the line. She says it's very important, to do with the missing child. She will only speak to you.'
'No it's fine, put her through…Donna it's Margot.'
'Margot it's back, the car is back.'
'Okay I'll be right up.'
'It's parked right outside this time. Shall I get the registration for you.'
'I'm five minutes away. Just watch it. I'll give you my number, call me if it moves.'
Margot would probably live to regret giving Donna her job mobile but needs must at the moment.
'George I have to go, do you want a lift home?'
'Na Mum's in a bad mood. Dad is pissed again. I'm going to stay out and look for Kyle.'
Could she leave a nine year old in the park at night? She thought of Kyle and Rory.
'Actually I have a lead. I might need your help.'
'Sick.'

Margot ran as fast as she could back to her car.
'Sick car,' said George as he jumped in the passenger seat.
Margot made him put his seatbelt on then sped off as fast as she dared with a child on board. She parked at the end of the street.
'Did you trick me into going home?'
'No, I need to see who is visiting Kyle's house.'
They walked up the street together. Margot typed the registration number into her phone. The curtains were shut, she couldn't see

anything.

'We can get round the back, you can see in from my street, follow me,' said George.

George was off, running back down the street, Margot set off after him. He turned the corner and set off up the next street. Margot was puffing now. George waited for her by a driveway.

'Keep quiet,' he said.

He headed down the short paved driveway and quietly opened a side gate. They both slipped through. He led Margot to the bottom of the garden. There was a tall fence but up against the fence Margot could just about make out a bench in the dark.

'We have to stand on the bench. If you stand on the arms you can see over. You can see into Kyles' house. There's no curtains in the kitchen window.'

They both stood on an arm each. The kitchen light was on. Shelly was hugging a man. Margot couldn't see much of the man other than a mop of ginger hair. As they separated George said 'That's Kyle's Dad.'

'Are you sure?'

'Yes. I seen him before when he picked Kyle up. He had a white van with Dan Morgan painter and decorator written on the sides.'

'Let's get out of here before we are seen.'

'You were hoping it was someone else wasn't you?'

'Yes.'

She didn't want to discuss the case with a nine year old. But it did look like Dan Morgan had stayed the night his son disappeared and Shelly was lying about it. She knew she had to tell her boss but she needed somewhere safe to leave George first. Was home safe?

'George if you go home will you be safe?'

'Yeah, I can sneak in, stay out the way.'

'You need to go home now, sorry.'

'Will you find Kyle?'

'I'm going to try my hardest.'

'Okay. Remember, don't tell Mum I helped you.'

'I won't. Thanks George.'

Margot watched him up the street. She then rang Luke and explained what she'd seen.

'Great work Margot but you should've gone home. Can you keep an eye on the car while I ring the boss? I'm guessing he's going to want them both arrested and forensic in the house.'

'Sure.'

Margot didn't want to just stand in the street. She decided to knock on Donna's door.
'Come in Margot, we can watch from the bedroom.'
Donna hurried her up the stairs.
'Bloody hell!' said Margot.
'You can borrow anything you want.'
'I wouldn't know what to do with most of it.'

Margot had had her eyes opened in the job but not this far. It was like some medieval torture chamber in pink.
'It looks painful.'
'That's the whole idea Margot. You would be surprised who knocks on my door late at night. It's not always who you think.'
'You are alright aren't you Donna?'
'No one has ever asked me that before. It pays the bills Margot. So what's happening?'
'I just have to watch for now.'
'Shall I put the kettle on then?'
'Please.'
'Tea or coffee?'
'Coffee please.'

After twenty minutes Margot's phone rang. It was DI Hall.
'Margot. Any change?'
'No, the car is still there.'
'An arrest team will be there in five minutes, stay where you are till they arrive. Then go home Margot. I mean it Margot, there is going to be plenty to do tomorrow. Including interviewing the parents. If you are tired that's when mistakes are made.'
'Yes Sir.'

Margot saw the panda car arrive at the front of the property. Three police officers squeezed out and knocked at the door. Shelly opened it after a while. She watched Shelly being led from the house in handcuffs. Where was her husband? Margot suddenly thought of the back garden. He must have run out the back. Her phone rang.
'Margot, they have the husband. He tried to leg it over the back fence. Go home Margot. If you don't I can't have you on my team. I can't have my staff running around on their own agenda off duty.

We will talk tomorrow. Final warning Margot.'
'Yes Sir.'

Margot sneaked out the back of Donna's house and retrieved her car. She did actually drive home. She couldn't sleep.

Margot

Margot drove into work early. Luke was already in. It was seven in the morning. Twenty-two and a half hours.
'Margot, we are interviewing the Dad now. He doesn't want a brief,' said Luke. Margot was excited. 'I'll lead. Boss just wants him challenged on his movements for now.'
'Okay,' said Margot following Luke out the office.
'Margot you can't go off on your own like last night. If anything had happened we wouldn't have known where you were. Besides, procedurally it causes a huge problem. We could get torn to shreds in court. No one will thank you if you screw up a conviction.'
'I'm sorry.'
'Come on, let's see what he's got to say.'

Margot didn't think Dan Morgan looked worried. He did look defeated though. Luke did all the introductions. He cautioned Dan and told him he'd been arrested on suspicion of child abduction.

'I'm sorry, we should have told you the truth. I didn't know she'd lied to you until I spoke to her just before you arrested me. She didn't see Kyle leave. I stayed the night. The alarm went off at 7.20, I turned it off and got dressed and left. We are considering getting back together, for Kyle more than anything. It's not that we don't like each other. It's hard to explain. We separated nine months ago and I guess neither of us are particularly enjoying it. So we agreed to give it another go. We didn't want Kyle or her mother to know as we weren't sure which way it was going to go. He was devastated when we split. I crept out. She fell back asleep, didn't wake till the school called. She just assumed Kyle left at his usual time.'
'We've just spent nearly twenty-four hours working from an incorrect timeline,' said Luke.
Dan started to cry. Margot in that instant didn't think he was involved.
'I'm sorry,' he sobbed.
'What about your phone?'
'I accidentally left it at Shelly's. I was halfway home when I realised what I'd done. I had to drop the car off, get the van and get to work I didn't really need it and I had to halfwayob I was at finished in a day. I didn't have time to go back and I was planning to go back that night anyway.'

'Why did you buy the car? You bought it two weeks ago, yes?'
'Mainly to save the miles on the van. Partly so Kyle wouldn't recognise it. And if I'm honest I was hoping it did work out for us and the van only has two seats. Shelly doesn't have a car, I was going to give it to her regardless of what happened.'
'Did you look in on Kyle at all when you were there?'
'I couldn't risk it. I wanted to. I should've.'
'So did you drive straight home then straight to work?'
'Yes. I had a quick breakfast at home, loaded the van and left.'
'Write down the exact route you took. One more thing - why did you run when police knocked at the door?'
'Shelly begged me to. She said they would think it was us if we were seen together, that you'd waste time trying to prove it was us. Which is exactly what happened anyway because the stupid woman didn't tell the truth. I didn't know you had come to arrest me.'

Margot and Luke waited while he wrote the route down. Luke read it out loud for the tape. They terminated the interview and put him back in the cell.

'I think that was the truth but he certainly had opportunity,' said Luke.
'He's not really the one that lied is he? Shelly didn't tell the truth at all.'
'He failed to mention he stayed with Shelly when he was spoken to yesterday. Or where he'd left his phone.'
'I get that but he was told his son disappeared on the way to school. I think he thought Shelly had seen him off.'
'Forensics are going through the house and car. The boss won't let him go anywhere before that's done. Let's head back upstairs and see the boss.'
'Luke I think we should take a look at Nathan's phone.'
'I agree with you on that.'

They found their boss in his office, they knew he had been monitoring the interview.
'I guess that explanation makes sense,' said John without looking up from the screen of the laptop he was watching. Luke told him about Nathan's phone.
'Agreed. Check that phone. Before you head off listen to the mother's interview. I've asked Karen and Matt to do it. She did want

a solicitor she's just finished consulting with her brief. She's been in there for an hour, a sure sign of guilt in my book. You can listen from here, I'm going to remotely monitor again.' They pulled some chairs around and crowded around the laptop. Margot struggled to see as the light reflected awkwardly off the screen. She kept bobbing up and down trying to find the sweet spot.

Shelly did look nervous. The introductions were done. When she was read the caution it was as if the life was being sucked out of her. When she spoke it was barely audible. Margot had to concentrate hard. The solicitor informed them a prepared statement was going to be read out first. The solicitor read it.

'*I put Kyle to bed at nine o'clock. Dan my husband arrived at around midnight. We are on a trial reconciliation at the moment having been separated for the past nine months. We were keeping that to ourselves for the moment. When Dan got up for work he knocked the alarm off instead of putting it on snooze. I thought I could have another ten minutes but I fell back asleep. I overslept. I checked on Kyle, he wasn't in his room. His school bag and uniform were gone. I assumed he'd left for school. I lied because I didn't want you to think I was a bad mother. I didn't check on Kyle after I put him to bed.*

My client wishes to cooperate, she will answer any questions.'

'Those are mostly the solicitor's words boss,' said Luke.
'I agree. Let's she how she handles the questions.'

'Has Kyle ever had to get himself ready for school before by himself?' Karen was asking the questions.
'No,' said Shelly. Shelly was giving her answers to Matt.

'That's a lie,' said DI Hall.
Margot watched closely. If it was, she was a good liar. She wondered why her boss was so sure.

'How many times has Dan stayed over?'
'That was the third time.'
'Did Dan leave his phone?'
'By mistake yeah.'
'Do you know where Kyle is?'
'No. I honestly thought he'd gone to school.'
'How would you describe your current relationship with Dan.'

'It's complicated. When we separated we had just drifted apart there wasn't a massive bust up or owt like that. Kyle missed his Dad. Money is tight, Dan pays the rent on my house. We didn't seem to be achieving anything by being separated, except being skint. We had been madly in love once. Dan is a good Dad. He's never been violent. Sometimes it's just better the devil you know.'
'Have there been any other men?'
'No.'
'You have never met anyone, not even for a date?'
'Dates but I didn't take any of them home. I was separated at the time.'
'It's not a criticism. We need to check them out that's all.'
Shelly looked at her solicitor who nodded.
'They were all from a dating app. If you give me my phone I can show you.'
'If you give me your PIN number we will check.'
She looked at her solicitor who nodded again.
'141214. Kyles date of birth…There's a lot because I didn't find the right one. I don't want you to get the wrong idea.'
'Any show too much interest in Kyle?'
'No.'

'What's she holding back?' said DI Hall.
'She would have lied about her age and probably said she didn't have kids,' said Margot.
'Quite possibly. Luke get that phone analysed on the hurry up please.'
'Already in hand boss.'
'Okay you two go and see this other kid, Nathan. Seize his phone if you have to. See if you can get it out of him first, save some time.'
'Will do. Come on Margot.'
'Sir, how could you tell when she was lying?' asked Margot.
'She can't keep her right leg still, watch. It stops when she lies or is considering her answer.'

Margot hadn't even noticed that. She still had so much to learn. She looked at the screen. Shelly's right leg was bouncing up and down as her foot flexed. Margot thought it looked like she was trying to drill through the floor. A habit so ingrained she didn't know it was giving her away.

Margot wanted to stay and hear the rest of the interview but even she could tell when a nine year old was lying. She knew Nathan had lied about the phone. She hurried out after Luke. They drove out to Nathan's house. As they pulled up Margot looked at her watch. Half past ten. Twenty six hours, although she now had to remind herself they didn't actually know what time Kyle left home.

Luke knocked on the door, it was answered by Nathan's Mum.
'Sorry to disturb you again. We think Kyle may have borrowed Nathan's phone.'
'Please come in.'
Nathan's mother marched them into the living room. Snatched Nathan's phone out of his hands and gave it to Luke.
'If you ever want that back you tell these officers the truth right now. Did Kyle contact anyone on your phone?'
Nathan started to cry. 'We booked a taxi on the app.'
'Jesus! Nathan, where too?'
'His Dad's. He didn't get in the taxi cause they called me asking where I was. I thought he'd changed his mind.'
'And you're saying this now,' snapped his mother.
'It's okay, we just need the truth,' said Luke.
'I was scared to say because they said they would still charge. Kyle was going to get the money off his Dad to pay the taxi. I'm sorry Mum.'
'I gave Nathan the app in case of an emergency. My Mum is very ill, in and out of hospital. Sometimes I just have to drop everything and run. That way Nathan would never be stuck. It was for emergency use only. I thought you were more sensible than that Nathan.'
'Kyle was sick of his mother sleeping with other men Mum. She'd leave him for hours on his own. I was trying to help. He was only going to his Dad's.'
'It's okay Nathan. What time did you book the taxi for?'
'Six. He said he had to get there before his Dad left for work.'
'From here?'
'Yeah, he had to pretend to be me.'
'I know the boss of the taxi firm. I used to work there before Nathan was born. So he was okay with me letting Nathan have the app. It was supposed to be a fail safe incase I had to rush and sort Mum so I knew Nathan could get somewhere safe in safety. I'm so sorry.'
'It's okay. I'm going to need to take a look at the app,' said Luke.

Luke tabbed through the app. The name of the taxi driver that was dispatched was there and confirming he had arrived at 6am. Trevor in a silver Skoda Octavia.

'Was that the only time he used your phone Nathan?'
'Yes I promise. And he didn't use it, I did it for him.'
'Okay thank you.'
Nathan's Mum apologised all the way out the house.

As they got back in their car Luke said 'let's go and find Trevor next.'
'Whilst we are here can we just pop up to Kyle's house? Forensic are still there aren't they?'
'Yes. Why Margot?'
'I just want to see if Kyle had an alarm clock and what time it was set for.'
'That's a really good idea Margot.'
'Luke, you and Tom, are you going to have children?'
'No I don't think so. It isn't that we haven't had that discussion, it's that we both want to focus on our careers for now. If we had kids one of us would have to give up their career for sure or we'd never be at home. Tom is enough for me. Tom would love to see you by the way, it's been a while. Why don't you come up for dinner with my Dad when this calms down?'
'I'd love to.'

They had reached Kyle's house. Luke collared a CSI as they came outside.
'Have you found an alarm clock in Kyle's room?'
'Not to my knowledge. I'll check.'
'We wondered if there was one what time it was set to,' added Margot.
Luke and Margot waited at the cordon for the CSI to come back.
'Yes, a travel alarm under the bed. Set to 5.30am. Turned off now.'

Curtains were twitching. Margot remembered the mother on her old estate who had been hounded out after she'd gone on a three day bender and left her two year old at home with her violent partner. The two year old had been murdered. The boyfriend sent to jail. Margot at the time thought she had deserved everything that happened to her. The shit smeared all over everything in her house. The dolls superglued to her windows. Even if Shelly was innocent, the sight of a cordoned-off house, white suits going in and out like ants removing brown bag after brown bag, was enough to make her guilty in the eyes of most. They wouldn't wait for a judge and jury. The estate would rise up against her regardless now. Even petty criminals like the Nolans clung to the moral high ground when a kid was missing probably dead.

'Margot you look miles away. Let's go and speak to Trevor. That was a really good shout by you on that alarm clock by the way.' Margot couldn't be happy. Kyle was with a stranger. Probably dead by now. Because he'd left thinking his Mum had found somebody else. He left to find his father who was sleeping in the next room unbeknown to him.

They headed to the taxi headquarters. A desk in a cramped office stuck to the back of a chippy. The smell of chips had crept in. Luke explained why they were there. The young girl on the desk called Trevor straight back for them. They waited in the office.
'I've found the job. I'll print it off for you,' said the young girl. 'Taxi was booked at 19.34 on the app the day before. Trevor logged as there at 5.56 and phoned the client at 06.05. Taxi was cancelled. Trevor billed them for the call out, but obviously we won't be charging.'
Margot was surprised with the young girl's efficiency. Margot had put cramped office, chip shop and taxi dispatcher together and come up with the vicar of Dibley's sidekick in her head.

Luke and Margot saw the Octavia pull up. They thanked the girl and headed outside. Margot immediately spotted the dash cam.
'Does the dash cam work?' Margot said pleased with herself for noticing.
'Yes, sorry I had absolutely no idea what was going on. I would have called you if I'd realised.'
'DS Luke Jones, DC Margot Jacks, we just need your help. Did you see anybody else around in the estate?'
'I don't think so. Take the dash cam, I can't say for sure. Nothing that made me suspicious, obviously I would remember that. I definitely didn't see the missing boy. Sometimes if you're not looking you don't see. I had no reason to be looking. Truth be told I was ready for my bed. That would have been a nice little job to finish the night. Sorry I'm not being much help.'
'We will need that dash cam. Can I take your full details?'

Margot wrote down his name and address and backed away to make a phone call. Trevor had no criminal record. His taxi licence was all in order. They thanked him and rushed back to their old station to view the dash cam.

Mo and Daisy were in. They all crowded round. The taxi was driven into the estate and was parked outside Nathan's house at 05.56. They watched as it waited outside, the picture didn't change, the only movement a piece of plastic that stuck out from the lid of a wheelie bin fluttering in the breeze. The taxi pulled off again at 06.05. It was then driven out of the estate, passing nothing but parked cars.
'So it looks like Kyle disappeared between his house and Nathan's. That's only about two hundred meters,' said Daisy.
'Or he never left the house. The taxi is pointing towards the bottom of Kyle's road. Nothing comes out of there. Kyle's road is a dead end. Any vehicle has to come out there,' said Luke.
'Or Kyle was early. Whatever happened, happened before the taxi got there,' said Mo.
'Or Kyle went over the back fence and into King street, then towards Nathan's. That would mean he'd come from behind the taxi. Anything coming out of King Street wouldn't be on the dash cam if the car turned away from the taxi at the bottom of the street. It didn't need to pass the taxi. The taxi driver wasn't much help himself,f he wouldn't remember one way or the other I don't think,' added Margot.
'If you're saying that Margot, for all we know the taxi driver could have picked Kyle up. Because the only thing the dash cam shows is in front of the car. Let's play it on.'

The taxi drove back to the dispatch station. The dash cam went off. Luke opened the next file. It started up ten minutes later and the taxi was driven to Trevor's home.
'Okay. It's unlikely he picked him up,' said Luke.
'He seemed really genuine too,' said Margot.
'Let's check, see what happened before. Maybe he had other jobs in the area he might have picked up something useful,' said Luke.

After watching the dash cam footage from 3am they were no further forward. Luke updated John.

'Guess we start taking a good look at all the residents then. Go over the house-to-house, find me anything of interest. I'm still not sure that kid made it off that estate. Obviously when the house-to-house was done our timeline was completely wrong. Put to one side anyone who said they'd already left for work. Great job you two. Forensic haven't uncovered anything suspicious so far. I'm going to have to let the mother and father go just as soon as they are done, if they don't turn up anything. Just the garden to do I think. Oh, and the dating app. You two have forty-odd, let's use her word – 'dates' - to follow up on. Margot was right - she's 26, not 30, and no kids. That does mean she probably didn't take them home as she said. Ties in with what Nathan said too, that she left Kyle to his own devices. Just go back and ask Nathan why Kyle decided on that particular day for me please.'

They did and Nathan said it was because Kyle wanted to get his prize for the best art project at school first. A small cup. Kyle had popped round to see if Nathan was alright after getting his teeth out, shown him his trophy and they put the plan into action. The mother confirmed that the time Kyle visited did coincide with the time the taxi was booked on the app.

'You know Luke, Donna entertains men. Perhaps we should ask her if anyone on the estate is a bit weird in that department.'
'Careful what you say to Donna, Margot, she's the worst gossip. But it wouldn't do any harm. Although there's not an obvious crossover between what Donna offers and paedophiles.'
'Is Donna such a gossip? Can you name one of her clients?'
'No. But I still don't trust her. She is an habitual liar.'
'I think she's had a bit of a shitty life. Why not pretend it was better than it was?'
'When did you get so friendly with her? I thought you tried to avoid her.'
'I did.'

Margot rang her and asked.
'Margot I'm not sure anyone who likes very young boys would come to me, I'm the wrong side of fifty.'
'So there's no one.'
'No. They all have their own thing and I do get odd requests but honestly Margot there's no one that I'm worried about in that way.'
'Thanks Donna'…You were right Luke, she doesn't know anyone.'

'It was worth a try Margot. Let's head back and go through the house-to-house that was done yesterday. Then start on this list of dates.'

Margot realised Rory was going to get sidelined again. In fairness to her boss, he'd driven out to Stamfordham and collected all the CCTV he could find for the night of the burglaries himself, because there had been no one else free to do it. Margot had seen it piled on his desk. She was thinking of offering to take some home and review it, however after her warning she probably shouldn't. She really wanted to stay on the squad. Besides Luke and her boss were right, you had to sleep at some point. She was really flagging now in terms of being able to concentrate. The thought of sifting through all the house-to-house. Then filling in the paperwork to get the details of the swipe rights made her sleepy just thinking about it.

Luke was running everyone through the PNC then passing the handwritten house-to-house sheets to Margot. Margot was reading them and putting everyone who could have been up early enough to have seen anything in one pile. The problem was that the officers attending hadn't always put the information she needed, because they were working from Kyle having left at 8.30. Not at home was written on quite a few. She silently cussed Shelly. Margot was struggling to understand why Shelly would lie when it was obvious to anyone the time he left home was vitally important.

John walked in.
'CSIs are done. One thing of interest - someone hid his school bag with his uniform in in the shed in the back garden,' he said.
'So he may have gone over the back fence and down the next street,' said Margot.
'Possibly.'
'If he did boss, it negates the value of the taxi dash cam. Kyle could have gone behind the taxi without being seen,' said Luke.
'Could he though? If he was that close to the taxi surely he would have made it to the taxi. Or the taxi driver notice a commotion,' said the DI.
'Actually boss we hadn't considered that. So he was most likely taken from the street behind his house. Or he was early and was taken before he got to Nathan's,' said Luke.
'This will be someone he knows, I'm convinced of it,' said the DI.
'If he hopped the fence he went via King Street. The house-to-

house wasn't done on that street. Although I can't imagine we will get much of a reception. Virtually the whole street hates the police,' said Margot.

'It also opens up a whole new line of enquiry. Perhaps Kyle saw something,' said the DI.

'Intimidation is more the Nolans style Sir. I can't see them taking a kid just because he saw drugs being dropped off or stolen gear being passed over the garden fence. That must be a daily occurrence,' said Margot.

'I agree with Margot on that Boss.'

'Guess you two will have to appeal to their better nature then. One way or another I need them spoken to. I'm letting the mother back in her house. The FLOs are accompanying her back. We need to know what clothes Kyle was wearing. I have a press conference to go to now. Revisit the house-to-house, revisit anyone who might have been about between half five and six, and add King Street. I want you two to do it. I think whatever happened happened really close to home. Before you do anything else send off that data protection form to get the information for the mother's dates, so we can make a start on that as soon as. The detective super is trying to steal us some more detectives from somewhere. It doesn't help half my squad are on standby for Crown Court from tomorrow. I need experienced detectives on this.'

Margot knew her boss wasn't having a dig at her. She knew everyone was flat out and the to do lists were getting longer and longer. She actually shared his frustration. Margot looked at the action tray, it was twice the size it had been this morning.

They headed out to redo the house-to-house. Another wasted two hours. Although they did find someone who left for work at half five. He saw nothing. Probably too early anyway. They knew they couldn't put off King Street for ever. They knocked on a few doors, no one was answering, probably because Colleen and her partner Kevin decided to sit on their sofa and drink beer. The sofa was in the front garden providing them with a view of the whole street. 'This is pointless Luke. I have an Idea, Let's write a letter, put it through the letter boxes with our mobiles on. That way if anyone wants to talk to us Colleen and Kevin will be none the wiser. That way their windows won't go out.'

'That's a really good idea Margot.'

They headed off to the station and printed out the letters. They returned to King Street. Colleen was not happy at being outsmarted. Especially by Margot. That was twice now. Margot held out a letter for Colleen.
'What's fucking in it?'
'We are asking for all the residents' help in trying to find Kyle.'
'We don't fucking know where he is. I know your game, you will be trying to pin the blame on us next. Take a good look at the mother. She's shagging half the town. If she didn't do it she might as well have done.'
Colleen refused to take the envelope. She turned and headed into the house, slamming her front door behind her. Margot let the letter fall over the fence. To her surprise Kevin picked it up.

Luke and Margot called it a day. They went back to their office and submitted everything they had to the incident room. Margot headed home. She slumped on the sofa and watched the ten o'clock news. Kyle had made the national news. She watched the press conference DI Hall and DSI Jasmine Walker were holding the press conference. They were good. Why wouldn't they be good? She'd seen countless police appeals for information over the years on the TV. It was different when you worked with the people doing them. Margot wondered why. She supposed because they were more human to you. They ate lunch, they broke wind.

Rory didn't make the main news. He did get ten seconds on the local news after Kyle had got another five minutes, an appeal for dash cam footage, CCTV footage and anyone in the area to come forward.
"Police are also appealing for anyone who has seen Rory Elliot to contact them."

Margot sat there. Should she ask Patrick for help? She remembered what Luke had said. Luke had never met Patrick, she had. She didn't doubt he could be in and out of people's houses without being seen. What if Rory was being held against his will? Abused as she sat there on her sofa. She didn't need to tell Luke. She rang Patrick.
'Patrick. We don't have the time to look for Rory properly. I'm worried. What if he's being raped and abused?'
'You want me to break into a few houses, see if anything jumps out?'

'What did you mean by you will help me if I help you?'
'If ever I get caught I will need you to get rid of any evidence. Don't worry, that hasn't happened yet. Every now and then I might need an address. In return I break in wherever you need me too. I know I can trust you Margot, you let me go for killing Mark. If you're like worried about trusting me all I can say is Frank trusted me. We looked out for each other. Frank always said there's plenty out there way worse than me. Occasionally I helped him catch the ones worse than me, when he was stuck like. You guys are shackled by too many rules and procedures. I'm not a monster Margot. I'm not going stand by and let a kid suffer. I've already checked quite a few houses. So if you want to deal with what I find I'm good with that. If you don't I'm also good with that.'

This was crossing a line and she knew it. Hadn't she already crossed that line when she'd watched Patrick kill Mark then covered it up? Hadn't her thought in that moment been to want to eliminate the Mark Rohans of the world? In what world was it right to kill or abduct a child?

'Okay I'm in.'
'I've found nothing yet. I'm in the village now. I'll let you know if I find a suspect.'
'Thanks Patrick.'

Margot immediately had second thoughts. Her life had just changed. She wasn't just a police officer anymore. She was also a criminal. Her Dad always said she'd amount to nothing.

Margot went to bed and tossed and turned. Paranoia was creeping in. Patrick was recording the calls to blackmail her. The NCA were recording the calls. GCHQ were recording the calls. NASA were recording the calls. She started to feel very hot. She was soon covered in the sweat of the guilty. Was it too late to call the whole thing off? Patrick was going to do what he did anyway. Surely it was better she dealt with the consequences not him. If Rory was found alive it would have been worth selling her soul for anyway.

Her phone rang. She jumped. She was actually shaking when she answered it.
'DC Jacks it's Kevin Wallace. Colleen Nolan's partner. I think I heard…I'm not giving a statement mind and this has to be confidential or I'm not saying.'

'Look Kevin we are not interested in what you were up to, all we are interested in is finding Rory before it's too late.'
'Who's Rory?'
'Sorry I meant Kyle.'
'I was up early to take delivery of something. I didn't see Kyle but I heard a car, bottom of the street. I heard it stop then I heard a scream which was muffled quickly. Then I heard the car speed off. I didn't see anything. I only heard.'
'What time.'
'Roughly ten to six.'
'Could you tell which way the car was travelling?'
'It sounded like it came into the estate from the town centre side, left the other way.'
'Could you give any idea of the car from the engine noise?'
'Not really. Sounded like a normal car.'
'You couldn't see anything?' asked Margot remembering you could see the whole street from their garden.
'No, delivery was at the back.'
'Thanks Kevin. Look, I know you won't tell me who made the delivery, but I need to talk to them. Pass on my number, they don't have to give a name.'
'I can't, if I do that then they will know I spoke to you.'
'Then find a way yourself of seeing if they saw anything and call me back.'
'Okay I can do that.'

Margot immediately rang Luke and told him what Kevin had said.

Luke

Luke got out of bed and rang John and relayed the message.
'Can he be relied upon, this Kevin Wallace?'
'He's a drunk, a handler, and a dealer. Normally no but what's the point of lying?'
'To deflect.'
'I think the obvious way to deflect is the parents. He doesn't have much in the way of brains Boss. He very much does what Colleen tells him.'
'The letter was a great idea but why didn't you put your number not Margot's? No disrespect to Margot but you just have more experience.'
'We put both our numbers. People open up to Margot more Boss.'
'Because she's really nothing like a police officer. I'm not having a go at her Luke, I wanted her on my team because she's different. She comes up with some really good stuff, sometimes. It's just if that's true that's the first evidence of abduction we have. To be fair I've favoured the parents up until this. I need to be a hundred percent sure he's not lying Luke before I about-turn. I need you to engineer a way of speaking to him face to face. Grill him.'
'Yes Boss.'
'Tomorrow get Margot to grab one of her old shift and try and alibi all those dates. You speak to Kevin, find out who else was with him and speak to him as well. Arrest them if you have too. I doubt we will get anymore detectives on this, two teenagers have just been stabbed to death by what looks like a gang of twelve. That's anyone we might have got at a push, lost to that. So as ridiculous as it is, that now leaves just you, Margot and me on Kyle Morgan and I haven't forgotten about Rory Elliot.'
'Are you still at work Boss?'
'Yes, although I was literally just leaving. I made a start on the CCTV.'

Luke knew that job should be delegated. But to who? There wasn't anybody. He looked at the clock, it was half past midnight. He crept back into bed. Tom had woken up.
'Sorry work, all sorted for now.'
'It's fine. Are you heading in early again?'
'Yes sorry, I'll try not to wake you.'

Margot

Margot drove to her old station. She was excited to be teaming up with Daisy again. She admired Daisy's resilience; after Mark had abducted her, she had insisted on coming back to work after only two weeks. Daisy was waiting for Margot.
'So have I understood correctly? They want us to interview forty-two good-looking eligible young men?' said Daisy, smiling as Margot got out the car.
'Yes.'
'What could possibly go wrong?'
Margot smiled back. 'And to make it easier they have all been asked to attend here at fifteen minute intervals.'
'Speed-dating, even better.'

'Boss wants us to alibi them all for the morning Kyle went missing. And to find out when they dated Shelly and how many times. What she was like, that sort of thing,' said Margot.
'Your boss still thinks it could be her then?' said Daisy.
'She certainly hasn't been ruled out yet.'
'What do you think?'
'I don't think it's the mother or father. Although Shelly does lie a lot.'
'I know she lied but I don't think it's her either.'

Margot had forgotten how small this interview room was. It was certainly going to be cosy. The first one walked in. He didn't look nervous. He was very good looking. He knew it too, thought Margot. He immediately started flirting with Daisy. Margot felt like the prudish chaperone from one of those historical dramas she'd started watching on the TV.
'Do you know what this is about?' she asked just like a prudish chaperone in a TV drama. Gary Bennett didn't even look at Margot. He smiled and spoke to Daisy. Whist flexing his pecs through his condom-tight T-shirt. He then showed off his biceps by running his hands through his hair.
'Yes the man on the phone said you needed to ask about my relationship with Shelly Morgan. I actually didn't know who you meant at first. Then the man mentioned the dating app. There was no relationship. It was one night only. She was just in it for the sex. She made that totally clear. She actually said she was just wanting

a good time and she wasn't looking for a relationship.'
'So did you have sex?' asked Daisy.
'Yes,' he said slowly licking his top lip. Christ, thought Margot. Daisy kicked her under the table.
'So where did you go for the sex?'
'Skate park.'
'Who suggested that?'
'She did. We couldn't go to mine because I live with my Mum and Dad. Only because I can't afford a flat yet. She said she lived with her parents too.'
'Did you know she had a son?'
'No, she said she was single with no kids.'
'Where were you Thursday morning from 5am to 9.30 am?'
'In bed. I got up at seven. Headed to college at a quarter to eight on the bus.'

They took down the details of the bus. Daisy saw him out and brought the next one in.

After another ten, the novelty of the speed-dating was wearing off fast. A pattern was developing. There was only ever one date, they met in the pub on the high street, left at closing, had sex, mostly in the skate park and never at hers. Everyone so far had said they were unaware she had a child. The only thing that didn't follow a pattern were the guys themselves. Margot couldn't help but notice how very different they all were.
'In all honesty, apart from not forking out for a babysitter, why not Margot? She's having more fun than I bloody am,' said Daisy.
'Let's not forget the main reason we are doing this is to see if any of the guys jump out. Perhaps she did date one of them more than once. Perhaps she did take one of them home. Do you think the fact she doesn't go for a certain type is odd? They are very different, that last one was nearly fifty.'
'No, I just think she's picking the good-looking ones. They are all a bit pretty for me. What's the husband like?'
'Ordinary really. Ginger like Kyle.
'I'll go get the next one.'

Daisy stretched her shoulders and headed out the room. She soon came back. 'Next one is a no-show. I could do with a cuppa. Let's ring him and take a break.'

Margot rang him, he was on his way in a taxi. Margot thought he sounded elderly. Margot and Daisy saw the taxi pull up just as they'd made a cup of coffee each. Margot and Daisy looked at each other. This couldn't be right. They headed outside to greet him.
'Hello. John Martin?'
'Can you speak up, I'm a little deaf?'
'Are you John Martin?'
'Yes.'

They helped him in. Daisy and Margot looked at his online profile picture. A thirty-something stared back at them.
'Do you know who this is?' asked Margot showing him the profile picture.
'No.'
'Do you live with anyone or have any carers Mr Martin?'
'I don't have any family left. Ben comes in twice a week to help with the shopping and cleaning.'
'We need to find Ben,' whispered Daisy. 'Look this is easy, why don't I carry on with this? You take Mo and find this Ben.'
'Are you sure?'
'Yes.'

Margot found Mo and told him she suspected someone had used John's details to create a fake profile. They took John home. Margot noticed how John immediately warmed to Mo. Mo was just one of life's good guys. Margot suddenly thought of Patrick. She was really regretting her decision in the cold light of day. She suspected Patrick had found nothing again as he hadn't called back. Mo soon had John settled in his home with a cup of tea.
'John, where are Ben's details?' asked Margot.
'In the blue folder.'
Margot hunted around for a blue folder. She eventually found it in the kitchen in a drawer covered by kitchen utensils. It was his care plan. A large sticker on the front said KEEP BY PHONE. She found the details of the care company and rang them. Margot spoke to the manager who as luck would have it wasn't far away. The manager said she'd come straight round. Margot showed her the profile picture when she arrived.
'Do you know who this is?'
'Possibly Ben, ten years and two stones ago. Why?'
'Someone set up this dating profile using John's details.'

'And did they use John's card to pay?'
'We haven't got that far yet. What's Ben like?'
'He's not been with us that long, just over three months maybe. He did have references. I've had no complaints but he's not interested in doing any extra hours. Most of my staff work overtime. We are desperately short at the moment. I've three off on the sick. He doesn't have to, but if you don't the visits get too short and if I'm honest our clients suffer as a result. I guess what I'm trying to say is I don't think he cares that much about the clients.'
'Where would we find John's bank statements?'
'He's online. John has full capacity. He's just not mobile. I'll ask him…John can you show the detective your bank account? You don't have to, but she just needs to check none of your money is missing.'
John put his PIN in and Margot checked his current account.
'When does Ben visit?'
'Monday at ten, Thursday at eleven.'
'What was the last thing you bought on Amazon John?'
'I don't have Amazon, can't be on with any of that. I like to see what I'm buying.'
'You didn't pay £89 to Amazon last Thursday?'
'No.'

Margot tabbed back through. 'Looks like it started about three months ago.'
'Shit,' said the manager under her breath. 'I'll check all his other clients. You will be wanting to know where he is right now?'
'Yes please,' said Margot.

Margot and Mo left John with the manager. They set off to go and arrest Ben. They eventually found him smoking a cigarette around the back of the client he was supposed to be visiting. Margot looked at him she thought it probably was Ben on the profile picture, but like the manager said ten years and two stones ago. They took him to the custody suite and booked him in.
The DI was waiting for her outside custody.
'Good work Margot. So he's on the sex offenders register, raped a nineteen year old female. I've dug out the file, he drugged the female on a date, helped himself after that. Met her on a dating site. Only got five years, out in two and a half. Nothing to suggest he's into kids though.'
'I think he's been stealing from the elderly people he was supposed

to be caring for, Sir. I think he also falsified his references, they weren't checked. He borrowed one of his elderly client's details to set up his profile. He's no catch Sir, he's slobby and he smells. I think given the other guys Shelly met she'd have just sacked him off, once she'd seen him and realised he was nothing like his profile picture.'

'Maybe, but his MO is to spike their drinks. If she'd stayed for a drink she might not remember the rest. She might have taken him home. I appreciate this could well be a massive distraction as far as Kyle goes but I can't ignore it. I'm going to get the FLO to ask her about him. See if she did take that drink. Can you get the timings of his visits to John from the manager, tie those into his order history from Amazon? Get a statement from John. I know we are stretched, but I think I'd rather we keep him for now rather than hand him off to local CID. Yes, I'm going to keep him until I'm sure he had nothing to do with Kyle. I'll interview with you later. Go and get enough evidence so we can at least charge him with the thefts from John and using Johns details on the dating site. I will get local to take over any enquiries to any theft or fraud from any other victims so we don't get bogged down. I at least want enough to get him back inside for breaching his licence. We need to search his flat, Margot go and grab some white suits from the CSIs before they disappear. They are in a briefing with DSI Walker, they should be nearly done.'

'Can I help Sir?' said Mo, who had been standing behind Margot.
'We need all the help we can get so yes. DI John Hall.' John held out his hand.
'Mo, Sir.' Mo shook his hand and smiled.
'Ah our taxi driver from Lucy.'
'Yes, Sir.'
'Well let's get stuck in, you go with Mo, Margot. I'll get the Detective Super; we are going to have to have the meeting I'm supposed to be having with her right now on the hoof. Do we have his phone?'
Mo held up Ben's mobile phone.
'Good.'

Margot could do with coming up for air. That wasn't going to happen. Margot and Mo rushed up to the office, grabbed some white suits from the CSIs, logged the phone into property, then rushed to the ladies' and gents' respectively. They drove to Ben's flat. They suited up outside. Mo was already fastening his, Margot had started by putting hers on back to front and was still trying to rectify her error. Hers was also more of a squeeze than she would like to admit. Margot caught her reflection in the car window, she looked like the Pilsbury Doughboy. She sighed. They put latex gloves on and shoe coverings. She couldn't help but think that Mo still looked like a policeman, even when completely covered from head to toe.

Despite the face mask, the smell of damp and takeaways hit Margot as soon as she walked into the flat. It didn't look like it had been cleaned once in the five months he'd been out of prison. Takeaway boxes littered where they had quite literally been chucked over the back of the sofa. The sink was full of dirty dishes; mould had started growing on them. Margot looked around. The glint of several new things caught her eye - a TV, a toaster, a pair of trainers. She poked her head in the bedroom; another newish TV. A laptop - she was definitely seizing that.

Detective Superintendent Jasmine Walker came in with DI Hall.
'Our man doesn't have a car, so do you really think he had something to do with Kyle, John?'
They were clearly mid-conversation, thought Margot.
'He could have used someone else's car, with or without their knowledge. To answer your question - probably not, but I'm not sure enough yet.'
'Should we put forensic through first then?'
'We will have a long wait, with twelve murder suspects' houses being searched as we speak. Let's bag up clothing and bedding and take a cursory look around. If we find anything that suggests Kyle was here we can call a halt and get them in. They won't thank us for processing this flat Ma'am, on a fishing trip for what could turn out to be...How many Amazon payments did you find from the old fellow's bank accounts Margot?'
'Seven Sir.'
'A small scale theft.'
'Okay, agreed. I'm more worried how many women he met through that profile.'
'Sorry Ma'am, I can't take that on too right now. I only have Luke and Margot on two missing boys. I can't action everything I should be actioning in the here and now as it is. I'm running the incident room by myself now and I shouldn't be running around searching houses and interviewing suspects.'
'I'll make some phone calls when I get back. Get the local CID to

look into possible victims. I guess as long as you get him for breaching his license he can't do anymore damage. Come on, let's get stuck in here, seeing as you've kidnapped me.'

The house search, despite burning valuable hours, revealed nothing of any interest as far as Kyle went. They seized all his clothing and bedding. And anything that looked new. Then all left to head back to the station.

Luke was sitting at his desk as they lugged the evidence bags into the office.
'How did you get on Luke?' asked John.
'I eventually tracked Kevin down. I arrested him for possession. The arrest was just a means to an end. He's scared of whoever it was he met that morning. He isn't going to give up his name for love nor money. My guess is he took delivery of a quantity of drugs. He said he has asked him if he saw anything and he said to Kevin he didn't. I believe him boss I think he really did hear the car and a scream. That time of the morning it would have been really quiet. How do you want it played from here on in boss? I was thinking keep him sweet give him a caution, it was just a bit of cannabis. Any house search is pointless now - any gear they did have will have been moved.'
'Keep him sweet. He obviously wants to help with the kid. It worries me no one else heard this scream though.'
'People would have been asleep. He said it was stifled really quickly.'
'Was this before or after he took the delivery?'
'Literally thirty seconds before.'
'So it can't be the delivery guy?'
'No boss, and I did get out of him the delivery guy was on a motorbike. He's adamant it was a car he heard. I've started to collect CCTV on the route the Dad took to verify his movements. Chances are the motorbike, and possibly this other vehicle Kevin heard, went the same way back towards Newcastle.'
'Keep going with that Luke.'

They stacked the bags on the floor of their office.
'Margot, Mo, go and get John Martin's statement and go and see the manager. I'll log the property and plan the interview. You know what you need Margot?'

'Yes Sir.'
Margot and Mo disappeared out the office.

The DI's phone rang. Luke watched his face contort.
'Luke, get rid of Kevin quickly. The arm of a child has been recovered in a field up near Scots Gap. Farmer has found it.'
'Shall I call Margot back?'
'No, I need those statements.'
'Daisy has just finished with the dates. She's more than competent to take those statements. Daisy is good. She can pick Mo up, drop off the interviews at the same time.'
'Okay, anything from the dates?'
'She said none of them jumped out. Thirty have verifiable alibis. The other eleven were home alone in bed. Then there's Ben in the cells.'
'You say she's good. Would she follow up the alibis?'
'She would. And she'd do a good job. She's Mo's tutor constable so you would have to sweet talk their sergeant.'
'I'll get the boss to do that. They're not going to say no to a Detective Superintendent.'

Margot

The farmer was on his quad bike waiting for them in a gateway to a field. A muddy collie dog started turning in tight circles on the back as they pulled alongside. Margot and Luke were in one car, the DI in another. Luke put the window down.
'Where's the best place to park?' he asked the farmer.
It looked like a quiet lane but sod's law as soon as they had stopped, a car had wanted to get past.
'Next field along, pull in the gateway. Ground is solid enough to get two cars in, only just mind don't go too far in or I'll be having to fetch tractor.'

Luke edged past the car and found the gateway. Luke reversed in too far. Margot laughed.
'He'll be having to fetch tractor now,' teased Margot. John parked in front of them. They all set off walking back to the quad.
'It's pretty remote, isn't it?'
'I'm guessing that was the idea Margot,' said the DI as he took in the surroundings too.

Margot looked at the waterlogged fields then at her shoes. She should have brought her wellies.
'Where is it?' asked John as they reached the farmer.
'See the tall ash.'
Margot could just see trees. A small copse bordered the opposite side of the field.
'Yes,' said the DI.
'It's got caught in the barbed wire of the fence, by the ash tree. My guess is a fox got a hold of it. You can see the teeth marks, must've tried to pull it free, torn the flesh a bit.'
'Have you touched it?'
'No. Was obvious it was a kiddie's arm. I seen the news about the missing kid Kyle Morgan. I figured I might have found a piece of him.'
'Why were you in the field?'
'I was checking on the lambs. I've moved sheep, figured you wouldn't want them in the field.'
'Where does the fox live?' asked Margot.
The farmer looked at Margot.
'Buggered if I know.'

'Okay, we'll take it from here. Just one more thing - is there better access to the woodland?' asked John.
'No, this is closest you can get.'

They set off across the field. Margot's feet were soon soaked. She was lagging, she felt like she'd taken to an ice rink. She feared if she speeded up she'd do her first ever triple salchow.
'Keep up Margot. Why did you ask where the fox lived?' asked John.
'I just thought he might have taken some other body parts home with him.'
'Actually Margot, I think they cache their food near where they find it. But it's not as daft a question as it seemed. The rest of the body could well be in those woods.'
How did her boss even know all this stuff? She chased the disturbing image of fox cubs being served human body parts out of her head.
'I'll get a cadaver dog up here once we've verified it is actually an arm.'

Margot didn't want to get any closer. She could see from where she was standing it was real.
'Okay forensic recovery. Search team. And cadaver dog. I'd say that was older than nine. Rory? Let's not jump to any conclusions. That initial cut - that's too clean for an animal, that's been done by something reasonably sharp. From the marks on the bone I'd say a saw.'
'Do you think whoever it was cut his arm off because he was burgling?' asked Margot feeling sick.
'I think we need the rest of him before we jump to any conclusions. Are you alright Margot, you've gone white?'
'I'll be okay.'
'Go back. Take my car and drive around the periphery of the woods. I just don't see this side being the access point. Check right around the woods for any CCTV.'
'Yes Sir.'
DI Hall threw her his car keys. Margot stretched to reach for them and promptly spun round and went flat on her face.
'Are you okay Margot?'
'I'm fine,' she said as she did an impression of Bambi on ice.

'I've never known a detective like her,' said John to Luke as Margot skated back across the field. Margot overheard.

Margot eventually made it back to the safety of the road. She found a tissue in her pocket and tried to rub the worst of the mud off her. The tissue was soon overwhelmed and started to disintegrate. Margot was left rubbing away with nothing, wondering where the tissue had gone. She opened the car and sat in the driver's seat and cleaned the mud off her face as best she could with spit and a finger. Her shoes slid all over the pedals. Luke and the DI hadn't fallen over. Hadn't asked where Mr Fox lived. Hadn't sung Whitney Houston at a pub brawl. She looked in the rear-view mirror. Luke had got the car stuck though. She felt better. She brought up Google maps. The farmer was right, the woods were closest to the road this side, but at the far side it looked like there was a dead-end lane. A better place to park surely if you didn't want to be seen disposing of a body. She set off with renewed enthusiasm.

She found the lane easily enough. It seemed a totally pointless lane, it didn't go anywhere. It just stopped at a gate to a field. She could see the copse of trees two fields away. She filmed a video on her phone. She looked carefully for tyre tread marks and footprints in the field. Everything was just too wet. The gate wasn't locked and was wooden. No chance of fingerprints. The heavy rain last night would have washed away any DNA.

She thought of Mark. Was the rain part of the killer's plan or had Rory been dumped beforehand? Was it Rory? Was it even male? Margot's quest for CCTV had been easy to this point she hadn't even passed a house. She headed off in the opposite direction to complete her loop. She came across two houses; she couldn't see any cameras but she thought it was at least worth asking.
'Hello I'm Margot,' she said as an elderly lady opened the door.
'I'm not interested.'
'I'm the police,' said Margot showing her warrant card. The lady took it off her and examined it, then Margot.
'You're covered in mud. Have you come about the badger baiting?'
'I fell over in the field. These shoes are my comfy ones, there's no grip on the bottom. What badger baiting?'
'Last night. I could see torch-lights in the woods. They come with shovels you know.'
'Did you see them?'

'I saw the torchlight, last night in the woods, are you not listening?'
'What time?'
'Ten. Bedtime.'
'How many torchlights?'
'Two. I rang my daughter.'
'Did you call the police?'
'Not much point, you never turn up.'

As Margot reached for her notebook and pen to write it all down, the old lady shut the door. Margot hadn't finished. Despite knocking again, the door remained firmly shut. Margot tried the handle, it was locked.

Margot tried next door. An elderly man in overalls opened the door.
'What's she complained about this time?'
'I'm sorry?' said Margot.
'You are the police aren't you?'
'Yes. But I'm just trying to establish if you have seen anyone driving down the lane in the last few days. The dead end just along the road.'
'She complains about my chickens going into her garden. What does she expect me to do, tell them they can't go? Last week she called you because I'd put a cardboard box in her wheelie bin. She'd already put it out. Mine was full. Where's the harm in that?'
'Is she new then?'
'No, she's been complaining for the last forty years.'
'Sorry, but this is important. She said she saw torchlight coming from the woods at ten last night. Did you see anything?'
'Can't say I did. That one's prone to imagination mind you.'
'So there wasn't torchlight, or you couldn't say?'
'Couldn't say. I don't look out my window every five minutes like Lady Muck to count the bleeding chickens.'

Margot tried the old lady again. She saw her look out her window. The door was opened again.
'What did he say?'
'That he didn't see any torchlight.'
'Huh.'
The old man came out into the front garden. Margot was momentarily distracted. The door was slammed shut again. Bollocks, thought Margot. No amount of knocking brought the lady

back. The old man pottered around trying to look busy pulling up a weed.

Margot decided she'd have to come back. She got back in the car and continued. She rounded a bend and was surprised she had completed her loop. She hadn't passed any other properties. She decided to go round again. She spotted the farmer on his quad, she waved him down.
'Are there badgers living in the trees?'
'Badgers aren't monkeys?'
Margot actually knew that.
'No, I meant do they have like a burrow in the woods?'
'Badgers live in setts.'
'So, is there a badger sett in the woods?'
'Aye. I can show you where the sett is, but a badger didn't take that arm.'
'I'm sure I can find it. I will have to wait for forensic to finish first though. Do you know the two elderly people in the cottages on the far side of the woods?'
'Aye. If they were the last people on earth they'd still rub each other up the wrong way.'
'She reckons she saw torchlight in the woods last night.'
'I'd take anything she says with a pinch of salt. She complained me cows were making too much noise last week. Week before, tractor had made the road muddy. Your lot know her. Even yous have stopped bothering to come out.'

Margot continued and stopped at the cottages again. She imagined herself in an endless Groundhog Day loop. She knocked on the door of the old lady. She answered.
'Sorry to bother you again but it's really important. Did you see any vehicles last night?'
'No.'
Margot heard flapping behind her. She jumped and looked round. A chicken had flown up onto the wall. She heard the door slam shut. Bollocks, thought Margot again. No amount of knocking worked. She was damned if she was going round again.

Margot edged past the chicken. It was the closest she'd ever got to a live chicken.
'Do you want to take some fresh eggs?' came the old man's voice from next door. Margot didn't want to appear impolite.

'Yes please,' she said.
The old guy handed her four eggs.
'Fresh today,' he said.
Margot said thank you. She carefully placed the eggs in the cup holders. They seemed to be covered in chicken shit. She wondered where a chicken actually laid their eggs from. She didn't know. She didn't feel she could ask the old man if chickens shat eggs. She decided she preferred supermarket eggs and contemplated throwing them out the window, only she didn't really want to touch them again. She drove back round. A CSI van had arrived as had two uniformed officers. She could see the officers talking to the DI across the field. She waited for the DI to walk back across the field.

'Anything useful Margot?'
'Maybe. An old lady thought she saw two torchlights last night in the woods at ten from her bedroom window. She thought it was badger baiting. I guess it could have been someone burying a body. Or perhaps it was badger baiters and their dog uncovered the arm. She's not the most forthcoming witness. The farmer and her neighbour said take what she says with a pinch of salt. There's no CCTV Sir. Just fields. There is a badger sett in the woods.'
'Okay, we'll bear that in mind. I'm heading back to the office. A search team is en route. Luke is going to stay and coordinate. You come back with me. Let's see how Daisy has got on, then interview this Ben.'
Margot handed the car keys back.
'Are those eggs in the cup holder?'
'Yes fresh today. They are for you Sir.'

They arrived back at the station. Margot's phone pinged. She could see it was a WhatsApp from Patrick.
'Sir, hI'm just going to head to my locker and change.'
'Good idea Margot. I'll speak to the FLO, see what Shelly said about the date with Ben. I'll touch base with Daisy and meet you in custody in fifteen. We don't have time to plan the interview, just sit tight Margot unless I nod to you, okay?'

Margot nodded and hurried to the locker room. Luckily it was empty. She looked at the WhatsApp. It was a picture of a bill for a new set of Mercedes car keys billed to Mr R Grant of Holly Cottage.

Why was Patrick sending her that? She typed in 'can you talk?' The app told her he was typing; she waited for the message to come through.

'No, but can use this talk later.'

'What does it mean?'

'That they had car keys stolen?'

Margot remembered his theory about taking the car. 'No cars stolen', she typed and sent.

'Not unusual to take keys but come back for car when done.'

Margot was struggling to follow his logic. 'Are you saying this person killed him?'

'No. A good burglar will cache the stuff from each burglary. So if stopped by police they are clean. Then when done retrieve all property including stealing car from drive.'

That did make sense. Why hadn't the person reported the burglary? Perhaps they didn't know they had been burgled, perhaps they thought they'd mislaid the keys. Had Rory come back to steal the car and they'd caught him? Mr R Grant, whoever you are. No, because you wouldn't need new car keys. So if you were just another victim, did that actually help in anyway at all?

'Does this help?'

'Doesn't look like he left village.'

I'd already guessed that, thought Margot. Then she had to concede Patrick had potentially found evidence to support her theory. Evidence she would need to officially come across. She thought of the fox cacheing it's food. So was the jewellery he stole, still there hidden somewhere in the village? She was going to ask Patrick to look, then had a better idea.

She changed and cleaned up. And waited for her boss.
'Sir I had an idea. The fox made me think of Rory burgling. Burglars often cache the stuff they steal don't they? Can I run a police dog around the scene of the burglaries, it might help establish if Rory left the village or not? I still want to do some house-to-house too

Sir.' Margot knew exactly which house she wanted to start on. Mr R Grant, Holly cottage.

'Good idea. Ready for this interview first. Shelly did stay for a drink. She said he looked nothing like his profile and she told him so, said she wasn't interested. She woke up the next morning in her own bed half dressed, with absolutely no recollection of how she got there. He wasn't there and she doesn't think he came home with her. It was two months ago. CCTV from the bar is lost after thirty days unfortunately. He opened the Amazon account using John's name, address and bank card. Got the parcels delivered to John's. Including the two TV's we took from the house. Doesn't look like he's taken anything from the other clients. A bit of cash maybe but we are on a hiding to hell trying to prove that. I'm guessing he will no reply. If he does we can't prove any rape at this moment in time. Or that he had anything to do with Kyle. We ask the questions and move on. Then we run with our strong suit the theft and the dating profile which breaches the condition of his licence. We get him recalled and hand it over to CID. If we get any evidence later we can revisit him.'

'Got it Sir.' Margot decided she'd just keep quiet.

DI Hall did all the introductions. Margot looked at Ben. He was letching at her boobs. Margot noticed his solicitor had moved as far away from him as possible and was sweating with her jacket still on. He did look really nervous though.

'Did you set up this dating profile?'
'No reply.'
'Two months ago on a Friday night you met Shelly Morgan in the Dog and Slippers. What happened?'
'No reply.'
'Did you have sexual intercourse with her?'
'No reply.'
'She remembers meeting you. Via the app. She accepted a large gin and tonic from you. Did you spike that drink?'
'No reply.'
'Did you ever meet her son?'
'No reply.'
'Kyle Morgan 9 years old. He's missing. Did you have anything to do with that?'
'No.'
'Where were you Thursday morning from 5 am to 9am?'

'Home.'
'Can anyone verify that?'
'No.'

They continued with their questioning about the profile and the thefts to which he no replied. The DI wound up the interview.

'What do you think Margot?' asked John as they walked back to their office.
'I think he's a boob man, Sir.'
'Sorry about that. I'd have asked Luke to interview with me if I'd have known he was going to gawk at you for the entire interview. The only question he answered was when we specifically asked about the kid. I'm trying to decide if that makes him more or less of a suspect in my mind. Get tech to go through the phone and laptop, see if he's ever shown any interest in young boys, please Margot. Do that first, then organise your dog and start your house-to-house please. I'll sort the paperwork for Ben. I'll ring the prison, see if he associated with any child abusers while he was inside. He could have just provided the information of course. Grab Luke before you start your house-to-house Margot. I don't want you on your own. You could be knocking on a killer's door.'

Margot had studied the map of the village. She needed a logical place to start that meant she could visit Mr R Grant of Holly cottage as soon as possible without it appearing suspicious to Luke. She also hoped he'd go for the two at a time approach to save time so she could speak to Mr Grant alone. Margot was waiting for Luke in the village.
'What do they think about the arm?'
'They pretty much just took it away. Search teams are still at it but they found your badger set and it hasn't been disturbed lately. There was evidence of old digging. The handler doesn't think there's anything else there. Dog's not interested.'
'So where's the rest of him?'
'No idea. Let's make a start. Where are we starting?'
'All the burglaries are to the West of the foster home. I thought we'd just start here seeing as this is where I parked the car.'
'How many do we have to do in total?'
'Seventy-two. Why don't we do two at a time? You do one side of

the road I'll do the other.'
'Okay but let's set up a WhatsApp. Message each other which house we are entering.'
'Okay I'll start this side. You start the other.'

Margot wondered how many of these houses Patrick had been in. She soon got to Holly Cottage. Much more house than cottage she noted. A sizeable house in a large garden. A garage that looked just like a mini-house was attached to the side of the house. Margot thought it looked just like mother house and baby house. She established Mr R Grant was a GP who lived at home with his wife and St Bernard, Colin. Colin was now drooling all over Margot's trousers.
'Do you mind the dog? I can put him in the kitchen if you don't like dogs.'
It wasn't the dog Margot disliked it was the drool, but she didn't want to offend.
'No it's fine. We are just doing some house-to-house regarding a series of walk-in burglaries. Has anything gone missing lately?'
'No. I'm sure we haven't been broken into.'
'It's small things - cash, jewellery, car keys.'
'Now you mention it, the car keys did go walkabouts. I searched high and low for them.'
'When was this?'
'Same night as the other burglaries now you say. A colleague of mine was broken into. I didn't connect it. I'll double check with my wife when she gets home from work, but I'm pretty certain she has had no jewellery taken and the car wasn't stolen.'
Margot remembered the three-car GP.
'The other GP Adam Hill, do you work together?'
'No we are at different practices but we've known each other for well over twenty years.'
'I'll need to take some details if that's okay. Do you have a bill for the replacement keys?'
'I do.'
'Can I see it please?'
'I'll dig it out, follow me through to the study.'
Margot was led into another big room, more man-cave than study. A pool table dominated. There was a large TV comfy armchair. And modest desk.
'Sorry I'm not the most organised, let me look for it,' he said as he looked through a large box of what looked like bills. He clearly

didn't have much of a filing system. Perhaps he had actually lost the keys. Margot looked at the photographs on the wall. An old man in waders proudly holding aloft a large fish held pride of place. The other photos were all of the doctor and a lady, his wife Margot assumed, with various reincarnations of Colin over the years. The Doctor looked to be in his late forties now. No children she concluded. She wondered if like her they had wanted children but couldn't have them.
'Ah found it.'
'Can I take it please, just in case I need it?'
'Let me run myself off a copy first if that's okay. Just in case I need it.'
'Go ahead.'
The doctor moved over to a printer in the corner of the room and made himself a copy.'
'Thank you,' said Margot taking it.

Margot had everything she needed. She left to find Luke. She looked at her trousers, she looked like she was an extra in a sliming scene from Ghostbusters.
'Anything?' she asked.
'Not so far. You?'
'I may have something but it could be nothing. A set of lost car keys.'
'You're thinking Rory may have stolen the keys?'
'He'd need transportation. He's been caught driving stolen cars before. But I don't get why the car wasn't stolen. The guy's got a St Bernard and a wife. The dog would lick you to death mind. I didn't meet the wife. He's a GP. Really nice man.' Margot felt manipulative as she'd said it. She didn't like with holding the truth from Luke. She'd made him a promise that they would always tell each other everything. But if Patrick was going to bite her, she didn't want Luke to be bitten too.
'Maybe he would have stolen the actual car later but didn't because he was already dead?'
'So it supports my theory then that it was a burglary gone wrong? That there's another property somewhere that was burgled. That the occupant caught Rory, and then something happened.'
'Yes. I'll ask for forensic to give the house a once over, because at the end of the day it could just be lost keys. Oh the boss just called your dog is on its way. And Ben shared a cell for three weeks last June with a man convicted of two counts of child abuse. Apparently

they became quite chummy after that. He was released two weeks ago. Staying at a bail hostel down in Middlesbrough so not that far away. Boss is following it up.'
'That sounds promising. You don't look that pleased.'
'Say Ben and this guy planned to abduct Kyle. You would abduct him on the way to school or at least somewhere you knew where he was going to be. They had no way of knowing he was going for a taxi at 6am. It makes no sense.'
Margot could see Luke's point. Luke seemed to be deep in thought for a while.
'Let's keep going with this. See how many we can tick off today,' he said after a while and headed off to his next house

Margot's phone rang as she walked to her next property. She didn't recognise the number.
'DC Margot Jacks,' she said.
'Hi it's Penny from the forensic science service. I have the results for the series of burglaries in Stamforham for you. DNA from your suspect Rory Elliot was present on the swabs obtained from the point of entries on two properties. Nothing from the other house, as in no DNA. He scratched himself on a window frame, slightly protruding screw to be precise, which drew blood. Sample SW3. I'm emailing you the full report now.'
'Thank you.'

Again it was nothing she didn't already know. But it was proof. Proof Rory had done at least two of the burglaries. She waited for Luke to come outside again. The dog handler arrived. Margot explained she needed her to search for stolen property. Jewellery and a set of car keys. She raised an eyebrow when Margot produced a map and showed her the area she needed to search.

She saw Luke come out the house opposite and she waved at him, he walked over to her.
'Luke did that arm have a scratch on?'
'Yes why?'
'That was the lab. Rory definitely did at least two of the burglaries; she reckons he scratched himself on a protruding screw.'
Luke brought up the photo of the arm. There was a perfect screw size scratch on the underside.
'It's him,' said Margot.

Luke's phone rang. Margot waited for him to finish the call.
'Boss wants me back to go and interview this paedophile with him. He wants you to go and see the home office pathologist who is examining the arm. We will have to come back to this Margot. Sorry, I know this means a lot to you. We are stretched too thin. And there's the smallest of small chances Kyle could still be alive. Boss wants a briefing after that. Come up with a plan of action.'
'Okay.'
'Try and get him to give you an idea of how the arm was severed what sort of tool we are looking for. Don't forget DNA for identification. And TOD.* A CSI will meet you there. Mortuary at the RVI.*'
'Will do. Catch you later then.'

Margot

Margot headed for the morgue. She suited up. She couldn't help but think the arm looked so small on the steel table all by itself. The fingers reflected in the polished surface giving the impression of two hands reaching towards each other. Margot wanted to hold his hand while the pathologist examined it.
'We need DNA for identification. We need to know what tool was used. And a TOD,' said Margot after she'd gotten over the initial shock.
'I haven't met you before, are you new to MIT?'
'Yes sorry I'm Margot. I should have introduced myself first. I was worried I'd forget to ask you something.'
'Ah Margot. Yes I've heard all about you. Well I won't be able to tell you much without the rest of the body. I'd say male, mid-teens. Arm was severed postmortem. First guess small, possibility electric, saw. When did he go missing?'
'About a week ago.'
'Hum, I'll take tissue samples to examine under the microscope. I'll swab the wounds and send them to the lab, they will be able to tell what animal got hold of the arm. Fox is the most likely in my opinion. I'll take swabs from the skin for you too. That's all I can give you just now.'
'What about TOD?'
'There's a possibility it may have been frozen. I will be able to confirm or refute that for you later.'

Margot thanked him and nipped outside to call Luke.
'Thanks Margot. Boss said get the swabs away to the lab straightaway.'
'No problem.'

Margot

Margot returned to the station to complete her paperwork for the swabs. She rounded the corner and was almost at the door to her office when she noticed Jasmine and the new Chief Constable addressing the rest of the squad. She ducked down. If she crawled forward on her hands and knees she couldn't be seen, and she could just head back down the far stairs and use another office. The trouble was her hands were full. She could use her elbows. It wasn't that far, ten meters or so. As long as she kept below the level of the glass she'd be fine.

Margot began to crawl on her elbows and knees. Hands full of all her's and Luke's notes from the house-to-house and a list of the exhibits from the post-mortem of the arm. She heard the door open behind her.
'Are you alright Margot?' said Jasmine.
Margot looked over her shoulder to see the Chief Constable staring at her. Margot's mind went blank. Later she came up with all sorts of plausible explanations. She'd dropped her paperwork. She'd lost a contact lens. Not that she wore them but who'd know.
'I'm fine. I'm checking for mice, Ma'am.'
'Why?'
Why was she checking for mice? She racked her brains.
'I'm actually checking for mouse droppings Ma'am.'
How was that any better? she thought. Stop talking please, she told herself.
'Why Margot?'
Margot glanced at the health and safety poster stuck on the wall.
'Health and safety Ma'am. The posters all say we must all take responsibility. Mice are very unhealthy.'
Margot stood up.
'This is one of my detectives Margot sir. She's working the two missing boys,' said Jasmine giving Margot an odd look.
'How's that enquiry going Margot?'
'There's a lot to do Sir. We have an arm... just one, the right one... As opposed to the left that is. We think a fox might be involved...
'Well don't let me stop you. Nice to meet you Margot. Again,' said the Chief Constable smiling.

Margot could literally feel the heat coming off her as she headed into her office. She got stuck into the paperwork so she didn't have to make eye contact with anyone. The pathologist rang her just as she'd finished.
'I thought you'd like to know. The arm was frozen. There is very little decomposition so the arm was not exposed to the elements outside for long. I'll have more later.'
'I suppose it might explain why he was cut up. So he'd fit in the freezer. It's all a bit odd though isn't it?'
She was expecting a reply but the pathologist had hung up.

Luke and the DI were going to be another couple of hours. She decided to get stuck into the CCTV for the night of the burglaries. The only camera that covered the road was from a private house. It was a good image. The only downside it was in the middle of the village. So traffic need not necessarily pass it. Margot suddenly realised they would have to go back and get the most recent CCTV as well. Seeing as the arm could well have been dumped last night.

She was tired. The upside at least was that she could sit at her desk for a bit, rest her feet. She started at 6pm when the foster parents said Rory left. She gasped; there he was sauntering down the main road. It was just getting dark. She noted he was dressed in black tracksuit bottoms and a black hoodie. Margot played it back several times. She found it hard to accept the image she was watching was now dead, probably killed later that very night. Cut up and put in a freezer. She was trying to note all the vehicles that drove past the camera but they were side views only. Vehicles weren't her thing. She was struggling to identify the makes and models. A couple of dog walkers went past. Margot watched on, struggling to keep her eyes open now the shock of seeing Rory had worn off. She kept having to rewind every time she reallsed her concentration had gone and she hadn't seen anything for a while despite staring at the screen. She was now at 9pm.
'Shit,' she said out loud. Several detectives looked round.
She rewound and paused the screen. A white van was driving down the road, with 'Dan Morgan Painter and Decorator' written on the side.

Margot tried to process what it meant. Why was here there? It was nowhere near his house in Whickham. Had he had a job in the area? She tried to connect the two cases. Dan runs Rory over and accidentally kills him. He panics and hides the body in the freezer of his house. Kyle does get to his Dad's and finds Rory's cut up body. Dan has to kill Kyle to keep him quiet. Was that possible? Margot remembered Dan in the interview. She just didn't think he could kill his own son. Besides his van had been examined. His house was searched. It was still a hell of coincidence. It had to mean something.

She should wait for Luke and the DI to come back. She looked at her watch, they wouldn't be long. She should keep watching. Margot's heart suddenly jumped into her mouth. She fast forwarded a few days to Wednesday night. Bollocks. There at half past midnight were her and Patrick walking past the camera. Margot regretted having such a distinctive shape. She started to panic. There was no reason anyone would look that far ahead from the night of the burglaries was there, not with everything else that was going on? She hoped Patrick hadn't been caught on any cameras on other nights. She rushed to the toilets. She felt physically sick.

She rang Patrick.
'Patrick we are on camera together walking down the main road the night I met you there. I'm worried you will be on more CCTV.'
'If I am they won't be able to identify me don't worry. We did nothing wrong that night. Just try and make sure you do the CCTV if you can.'
'Rory is dead. He was kept in a freezer. Cut up with an electric saw. Have you seen anything like that?'
'No. I'll bear it in mind.'
'You can't go back tonight Patrick. So far we only have an arm. If more of him turns up we will get more CCTV.'
'Okay I'll stay out of the village for a bit.'

When she got back from the toilets Luke and the DI were back. She took a deep breath.
'Sir I need to show you something. I made a start on the CCTV.'
She showed them.
'Bloody hell. That can't be a coincidence,' said John.
'Where was the property he was decorating Boss?' asked Luke.
'Jesmond, but that was just a day job. I don't think we actually asked about any other jobs given it was outside the timeline. This is 9pm on a Sunday what's he doing there then, and he's heading away from his home address? I don't know what it means, but you

two go and ask Dan Morgan about it now face to face.'
'We need the CCTV from the same camera for the night the arm was dumped too Sir. There's absolutely no guarantee it captured anything, but I don't mind checking it Sir.'
'Go and pick it up tomorrow Margot.'
Margot breathed out.

'So what happened with the sex offender?' asked Margot as they headed down the stairs to the car.
'He provided an alibi for the actual abduction. Local CID are running it down for us. He's so normal Margot. I mean that not in a good way. He's clever, charming even, he's a groomer. Who knows what he's been thinking and planning in that cell?'
'Is his alibi strong?'
'Yes and no. He reckons he was enjoying an early morning walk. The bail hostel has CCTV. He said he signed out at 7am and that will be on camera. After that he wandered around on his own, all day as he does every day. Time wise he couldn't have done the abduction. That's not to say Ben didn't do that part on his own. He's been sleeping each night at the hostel. Again we will verify that but if he hadn't then he'd have been recalled. I guess he's still in for now regardless. They are checking the call log for the hostel phone to see if he contacted Ben after his release.'

They drove in silence to Dan's house and knocked on his front door. He came to the door in tracksuit bottoms and T-shirt, bare feet. He looked like he'd just woken up. The sight of Luke and Margot seemed to be a complete shock for him.
'Have you found him?'
'No sorry. Can we come in for a few minutes please?' said Luke.
'Please come in. Excuse the mess.'
He showed them into the living room. Margot noticed all the pictures of Kyle and Shelly.
'Where were you on Sunday? The Sunday before Kyle went missing.'
'Working mostly.'
'On a Sunday?'
'I can't turn work down at the moment. Things are tight, Shelly only works three days a week. I'm paying a mortgage, the rent on Shelly's and double bills. It was a really good job. Five days in total. I worked Saturday through Wednesday on it. Why? Is it important?'
'Where was it?'

'Big house in the countryside outside of Stamfordham.'
'What time did you finish?'
'Late. Just before nine. I dropped Kyle back at home then went home and was back at five in the morning the next day.'
'Kyle was with you?'
'Yes it was my weekend to have him. I know it sounds like a shit weekend coming to work with me but he actually had a great time. The garden and house was massive. And part of my job was to feed the owners cats. They have three. Kyle is obsessed with cats. He played with them for hours in the house and garden.'
'So the owners were away?'
'Yes they wanted all the window frames painted. The kitchen. Master bedroom and living room. Like I said it was a massive job. My mate Frank was supposed to do it but put his back out. He recommended me. There's no way I could turn it down. I promised I'd make it up to Kyle but in the end he had a great time. I literally didn't see him from the time I got there to the time I finished. He wanted to come back with me on Monday. I said no of course he had school.'
'Did Kyle mention he'd seen anything?'
'No why?'
'Another boy is missing. Older than Kyle. He went missing Sunday night from Stamfordham.'
'The boy with the foster parents?'
'Yes you know him?'
'No. I saw it on the news. I don't normally watch the news. But with Kyle missing. I just thought he'd run off. All the news said was concern is growing for a missing teenager who left his foster parents house on Sunday. I don't even think they said Stamfordham. They showed a picture and asked anyone who had seen him to contact you. Do you think it's connected?'
'We have to consider it. But that's just one line of enquiry amongst many.'
'I don't see how it can be. Kyle never left the house or garden. The property is a canny way outside Stamfordham.'
'Are you sure he never left the garden?'
'Kyle is a good kid. I told him not to leave the garden so he wouldn't have done. He knows there aren't many rules as far as me and him goes but what rules I make are non-negotiable.'
'You may well be right, but I think I'm still going to need to check out that house.'

'Sure. I'll write the address down for you. You're not thinking I had anything to do with his disappearance are you? I didn't see him. The other kid that is.'
'No. We just don't like the coincidence of Kyle being near where the other boy disappeared from on the night he disappeared.'
'I just don't see how it can be connected. Shelly doesn't know I took Kyle to work all weekend by the way.'
'Why didn't you tell her?'
'It's not so much Shelly as her bloody mother. I was never good enough. She just makes me feel totally inadequate. The people on the estate think it's Shelly you know. She's gone to stay with her mother. There was shit shoved through the letter box and smeared on the windows this morning. They'd wrote murderer in shit on the window, MURDRER to be precise. Do you think she had something to do with Kyle disappearing?'
'Do you?'
'I don't know. I didn't think so. It's just she was behaving very oddly this morning.'
'How so?'
'She was distant kept pushing me away. Arguing over everything. I left in the end. Drove round looking for Kyle.'
'We will keep in touch.'

Margot waited till they were in the car before she spoke.
'Do you think we should have told him Rory was dead?'
'Not til we know it's Rory for sure. We need DNA confirmation. You're right though Margot, with what we just told him we should give him a heads up before he hears it on the news. What do you make of Shelly's behaviour - suspicious or worried parent?'
'She's also probably wondering if Ben might have raped her. She will be worrying if she brought her son's abductor home with her. Right now she has a lot of reasons to be falling apart.'
'You're right. I'm still not sure about her though. Let's check this house out on Google maps.'

Five Acre House did indeed look like a perfect kids' playground from above. It wasn't overlooked by other dwellings. The house was surrounded by a garden full of trees and even a small maze by the looks of things. Probably about five acres of garden. Hence the name they assumed. Beyond the garden was the road at the bottom and just fields on the other three sides.
'First thing tomorrow let's go there in daylight. I'd say it was a good

five miles from the village. I can't see Rory walking there. It's not near another property. The only thing is the road,' said Luke.
'Are you thinking Kyle saw Rory in a car?'
'Just say for a minute he did. Then he could potentially identify the killer t- hey track him down and take him. The Dad's van is distinctive. He stayed Wednesday night don't forget. The night he finished the job, what if they followed him to Shelly's? Then the killer just waits. Kyle leaves and is grabbed.'
'Why not take him there and then?'
'Rory wasn't dead. They hadn't planned to kill him?'
'I guess it kinda makes sense. Accept that sounds very organised. And not at all like two members of the public that accidentally killed a burglar.'
'You have a point there Margot. Perhaps the burglary gone wrong is not what happened. Rory dealt drugs too. Why did you say two people?'
'The old lady said there were two torches.'
'We need to revisit her at some point too. I'll let the boss know. Then let's go home. I don't know about you, I'm exhausted.'

Margot drove home. She must be tired given how little sleep she'd had but her head was a tombola of ideas being shaken around. She thought if anything they were further from knowing what happened to both Kyle and Rory than when they started. She looked at her watch as she pulled up to her house; a quarter past eleven. She needed to try and sleep - in less than eight hours she would be back in work on what should have been her day off. What should have been a lovely trip to Whitley bay with Mervin. She could do with trying to assemble her thoughts. She wondered if he'd still be up.

She texted him. He rang straight back.
'I was just enjoying a nightcap. I take it you are definitely working tomorrow?'
'Yes sorry.'
'Not to worry; the nature of the job. Another time.'
'Actually I wanted to get your opinion on something'
'Fire away.'
'Firstly Rory goes missing sometime after 6pm on Sunday night. We think he did at least four burglaries in the village where he was staying with foster parents, then he disappeared. I had a dog handler look for the proceeds of those burglaries but she hasn't

found them yet, although she hasn't quite finished. Then Kyle disappears almost immediately after leaving his home address at around 6am on Thursday. He had booked a taxi to go to his Dad's. A very unreliable witness who was taking delivery of some drugs over the garden fence thought he heard a car and stifled scream. Then Kyle's Mum was probably drugged and date-raped by a sex offender who shared a cell with a child abuser. And to cap it all Kyle's Dad was decorating a house right near where Rory went from, with Kyle in tow. We are going to the house first thing but Kyle might have seen Rory and his abductors. Rory is dead - we have his arm, abandoned in a field up near Scots Gap. But no sign of the rest of him and he was kept in a freezer. Rory also deals drugs.'

'That's quite some case Margot. You need to pursue all the lines of enquiry. Sometimes it takes a while for the shape of a case to form. It can seem like you are trying to do a jigsaw puzzle with no idea of what picture you are trying to make and with most of the pieces missing. My advice - don't favour one line of enquiry over another; attack then all. Let the actual evidence direct you. John is the best boss you could hope for Margot. Trust him and learn from him. You will be a great detective one day Margot, but you must remember you are still learning. This isn't all on you.'

Mervin was right. She was the most junior of junior detectives. All she had to do is play her part. Let her boss worry about the bigger picture. Only it wasn't that easy. Margot felt the full weight of the responsibility on her shoulders right now.

They chatted for a while about what else was going on in CID. She could tell Mervin missed the job. She knew he'd be thinking about her case as well now. It was in his blood. Fifteen years of being the boss. A Detective Superintendent on major crimes. He was always fishing for titbits.

She eventually made herself a hot chocolate and headed to bed. It felt like she had fallen asleep minutes before the alarm went off. She hauled herself out of bed and into the shower. She really needed to do something about this shower, it was pathetic. Only a miserly amount of water reached her skin. She would ring a plumber later and treat herself to something like Luke and Tom had in their spare room.

She thought of Shelly. She didn't like her. She had admittedly been jealous in the past of anyone who had kids because she couldn't.

But she was over that, wasn't she? Especially since Emma and Adaeze had moved in next door. Emma had just learned to walk. Adaeze was glad of an extra pair of eyes. Emma loved Margot. Was she angry because she'd felt sorry for Shelly when they'd first met but then she found out she had lied? And worse left Kyle in the house on his own when she - let's face it - went out for sex. She just wanted to shout at her, why would you even do that? If she'd had a child she would have never have left them alone. A child to her would have been the most precious gift. She would have wrapped that child in a protective bubble wrap of love. Don't go near the edge. Don't touch that. Don't talk to anyone. Don't go on the internet. Don't run in case you fall over. Don't be a child. Would she have been a terrible mother? More prison wall than bubble wrap.

She wouldn't have left a nine-year-old on his own of that she was sure. Yet nine-year-olds in Kenya were out herding goats all day. She'd seen it on the Discovery Channel. She remembered Adaeze's gentle words to her the other day when she'd snatched Emma away from a stinging nettle and made her cry: 'Margot she doesn't understand why you won't let her play with that. Let her learn a few things for herself. She will remember they sting forever. We are here to protect her from the bigger dangers in life. I want her to be curious, to learn things for herself as much as possible.'

Margot thought about that now in the shower. Parenting must be complicated. She eventually came to the conclusion that unless you'd lived that life you shouldn't judge it. Her own parents were a classic example of how not to, or to be fair it was mostly her father. The problem was he dominated the house, there were large parts of her childhood where any memory of her mother was completely absent. Nobody can get everything right, it's impossible, she eventually concluded. She still didn't like Shelly.

She knew her boss was looking closely at Shelly. He had sat and read over every one of the interviews Daisy had completed. Shelly was a good liar. What is it they say - practice makes perfect. Margot knew if she wanted to be a good detective she had to make sure her likes and dislikes were not clouding her judgment. However as she dried herself she still wasn't sure if Shelly had told the whole truth yet. Despite all that she still didn't think Shelly had done anything to Kyle. Although doubts were now creeping in on that front.

She looked at the bedside clock. Damn, she thought. She was now running late having spent far too long ruminating in the shower. She hurriedly got dressed, threw some make-up on and rushed out the house. She realised she'd left her job phone. She rushed back in for it. She'd just missed a call from Donna. She sighed and rang her back.

'Hi Donna.'
'Margot I have some gossip for you. You are not going to believe this. Shelly Morgan and Kevin Wallace were seeing each other.'
'When? Are you sure? Who told you that?'
'He's been literally hopping over the garden fence.'
'Was he seen?'
'Yes three weeks ago.'
'I need the name of the witness Donna.'
'Mrs Hind from two doors down. That didn't come from me. Oh and it was Colleen who wrote Murderer on the window in shit. Have you seen the Facebook page?'
'No.'
'Have a look. It says Shelly was arrested for the murder of her kid, there's a picture of her leaving her house with Colleen's artwork in the background. Some of the comments are pretty brutal as to what should be done with her. One said she should be tied up in the town square so the whole town could rape her one by one. Someone else then said: the whole town's slept with her anyway. Then someone else replied: if you slept with this tramp best get yourself checked for STD's.'
'Why would people be that mean?'
'People are mean Margot.'

Margot now felt bad for hating Shelly. The people who wrote those things hated her too.

She arrived in work. She spotted her boss and told him what Donna had said. She showed him the Facebook page.
'Contact the administrator of the page. Get those posts taken down please Margot. Then go and find Luke and go and see this Mrs Hind. If that's true then I question Kevin's motives for mentioning the car and the scream. Luke told me about Five Acre House, visit

that on the way back.'
'Where is Luke?'
'Having a chat with the intelligence officer. Seeing who Rory was associating with.'

Margot grabbed Luke and told him the revised plans.
'Did you get anything from the intelligence officer?'
'He's going to task some informants. Nothing that useful as it stands. There was no doubt Rory was dealing and regularly, but he's bottom end of the chain as far as we know. That fight you walked in on at the Three Stars - which was pretty much Carr HQ - started when a rival dealer came in with ten of his best mates and started pushing his gear in there. It was a blatant challenge. The resident gang soon got wind of it and came mob handed. That area was firmly under the control of the Carrs. Angus Carr was recently convicted for supply along with his main men. The brother Denny is now in control but he's seen as a bit of a limp lettuce. Looks like the Donahues are trying to grab as much as they can while the Carrs are in chaos. The stunt at the Three Stars was pretty much a declaration of war. And the three guys battered to death in the last twenty four hours is probably the opening salvo.'
'Did Rory have anything to do with any of that?'
'Nothing at all that we know of.'
'Perhaps the Donahues were trying to scare Rory off, he was effectively working for the Carrs and something happened.'
'Maybe if he was actually physically dealing on what they now consider to be their patch they'd certainly threaten him. I can't see them tracking him down out to Stamfordham. He's small fry. Not worth the risk or effort. Besides this war kicked off after Rory disappeared. The whole freezer thing isn't the Carrs or Donahues usual thing. We can't rule it out Margot but it's not making sense to me yet.'

They pulled up outside Mrs Hind's. The curtains were still shut. Margot looked at her watch, it was still early she supposed, 8.30 am. They knocked on the door.
'Who is it?' came a timid voice.
'Police,' said Luke.
The door was opened. The lady was fully dressed. Margot had been expecting someone in pyjamas.
'Come in.'
They were led into a living room. Mrs Hind made no effort to open

the curtains. She saw Luke looking at them. It was dark in the living room.
'Sorry the press have been ringing the doorbell constantly. Taking pictures of the Morgan's house. I didn't want to be in the pictures. Is this about Kyle?'
'Yes. There is a rumour going around that Shelly and Kevin Wallace were seeing each other. Can you throw any light on that have you ever seen him going into her house?' said Luke.
Some people just can't lie thought Margot. Her face told them everything. Luke had noticed too.
'Do you want to tell me what you saw?' said Luke.
'I can't give a statement. My house practically backs on to Colleen's.'
'We just need to know what you saw at this point.'
'I saw him hop over the fence about three weeks ago into Shelly's back garden. I saw the garden light up like it does when the back door opens and closes. I thought it couldn't be. No one in their right mind would cross Colleen like that. So I ran to the front of the house. He didn't go into the street. I watched. Sure enough half an hour later the back door opens and closes again. Then Kevin emerges and jumps back over the fence. His hair was wet. Like he'd had a shower.'
'That was the only time?'
'Yes. I didn't say anything to anyone. Then I mentioned it to my husband. He said not to tell anyone. I didn't tell a soul. So it's common knowledge then?'
It will be now Donna knows, thought Margot. Then suddenly realised how Donna knew. She felt sorry for Mrs Hind. She clearly had no idea her husband liked pink.
'May be not common knowledge, but it has been mentioned. We thought we'd try the neighbours see if we could confirm the rumour,' said Margot.

They excused themselves.
'What was that about Margot?'
'The husband… Donna.'
'Oh.'
'So Kevin might have lied. It might have been Shelly all along.'
'Possibly. It's only him that heard that scream. Maybe there was no delivery, no scream. I don't know Margot, he seemed really genuine about that when I spoke to him. I couldn't see a motorcycle on the CCTV when I verified Dan's timeline. But that in itself is

meaningless - there's more than one way out of there. We've asked Division to seize all CCTV from all routes out but I'm not even sure how far they have got. There simply aren't enough hours in the day at the moment.'

'Come on, let's head to Five Acre House. And then pick up the CCTV from Stamfordham before something else happens. I just really want to see that house.'

'Me too.'

As they approached they could see a gardener in the garden mowing the lawn on a sit down mower.

'Well that answers the first question. You can clearly see the road from the bottom of the garden. In theory Kyle could have seen something,' said Luke.

'Should we go in? I don't know why but I'd like to see round the house.'

'I'm not sure we will achieve anything but seeing as we are here we may as well. Thinking about it I guess we should check whether anything is missing.'

'We should check the freezer too.'

They turned in and drove up the drive. A tanned lady answered the door. Skin leathered by countless holidays somewhere nice. Margot noticed she peered rather than looked. She was also impossibly thin. They showed their warrant cards.

'Sorry to bother you. DS Luke Jones, DC Margot Jacks.'

'Luke, Margot, is that you?' came a familiar voice.

Caroline poked her head round the door.

'Caroline! What are you doing here?' said Margot.

'Lucinda is an old friend. I'm reconnecting over coffee and a rather lovely lemon drizzle. More to the point, what are you two doing here? This is Luke and Margot that I told you all about Lucinda.'

'Oh how exciting. Please join us for coffee and cake.'

They were led into the kitchen. Margot looked at the cake and quickly caved. Luke explained why they were here.

'How awful. Please look round if you think it will help.'

'You definitely haven't been burgled?' asked Luke.

'No. At least I'm pretty sure I haven't. It's a big house.'

'It's normally jewellery.'

'No that's all kept in the safe. I keep a few cheaper pieces on my dresser but they are still there.'

Caroline and Lucinda invited themselves along for the search. Lucinda raised an eyebrow when Luke checked the chest freezer in the garage.
'Has anything in here been disturbed?' asked Luke.
'No I don't think so. I don't remember exactly where everything should be but I know those venison steaks and pheasants were definitely on the top.'
The freezer was full. They headed out into the garden and walked towards the road. Margot studied a car going past. You could see right in. If Kyle saw something, chances are they saw him. She looked back up the garden towards the house. Only the top floor was visible. Margot all of a sudden realised her logic was deeply flawed. Tiredness causes mistakes, that's what her boss had said.
'Luke it would have been dark. We forgot to factor in the dark. In the dark you wouldn't see anything.'
'You're right. So for our theory to work something must have happened.'
'Someone knocked the wall over while we were away. The paddock opposite is ours. It was just minor and we have already repaired it,' said Lucinda.
'Can you show us where?'
'Of course. Let's walk round - my days of jumping the wall are long gone.'

They walked to the drive and onto the road.
'Just there, just along from the drive,' said Lucinda pointing towards the spot. Only the flattened grass and a couple of tiny fragments of greyish bodywork evidenced the collision now. Luke collected the fragments of bodywork from the verge and placed them in an evidence bag. He looked back to the drive. A tabby cat jumped over the wall from the paddock, crossed the road and walked up the drive.
'What are you thinking Luke?' asked Margot. She knew that look well by now.
'What if Kyle ran out into the road, maybe following the cat, a car swerves? Crashes into the wall. Kyle sees Rory. Kyle runs off. He doesn't tell his Dad because he's promised to stay in the grounds and he's just caused an accident.'
'It's possible. His Dad said he was cat mad. He maybe tried to stop the cat going onto the road. The car would be going the right way. Away from Stamfordham if it crashed after the drive. It definitely wasn't reported, I checked all the incident logs for the night Rory

disappeared.'

'So the damage would be to the offside of the car. Where were they going though? That's away from Newcastle. They were going north.'

'We can't prove any of that happened though can we?'

'No. But I'd say someone tried to clear up here after the crash. They only missed two tiny fragments.'

'That wasn't us we just rebuilt the wall,' said Lucinda.

'We couldn't prove Mark did all those other murders but we know he did,' said Caroline.

Margot still wasn't sure about that. And Caroline was prone to jumping to conclusions. Margot did think Luke's theory was more than possible though. They searched around in the verges until they were satisfied they had everything. Then headed back to the house for more cake and coffee. They eventually had to say their goodbyes.

'Can we just stop and get the CCTV? I said I would be there ages ago,' said Margot.

'Yes, let's time from here to the village while we are at it.'

Margot timed. Ten minutes. Although she couldn't see how that would help. Because they didn't know what time the accident was, let's face it they didn't know what day. Maybe it would help later. Too far to walk though for sure. She also realised the CCTV might not help either. If the car came and went the same way it probably didn't even pass the camera. Assuming it picked Rory up somewhere near where he'd done the burglaries. Although if it had first come from Newcastle it should have come past the camera. However as they couldn't get registration numbers it wasn't going to get them anywhere quickly. The problem with the village was that there were four ways in and out, which quickly branched into a myriad of single track lanes and permutations.

'We really need a breakthrough, don't we?' said Margot sighing.

At that moment her phone rang. She crossed her fingers. It was the pathologist, the arm belonged to Rory. She already knew that. Luke looked expectantly at her.

'Arm is Rory's. DNA confirmed.'

'You make your own luck in this job most of the time Margot. Let's keep going.'

'Shall we finish the house-to-house whilst we are here too?'

'I'm going to touch base with the boss, then if he's got nothing else for us, yes.'

Margot picked up the download of the CCTV which was all ready for her. The lady looked like she had been waiting for Margot. She was smartly dressed and hovering in the hallway, car keys in hand. Margot suspected she'd probably made her late for something.
'Sorry I have to rush. It's all there as requested. I was talking to Margaret this morning, she's elderly, I keep an eye. I mentioned you kept coming for my CCTV. It may be something or nothing. Her eyesight isn't what it used to be. She said a man walked through her garden last night. That's her address.' said the lady handing Margot a piece of paper as she squeezed past her and picked up her coat from the end of the bannister. Margot got the hint and followed her out the front door.

She'd told Patrick not to go. Did he go anyway, she wondered? Besides, if it was last night what if anything could the connection be? She looked at the address. What was the harm in going? She was surprised when she looked at Google maps; the address backed onto Rory's foster parents' house. Perhaps it was connected after all. She told Luke and they headed straight round.
'Hello Margaret, I am DC Margot Jacks, this is my colleague Luke. I understand you had a prowler last night.'
'I did but I didn't call you. I didn't want to be a bother.'
'It's okay, we were in the village anyway. What time was this?'
'Two thirty in the morning. I couldn't sleep. My hip. I heard the gate squeak. I peeked behind the curtains and a man was standing by the hedge looking at the house opposite. He turned round and I had to hide. I was too scared to look out again after that. I just sat on my bed until it got light.'
'We don't mind if you call us out,' said Margot. 'It's our job. We like to know who's moving around at that time of the morning. What did he look like?'
'I couldn't find my glasses and I didn't want to turn the light on. So I don't know. It was just a shape really.'
'Fat, thin, tall, short?'
'Quite tall I think.'
'Can we check your garden?'
'Can you see yourselves out, my hip really doesn't like this damp cold weather.'
'Of course. Call us if it happens again though please.'

'What do you think Luke?' asked Margot as they stood in the little garden.

'I'm not sure. You can clearly see the upstairs of Rory's house over the hedge. Where was Rory's room?'

'I don't know. I've never actually spoken to the foster parents. There hasn't been time. Mo said they were good people and Kyle was on that CCTV, leaving just like they said.'

'Did Mo search his room?'

'Yes. And no mobile phone. According to the social worker he didn't have one. On account they took it off him because he was using it to deal drugs. That was four weeks ago.'

'We still need that phone. And he would have got himself another phone I'm sure. A burner probably.'

'Maybe not. The fence said Kyle rang him from the foster parents' to say he was running away.'

'Did you confirm if that was a landline?'

'No. Sorry I just assumed.' Margot realised she'd made a mistake.

'It's okay Margot. You have done a good job on this so far considering how little time you've had. But this is now a murder enquiry. We check and double check everything. Let's go and see these foster parents now. Besides I'm guessing the boss will want them to know about the arm being Rory's. I'll quickly run it by him.'

They knocked on the door. It was opened by Mrs Ward. Luke did the introductions.

'Please come in. Any news?'

'Yes. Unfortunately we believe Rory has been murdered. An arm has been recovered that has just been confirmed as his.'

'Oh God. Just an arm? Do you know how he died?'

'No not yet. We need to ask you a few questions. Was Rory in contact with anyone?'

'I'm sure he was, but without my knowledge. He had only been with us two weeks. I've been fostering for over twenty years, Detective. Rory was never going to stay put here. Social services were trying to put a little distance between him and his friends. Given his friends are all heavily involved in using and selling drugs. Forgive me for being cynical, but fifteen miles was never going to be enough. To get through to a kid like Rory takes a lot of time.'

'On Sunday before he left did he phone anyone from here?'

'I don't think so. Although I can't be sure. I was cooking dinner. Sunday is always treat night so it was homemade pizzas. Rory had anger management issues. He is taught online. Given he's been expelled from his school. We had had an argument about him doing his homework about five o' clock. He stormed up to his room. Then he shouted he was going for a walk to clear his head, that was about six. The last thing I shouted after him was 'pizza's at seven'. Seven o'clock is also the time we agreed with social services he should be in the house. I rang them when he wasn't back. They said give him to half seven if he wasn't back to ring you and report him missing. I rang you at quarter to eight. An officer from nightshift attended at about half ten to take the report.'

'Do you mind if I check his room?'
'You can. Although I've been in and cleaned.'
'Did he take anything with him?'
'No. He hardly came with anything. Social services provided a laptop for lessons that's still here. In terms of personal possessions he didn't really have anything.'

The room was nicer than Margot had expected. For some reason she was thinking Victorian workhouse and ravens. There was a Newcastle United bedspread and posters. A TV. A huge bean bag.
'They said he was a big Newcastle fan. We did our best to make him welcome.'
Margot and Luke looked out the window onto the old lady's garden. Luke opened the bedside drawers then checked the wardrobe.
'We will need the laptop social services gave him.'
'Of course, it's under the bed. The drawer pulls out.'

The only thing in the drawer was the laptop. Luke lifted it out and felt around inside the drawer.
'Just one other thing - was anyone hanging around that shouldn't have been prior to Rory going missing?'
'No. At least I don't think so. And normally if someone so much as parks funny it's all over the Neighbourhood Watch WhatsApp group.'
'Okay thank you. We will leave you in peace,' said Luke.
Margot knew the Neighbourhood Watch clocked off at bedtime.

They headed back and sat in the car. Luke rang the DI again and told him about the figure in the garden. Margot tried to think what it could all mean.

'Boss wants us to focus on the angle Rory upset someone, and Kyle saw Rory's abductors. Given the prowler last night he's wondering if the prowler is trying to retrieve something. Oh, and your dog handler didn't find the proceeds from those burglaries that Rory committed on the night he disappeared. He wants us to search the foster parents' house thoroughly, top to bottom, garden and all. He sending a drugs dog over.'

Margot felt terrible as they knocked on Mrs Ward's door again. Luke explained they were working off a theory that Rory may have hidden something that didn't belong to him. She didn't seem to mind the intrusion. It occurred to Margot that if they were right she'd probably want whatever it was out of her house anyway, given it probably got Rory killed. It also occurred to Margot the figure in the garden could have been Patrick and this could be a wild goose chase. She headed to the bathroom and locked the door. She messaged him. He replied straight away: 'not me.'

Despite the drugs dog climbing over, under, into and onto everything, sniffing, tail wagging impossibly fast, all it found was a small bag of cannabis hidden in the mattress. Luke and Margot searched the whole house. Nothing. Margot looked at her watch; another two hours and no further forward.
'Wouldn't he have taken whatever it was with him anyway,' said Margot.
'Very probably Margot, but we couldn't assume that.'
'So what next?'
'Let's head back to the station. We can see if the FIO* has turned up any whispers. I think we need to make a start on the CCTV too.'
'I don't mind doing that - seeing as I've already started it I know where I'm at.'

Margot

'Margot you will be pleased to know I've found someone to do the CCTV. Tracy - she's a detective from Division on light duties. I've already set her away,' said John, just as Margot opened the door to the office. Margot tried to look normal but ended up sashaying into the room like the exiting queen on Rue Paul's Drag Race. The DI looked at Margot and shook his head.

She sat at her desk. She should come clean now, it would be better, wouldn't it? She stood up intending to go and find her boss. Then it struck her if she came clean now it would look like she had only come clean because she had too. Because she was about to be caught out. She sat back down. The camera only showed them walking down the road. Like Patrick said, at that point they hadn't done anything wrong. She hadn't hid the fact to Luke she'd sought Patrick's advice. She didn't want to drag Luke into this. She was starting to feel sick when Luke walked in.
'Are you okay Margot?'
'Yes just tired I think. Anything from the FIO?'
'Not really. The turf war is hotting up but silence on the Rory front. I'd like to talk to the guy that ambushed you in the back alley.'
'I don't know who he is.'
'I've a possible from the FIO. A handler who used to do a lot of business in the Three Stars before everything kicked off.'
'Shall we go now?'
'Early morning wake up call I think. I have an address, I'll give uniform a shout for a bit of back up. I'll run it by the boss first.'

Luke walked over to John's office and shut the door. Margot imagined they were talking about her. When Luke emerged looking concerned she was nearly sick there and then.
'Everything okay?'
'Yeah.'

Margot waited for more but Luke just forced a smile and said 'boss wants us to speak to that old lady who saw the torchlights in the woods. Come on, let's head up there now.'
Margot's legs felt wobbly. Her mind kept going backwards and forwards like an indecisive pheasant crossing the road. Come

clean. Say nothing. Come clean. Say nothing. Say a bit. Say nothing. Say something.

They arrived at the lady's cottage.
'What's she called Margot?' asked Luke.
'I don't know. Sorry. She's a bit odd. You try, I wasn't really getting through. There is a bit of an ongoing feud with the old guy next door. Local have stopped attending because she calls about his chickens in her garden and such like. So we are not exactly flavour of the month.'

Luke knocked on the door. It was half opened.
'He's got some cheek I'll give him that. I warned him plenty of times about those cows making too much noise. No harm done, all I did was open the gate, let them out. Let them make that noise somewhere else. No crime in that.' The door was slammed in their faces. Luke knocked again.
'She won't answer it,' said Margot.
'What was that all about?'
'The farmer's cows - she complained about the noise they make first thing in the morning.'
'Is she…all there?'
'I don't know. Both the farmer and neighbour said take what she says with a pinch of salt. Although the neighbour certainly stokes the fire,' said Margot.
Luke knocked again. He shouted through the letter box. 'We just need to ask about the torch light you saw.'
'The badger baiters,' added Margot stooping to shout through the letter box too. They both stood there.

'She's really not going to answer is she,' said Luke more by way of statement than question. Margot shook her head.
'I feel we've had a completely wasted day,' said Luke.
'Not completely. We know whoever took Rory probably damaged their car. Can we do anything with those bits of bumper?'
'Do we though Margot? It's all supposition at the moment. We have absolutely nothing concrete. I'll see if the boss will authorise sending the fragments of bodywork away, I can't see it, let's face it, it could just be a drunk driver for all we know.'

They must have something concrete, but Margot went through everything in her mind. They didn't she realised.

Margot

She drove home still worrying about the CCTV. There was really only one person she could ask what to do. The person who already knew. She sat in her kitchen and called Patrick.

'Patrick I'm really worried about the CCTV. My boss has given it to another detective to do. What if they find you on the CCTV?'
'I told you they won't ID me. I'm pretty sure I avoided all the cameras anyway.'
'But you and me are walking down the road together.'
'And you were doing your job investigating a missing child. If anyone asks, you left a message for me to meet you there to ask if I knew who his handler was. I didn't. That's a completely legitimate line of enquiry.'
'Okay. Have you heard anything else on the grapevine?'
'No but I haven't been asking. I can nip back and talk to his handler if you want, I think he's been asking around.'
'No need, I've got that in hand.'
'Don't worry Margot.'
'So do you think I should mention we are on the CCTV?'
'No. That makes it look like you think it's worth mentioning.'

Margot thought she understood what he meant. She said goodbye. She'd lost her appetite, a sure sign she was still worrying. She heated up some tomato soup and just about managed to eat half of it. She moved to the sofa and grabbed a pen and paper. She wrote down all the important things they had found out and put circles round them. She kept drawing a circle round one: Kevin and Shelly? The circle was becoming thicker and thicker.

Margot fell asleep on the sofa. She was woken by her phone ringing. It was 1a.m. She looked at the screen, it was Donna.
'Margot I need your help. Kevin Wallace has had a heart attack. He's dead.'
'How do you know this?'
'I'm looking at him.'
'Call an ambulance.'
'I can't, he's in my bed. Colleen can't find out.'
'Donna you can't cover up a death.'

'I'm not covering up a death. He just can't be naked in my bed when he's found.'
'Are you sure he's dead, have you tried CPR?'
'He looks dead.'
'Donna I have to call this in.'
'Please Margot, you know what she's like. She will burn my house down with me in it.'
'Start CPR, you might be able to save him, I'll call an ambulance. I'm on my way.'

Margot dialled 999. 'Bloody hell Donna,' she said out loud as she rushed out to her car.
'Which service?'
'Ambulance.'

Margot arrived to see Kevin being put into the back of an ambulance, face hidden under an oxygen mask. Donna was standing in the door. Curtains twitched up and down the street.
'Is he dead?' Margot asked Donna.
'I'm not sure. They said something about ventricular fibrillation. I don't know if that's good or bad.'
Margot didn't either.
'What happened?'
'He came knocking. He'd been on the coke that much was obvious. He said Colleen had thrown him out, she'd found out about Shelly. I felt sorry for him, I let him in. I took him upstairs. One thing led to another. He was on top then he kind of fell off. He was clutching his chest. The look on his face - it was so desperate Margot, like he knew that was it. I called you straight away. I did the CPR. The ambulance crew said I did well. They shocked him and they have just put him in the ambulance.'
The ambulance put the blue lights and sirens on and sped off, making both Donna and Margot jump.
'Donna I have to let my boss know, Kevin is an important witness in Kyle's disappearance. I'm sorry.'
'It's alright Margot. The cat is probably already out the bag. I honestly thought he was dead.'
'Sorry I have to ask - was he a client?'
'No. We were a thing a long time ago before Colleen. I never let him in when he was with Colleen, only when he wasn't. I think he regretted getting involved with Colleen.'
'He told you that?'

'No he didn't need to. How does that song go? "You can check out any time but you can never leave." Being part of the Nolan clan is like that. He was stuck. You know what Colleen and her brothers are like Margot, in her mind he would always be hers.'
'Can you stay somewhere else Donna?'
'I have nowhere else to go Margot.'

Margot moved away and rang Luke and explained what had happened.
'Are you sure it's medical only Margot?'
'Donna said he'd been on the coke.'
'Okay I'll ask Division to attend. We at least need to search her house, make sure she didn't supply the drugs. Why did she ring you Margot?'
'I think she panicked. She didn't know what to do. I rang the ambulance so she could do CPR.'
'Okay stay there with her until Division arrive. Then go home.'

Margot did. She felt a little guilty about abandoning Donna as she drove home. Donna could look after herself, she told herself by way of making herself feel better. Margot didn't really want to be her friend. She wondered if she was being too mean. Before Margot joined the police she hadn't had friends either. She hadn't liked it. Perhaps she should make more of an effort. Perhaps she shouldn't - as a police officer she would have to declare any association with Donna. How could she be a friend under those circumstances?

Margot arrived home and immediately headed to bed. The clock on her bedside cabinet said 3am in radioactive green letters. Her alarm was already set for 5am. They were knocking on the fence's door at 6am. Margot felt overwhelmed. She started to cry. This was impossible, she was exhausted. She didn't sleep.

Margot

DI Hall was waiting for her as she yawned her way into the office. 'Margot you didn't need to attend last night. You should have just called it in. Attending incidents when you are off duty isn't something I can condone. Especially when a key witness is involved. Call me or Luke first if you are unsure what to do. I don't want to put pen to paper and give you an official warning, but if it happens again you are going to force my hand.'
'Sorry Sir.'
'Why did you go?'
'Donna was scared, I don't think she has any friends.'
'Margot you can't be her friend, you must be impartial. You have to be a detective and only a detective. Kevin Wallace is in ICU and it doesn't look like he's going to make it. Which is unfortunate to say the least because we needed to speak to him again.'
'Donna said Colleen knows about Shelly. And she must know about Donna by now. She will do something Sir, I don't think either of them are safe.'
'Do you really think she will try and kill them, Margot?'
'I think she will do something crazy like burn their houses down.'
'Why?'
'It's just who she is, Sir.'
'Okay, I'll issue Osman notices* to Shelly and Donna. Division can keep an eye and have a word with Colleen. Come on, let's go and put this door in, if nothing else we should recover drugs and some stolen gear. Bring the list of the items Rory stole from Stamfordham, I want to make damn sure those items aren't there.'
'Yes Sir.'

Gavin Mason's house was on the top floor of a block of flats. Probably by design the lift didn't work and the stairs were an obstacle course of shopping trolleys. Plenty of time to get rid of whatever stash of drugs he had. Luke knocked on the door, warrant in hand. The door was opened straightaway by a smiling Gavin. The drugs dog despite going ballistic found nothing. Neither did the search team.
'He knew we coming, that's for sure,' said John to Luke and Margot.
'I don't see how he could have,' said Luke.
'Margot do you think this is the guy that you spoke to in the alley?'

asked John.

'I'm not sure. It would help if I actually spoke to him Sir.'

'Go and speak to him. He might speak to you. If he doesn't, Luke you try next.'

Margot headed into the kitchen where he was sat at the small table.

'Thanks for the tip off Margot,' he whispered.

What tip off, thought Margot. Patrick! Shit. At that moment Margot felt like she was in an iron lung where someone had sat on the dial and all the air was being sucked out of her. Her stomach developed a heartbeat. Then she suddenly became very hot, she itched under her arms.

'Are you okay?' Gavin asked.

'Yes, is it warm in here?'

'No bloody freezing. Are you having one of them hot flushes? Me Mum gets them. She says it's cos of the bloody menopause.'

Margot wondered how old Gavin thought she was. The lack of sleep wasn't helping her complexion, but even so did she look old enough for the menopause? She consoled herself with the fact Gavin probably had no idea how old you had to be, and some people did start at 43 or younger. She tried to pull herself back to the task at hand.

'Gavin, Rory has been murdered. So far we have only recovered part of him. I really need your help. Had Rory fallen out with anyone? Was anyone after him? Did he maybe take something from someone? Shortchange a dealer maybe?'

Margot noticed Gavin looked really upset. Perhaps she should have broken the news a little more sensitively. He didn't say anything for a while. Margot was about to ask another question when he spoke.

'No. Rory was okay you know. He used, used since he was six. He swapped the stuff he stole for drugs. Used most of it, if he had any left he'd usually sell it in The Three Stars.'

'So you're saying he wasn't dealing dealing. The drugs he sold were effectively his already.'

'Yeah.'

'Could he have been holding drugs for someone? Or money?'

'I don't know everything he did, but I know if someone was looking for Rory they would come ask me where he was.'

'Why?'

'Rory is my cousin. He's family. I looked out for him.'

'Was Rory close to anyone else?'

'Only Aidan Daniels, but he OD'd a week ago on Ket*. Couldn't

leave his flat without pissing himself in the end.'
'Was Rory on Ket?'
'Probably if Aidan was. He asked me for it, I said no.'
'You don't sell Ket?'
'I don't sell any drugs,' said Gavin smiling. 'Look he was my cuz. I wouldn't give him Ket.'
'Do you think he was using Ket though?'
'Probably. I hadn't seen him as much as I usually did lately; we kinda fell out over Aidan. I knew he was hanging out with him and I told him divn't. When social services put Rory out in Stamfordham I was secretly happy cause Aidan was bad news for Rory. All he did was go from fix to fix and walk round like the living dead in between. Then he calls me and says he hates it at the new foster parents cos it was really boring and he'll be round later. He never showed. I asked around everywhere and nay one had seen him. I knew sommat had happened.'
'The number he called you on, was it landline or mobile?'
'Mobile, the one I give him for emergencies.'
'I'll need that number.'
'Sure but it's been dead since that night.'
'Gavin do you have any ideas at all?'
'I doesn't. That's why I told yous that night he was missing. Cause I wanted yous to take it seriously. I knew you would just think he'd run off again otherwise.'
'Okay thanks Gavin.'
'I can't be talking to you but if I hear anything I'll tell Patrick' he whispered.

Margot hoped Luke and her DI couldn't hear any of that. She needn't have worried, they were busy going through the bins in the communal area. A lone uniformed officer was standing guard on the door. She went down to relay what Gavin had said, leaving out the bit about Patrick of course.
'Okay Margot let's take that at face value for now. It's a blow-out here. Go and check this Aidan's flat, make sure Rory isn't holed up there or overdosed on the floor, then reconvene at the station. Let's go over where we are at, come up with a plan of action for today.'

Margot and Luke drove to Aidan's flat. The housing association were in the process of putting everything inside in a bag to incinerate. The two guys with the unfortunate task were wearing full PPE including respirators. Luke collared one of them.

'DS Luke Jones. Was the place secure when you arrived?'
'Yeah, we boarded it up after the occupant overdosed. Was still boarded up this morning. No one in their right mind would have broken in here mate.'
Luke made a quick phone call.

'He was found on the Friday before Rory went missing. Although he had been lying undiscovered for a few days. So if it was boarded up after his body was recovered, Rory didn't come here.'
'Gavin said Rory used drugs. I get the impression Gavin only gave him cannabis. I think Rory was selling his excess cannabis and using the cash to buy harder drugs. We should track down the person supplying him with the harder drugs. Gavin suspected Rory had started on the Ketamine.'
'Are you thinking Aidan's dealer?'
'Maybe. Gavin doesn't know of anyone who was trying to find Rory. Perhaps he was out of the loop. Perhaps Rory owes Aidan's dealer.'
'It's a possibility. The questions certainly need to be asked. Rory had got himself into something, that much I'm certain of. Did Gavin say how Rory knew Aidan? This is Forrest Hall, a canny way from Gavin in Blakelaw.'
'Rory was in foster care all over.'
'True. And I'm guessing Gavin wouldn't know what's happening on these streets. It's a good idea Margot. I've got a mate that works here, let me give him a quick ring.'

Luke made another phone call.
'Apparently a good place to start would be Nibbles. Josh Dennis. Taxi driver.'

It didn't take Luke and Margot long to find Nibbles. He was parked outside the kebab shop. Margot rarely met anyone she could beat in a foot race but this would no contest. Nibbles flesh actually wobbled in a wave around his body when he moved. His face was almost lost to his weight.
'How shall we play this?' asked Margot.
'I bet if we searched that taxi we'd find something, but I'm also guessing he'd lawyer up and we'd get nothing out of him but at least we could search his house. I can't see a better way at the moment.'
'If he's selling Ketamine to kids, I think we should arrest him

anyway.'
'We can't prove he sold to Rory and Aidan was eighteen.'
'He may as well have murdered Aidan.'
'Okay I'll get the boss to check we are not standing on anyone's toes and then we will search the taxi.'

Just as Luke called the DI Nibbles got back in his taxi, kebab in hand and drove off. Margot took the phone off Luke and Luke started to follow the taxi.
'Sir we are following Nibbles, can you check if he's subject of any ongoing op please?'
'Margot who is Nibbles?' asked John.
'Josh Dennis. Taxi driver. Possibly Aidan's Ket dealer. He's eating a kebab at the moment.'
'Stand by… plenty of intelligence to suggest he is dealing but the taxi has been stopped several times and nothing found. He's not currently subject of any op.'
'Okay thanks Sir…Did you hear all that?' Margot asked Luke as she hung up.
'Yes. Let's just follow for a bit, we can't stop him in a plain car anyway.'

Nibbles drove about two hundred yards from the kebab shop, stopped by the small mini-mart and picked up a fare. A hundred yards further down the road the fare got out. He then did a u-turn.
'That was odd. Turn around quick Luke, we are going to lose him.'
'I can't turn round here, he'll know we are following him. Besides I think I know where he's gone.'
Margot didn't have a clue. Luke drove further on then turned and headed back.
'As I thought,' said Luke. The car was back outside the kebab shop. Luke drove past.
'Aren't we going to search the car Luke?'
'No point Margot. The drugs are in the kebab shop.'
The penny finally dropped for Margot.
'I'll get the boss to get a warrant for the kebab shop. Division can hit it tonight,' said Luke.

Margot realised it was going to be another late night. She really needed a week in Majorca never leaving the poolside. The excitement now over Margot was struggling to keep her eyes open on the drive back to the police station. The next thing she knew

Luke was shaking her awake and they were parked in the bays in the compound of the police station.

'Sorry,' she said.

'Margot you look exhausted. I'll have a word with the boss. Go home early tonight, get a good night's sleep.'

'No I want to help. We will need to interview the drug dealers from the kebab shop.'

'In the morning Margot. The drug case will need to be dealt with first. At the moment we have no evidence they were involved with Rory. Firstly we need to find out who is involved. What vehicles they have access to and if any of those vehicles are on the CCTV.'

'Or damaged,' added Margot starting to worry all over again about the CCTV.

Margot's mind wouldn't focus as she sat with the DI and Luke thrashing out lines of enquiry. When the DI closed the meeting with 'okay I think we know what we have to do', Margot didn't have the slightest idea.

She walked out with Luke.

'Are you okay trying to have another go at the old lady, Margot? While I pull the file on Aidan's death.'

'Sure.'

Margot set off for Scott's Gap. It was never a good sign when you arrived somewhere and couldn't remember getting there. The old lady was in the garden. Great, thought Margot, I'll stand between her and her door. Margot noticed she was scrubbing chicken droppings off her path with a brush and bucket of soapy water.

'See. See. It's a health hazard. I've read all about bird flu, humans can get it. Did you know that? Perhaps you will take me seriously when I'm dead.'

Margot just wasn't in the mood.

'I'm sorry I don't have time to deal with the bloody chicken shit. I just don't have enough hours in my day. And I've wasted enough of those hours trying to speak to you. The reason I can't deal with your chickens is because a child was murdered and another one is missing. I just care more about kids than chicken shit.'

The old lady looked at Margot.

'I don't know anything about that.'

'But you might. The torchlight you thought was badger baiters - it wasn't badger baiters, it might be connected.'

'I didn't see anyone. You can see how far away the woods are, it was dark.'
'Where exactly were the lights?'
'In the woods, smack bang in the middle, big torches they lit up the whole trees. I called my daughter and then I shut the bedroom window and closed the curtains, turned the light out and went to bed.'

Margot looked at the woods. If she could see the torchlight, could they have seen the light go out? Would that be enough to spook whoever it was?
'Are you sure it was two separate torchlights?'
'Yes one was still, the other moved around.'
'Did you ever see both move at the same time?'
'No. One was just a light, the other was running around like a crazy person was on the end of it.'
Margot tried to concentrate and work out what it could mean. Had the person suddenly realised the arm was missing and panicked. She decided to take a walk up to the woods and immediately cussed, realising she'd not bought sensible footwear again.
'Do you have a pair of wellingtons I can borrow?' she asked.
'Inside the door, help yourself.'
There were a selection. Margot chose the pink pair.
'Do you like them?' the old lady asked.
'Yes.'
'Keep them, they are hideous. My daughter bought them for me.'
'Thank you.'

Margot drove to the head of the lane and set off across the fields. She squelched through the mud with ease. She grabbed hold of a fence post and stood on the bottom wire of a barbed wire fence and immediately started to swing back and forward. She held on tighter and rather hopefully flung one leg over. She slipped and ripped her trousers. A triangle of fabric hung between her legs. Bollocks, thought Margot, noticing her thigh was also bleeding. She soldiered on.

She wasn't sure exactly what she was looking for. The woods after all had been searched. She headed for what she reckoned was the middle, she couldn't see the old ladies house for the trees. Middle wouldn't be middle-middle she realised. It would be edge-of-woods-middle. She headed back to the edge of the woods. The cottages were clearly visible across the fields. She searched around for signs of digging. For an arm-sized hole. Her foot suddenly disappeared from under her. She excitedly removed the dead leaves and branches. A small grave was revealed. She took a photograph. Did this help? It was arm-sized so had the person only had the arm? Margot tried to picture what had happened. The person put the arm down to dig the hole. Set up a torch to illuminate the hole. Finishes digging goes to get the arm from where he put it down and it's gone. He grabs the spare torch from his pocket and looks for it. So it could be just one person after all thought Margot. It certainly didn't look like the fox had dug it up it looked like someone had hurriedly kicked stuff in the hole. Did any of this actually help? She rang Luke and sent him the picture.

'With the time elapsed and weather, I doubt forensics will get anything but I'll run it by the boss. Hold on,' he said.

Luke rang her back 'Boss said preserve the scene wait for forensic. He doesn't think there is a cat in hell's chance of anything, but we have to try.'
Margot waited. She was getting cold, the draught round her crotch not helping. She couldn't go back to the office like this. Perhaps the old lady would lend her something to wear. Although Margot had to concede they were totally different shapes. Eventually CSI's arrived. Margot had discovered if she kept her legs clamped together the tear didn't show. She stood rooted to the spot whilst she briefed the CSI's. Then shuffled away making another complete hash of climbing over the barbed wire fence. She ripped the back this time.

Margot headed back to the old lady's. She was bound to have a sewing kit. The old lady was back inside. She knocked on the door. At least she answered.
'I've ripped my trousers, do you have a sewing kit?'
'Those are ruined. I have a skirt you can borrow.'
'I don't expect it will fit me.'
'Did I say it was mine? It was my mother's, she was your size.'

Margot looked at the skirt as she pulled back into the police station. She wondered if she could make it to her locker without being seen. Unlikely. She was dressed in the most ridiculous skirt she'd ever seen. The old lady's mother must have been colour blind, obsessed with period dramas and never went out, Margot concluded. She wished she'd kept her ripped pants on. She would have changed back but the old lady had already binned them. She had an idea she rang Luke.

'Luke, are you in the station? I need you to get me a spare pair of trousers from my locker.'

'Sorry Margot, I'm speaking to the officer who attended Aidan's sudden death. I'm not in the station.'

'Not to worry.'

Margot sighed. She got out the car and rushed to the door. It opened before she got there. The Chief Constable was just walking out.

'Hello Margot, why are you wearing that skirt?'

Margot's mind went blank. Never a good sign.

'There's definitely mice in the station Sir,' said Margot as she ran through the door. Gathered up her skirts and ran as fast as she could up the stairs to her locker.

She wrestled the skirt into her locker and hurriedly shut it in before it sprang back out. She couldn't help thinking the old lady had got the last laugh. She headed to the office.

'So Margot, I guess your hole strongly suggests she was telling the truth about the torchlight. Can you to do a CCTV sweep? All routes in and out of those woods, find me a camera on all routes if you can. We probably have a reasonably accurate timeline to go off if she went to bed at ten. Good work Margot. Have you changed your trousers?'

'Yes boss, I snagged them on barbed wire.'

'When you've done that go home Margot. Get some sleep. Start fresh in the morning.'

'Thanks Sir.'

Margot was pleased to head back out. She could return the skirt at the same time. She released it from her locker, manhandled it through the station like a drunk under arrest and shoved it in the boot of the car.

CCTV was thin on the ground. Margot managed to find a couple of doorbell cameras and one mounted on the side of a farm outfitters. It was far from the CCTV net the DI was hoping for. She downloaded everything and headed back to the station. She was about to start watching them when the DI came through.

'Go home Margot. Give them to Tracy to do as well.'
Margot looked at her watch. 6pm. She had put a full shift in already, but she felt guilty for leaving. She had to admit she desperately needed a good night's rest though. She headed to find Tracy. She didn't know her. She found her stuck in the digital evidence suite, coffee cup in hand. She was watching the screen Margot recognised the view. It was the camera her and Patrick had walked past. Tracy looked very efficient.
'Hi I'm Margot. Sorry, more CCTV for you.'
'It's okay, the Boss has already briefed me. I'll prioritise this.'
'Anything interesting so far from the CCTV the Boss collected from Stamfordham?'
'Just logging everything, nothing exciting as far as I can tell. I've got a tame traffic officer helping me out. Identifying make and models of the vehicles.'
'Great. What days are you doing?'
'Just the Sunday he went missing so far is done. I'm now doing the night the arm was disposed of.'
'Okay thanks. What about the prowler at the back of Rory's foster parents?'
'On my list.'

Margot headed out. She drove home. She plonked in front of the TV and tried to eat a microwave meal, she barely touched it. She couldn't concentrate on the TV. She normally liked The One Show. She went in search of chocolate. She opened the cupboard. She spotted her sleeping pills still in the police evidence bag Metcalfe had put them in. The use-by date would have long passed. She knew she wouldn't sleep without them tonight despite the exhaustion. She didn't want to go back to those days. She opened a bottle of wine and watched more TV.

She had a bath. It was only half past eight but she decided to go to bed. She lay there for an hour worrying about CCTV, about Patrick tipping off Gavin, of where Kyle was. She got up and took the sleeping tablets out of the evidence bag. She took three and flushed the rest down the toilet. She got back into bed and she did sleep.

The 685 to Newcastle was driving over the river bridge at Corbridge when the passengers on the top deck noticed a body floating down the Tyne. Face down. A pink puffer jacket and pink leggings all that was visible. There was a flurry of activity on mobile phones. Chris Greener, a part-time fireman, ran down the stairs and demanded to be let off the bus. He rushed to the wall of the bridge and watched the body float under. Too much water to even think about attempting any sort of rescue. He bolted behind the bus which was just setting off again and watched the body, rocked by the current, speed from under the bridge. He rang 999. He ran to the south bank of the river and tried to chase after the pink body. As he broke free of the trees onto the grounds of the Tynedale rugby club he saw pink again. He quickened his pace. The body was heading for some debris in the river next to a small island. The puffer jacket snagged on a branch. He waited for the emergency services to arrive.

Margot

Margot woke up. She didn't exactly feel like she was raring to go. Had it not been for the bottle of wine she might well have felt better, considering she'd been out for the count for ten hours. She glanced at her phone. Three missed calls from Donna. She headed for the shower then straight to work without breakfast, eager to find out all about the kebab shop.

Luke and the DI were already in.
'We hit the jackpot with the kebab shop Margot. The bosses are over the moon,' said Luke.
'Have you asked about Rory yet?'
'Not yet. They should be getting charged with possession with intent to supply shortly. CID are just waiting on authority from the CPS. Then it's our turn. Unfortunately none of the vehicles we know they have access to were caught in Stamfordham on the CCTV. Not even any of their taxi driver dealers. So we can't arrest them, there's absolutely nothing to connect them to Rory or Aidan.'
'They won't talk to us will they?'
'I doubt it. But their reaction might be interesting.'

Margot checked her phone. Donna hadn't left her a message. She'd rung three times around 3am. Margot couldn't be her friend. She didn't call her back. Margot and Luke twisted in their chairs until they got the thumbs up to speak to the kebab shop owner and staff. Then at the last second the DI swooped in and said he'd go with Luke. Margot was really disappointed.

Luke

The gaoler opened the cell door. Luke peered in.
'DI Hall, DS Jones. We need to ask you about a missing child. Rory Elliott, do you know him?' said John from behind him.
'Where's my brief?'
'In bed I should think. He was up half the night with you. It's a simple question, you are not under arrest. Do you know him?'
'No.'
'Aidan Daniel's friend. Fourteen-year-old foster kid.'
'I don't know him.'
They shut the cell door.
'That one wasn't the least bit worried,' said DI Hall.

They tried the other two. Both said they didn't know him.
'I actually believe them Boss.'
'Me too, they weren't the slightest bit worried. So according to the word on the street no one was looking for Rory. Where does that leave us?'
'I guess back with the burglary that went wrong.'
'Take a good look at Gavin for me too. That flat was too clean.'
'Would he draw attention to himself by ambushing Margot the way he did Boss if Rory had actually made it to his place? And what about the man watching the foster parents house?'
'You are probably right. Ask around anyway. He was too smug the morning we searched his flat. Speak to him without Margot being there.'
'Why Boss?'
'I think he sees Margot as a soft touch.'
The DI's phone vibrated.
'Tracy. She's got something,' he said.

Luke and the DI headed up to the digital evidence room.
'What have you got Tracy?' said John.
'Car on the camera from the farm fitters that Margot found. Image is not great because the camera isn't set up for the road, it's dark and there's no street lighting. I'll show you. It's a dark Range Rover I think. No view of the driver. Goes past the camera towards the woods at 21.35, back at 22. 29, at least I think it's the same vehicle. Of course there is no guarantee it went anywhere near the woods. This camera is a good ten minutes away and you would have to turn off that road.'

They watched, it was frustrating the camera was clearly positioned to record anything driving down the drive. All it showed was the bottom half of a car flashing across the screen, headlights and taillights further distorting what was already poor quality CCTV.
'Where is this camera?' asked Luke.
Tracy brought up google maps. 'Here I think, check with Margot.'
'Why Luke?'
'Well if you were coming from Newcastle and you knew where you were going there's a quicker way to get to the woods. It's just if our theory about Kyle seeing Rory in the car is right, they weren't taking Rory back to Newcastle then either. Whoever it was was heading north, away from Newcastle. If he was in a freezer that suggests somewhere with power. I'm even more convinced now our theory Rory fell foul of the drug dealers is completely wrong.'
'Oh, and I have your prowler walking down the street. Let me get it up for you,' said Tracy 'Don't get too excited Boss. It doesn't capture his face.'
'That's Dan Morgan, Kyle's Dad,' said Luke.
'I think you're right Luke. What the hell was he doing out there at half one in the morning?'
'Probably looking for his son. He knows about Rory.'
'Go and speak to him, verify it's him. Christ.'

Margot

Margot was waiting for Luke.
'I think the prowler was Dan, we need to verify that with him,' said Luke.
'And the drug dealers?' asked Margot.
'They said they don't know Rory. I'm inclined to believe them but it's still an open line of enquiry.'
'So we are back to burglary gone wrong.'
'I think so. Possibility a Range Rover might have dumped the arm. Dark-coloured, caught on the farm fitters' camera.'
'The GP had a Range Rover although it was white. They had three cars actually.'
'It definitely wasn't white. I'll show you the image when we get back, but first let's go and see Dan.'

Dan was at home.
'Dan is this you?' Asked Luke showing him a still from the CCTV.
'Yes.'
'What we're you doing in Stamfordam?'
'What do you think? Looking for Kyle.'
'Did you go to the back of the foster parents' house, through a private garden?'
'Yeah. Arrest me if you want.'
'You can't do that. We've just wasted another two days trying to find out who that was, in case he was connected with your son's disappearance. You are not helping.'
'He's dead isn't he?'
'I haven't given up hope yet,' said Luke.
'They told me the other kid is dead.'
'Yes that's true. How did you know where the foster parents lived?'
'Frank, my mate. I figured they would need a painter and decorator if they had lots of kids going through. I was right, Frank knew them.'
'You need to leave this to us Dan.'
'And how's that going? I'm sorry, I know you are trying your best but I've had absolutely no progress report from you at all. So I'm assuming you have sweet FA. He's my son, if you think I'm going to sit on my arse and do nothing but wait you are wrong.'
'Then at least tell us what you are doing.'
'Surely that goes both ways. Unless you still think it's me. "We are doing everything we can" doesn't wash with me. Tell me what you are doing.'

'We can't.'
'Why not? I'm his Dad.'
'Because I know you will seize on everything I say. We have several lines of enquiries on-going, not all of those will end up being relevant. When we have something factual that we can disclose without jeopardising any potential court case I will tell you.'
'So you do have FA.'
'We are following up several lines of enquiries. I'm not going to lie to you, we could do with a break.'
'Fine. If you tell me the truth about Rory, I'll tell you if I find out anything and I won't go wandering around at night. I know those other detectives were holding back. They wouldn't tell me where Rory was found or how he was killed. I have a right to know.'
'Sorry I'm not going to negotiate with you over confidential details in a case. There are reasons we withhold information, it helps us catch killers.'

Margot realised she'd have spilled everything to Dan if she'd been sent on her own. Once again she was reminded of her inexperience. As soon as they were outside Luke rang John.
'Boss we are going to have a problem with Dan. He's taking matters into his own hands. We are losing him.'
'I've just been updated by the FLOs, he's stopped engaging with them too, mostly down to Shelly. I'll get two new FLOs in for just him. Apparently he and Shelly are not speaking at all now. It was him I take it.'
'Yes Boss.'
'Is Margot there?'
'Yes Boss.'
'I need to speak to her. Donna's body has just been pulled out the Tyne at Corbridge.'
'Was she murdered?'
'Too early to tell. Obviously it's been treated as suspicious given the Osman notice.'

'Was who murdered?' asked Margot. Luke gave her the phone.
'I'm sorry Margot, Donna's body has just been pulled out of the Tyne,' said John.
'Colleen must have got to her. She called me last night three times, I was out for the count, I didn't even realise. She didn't leave a message.'
'Are you okay?'

'I think I might have let her down Sir.'
'She could have called 999 Margot.'
'What if she did it herself? Maybe I could have stopped her.'
'Margot we don't know anything yet. I just wanted to let you know. And ask you to pop back when you can.'
'Okay we'll be back soon.'

'What about Kevin?' said Margot to Luke.
'What about him?'
'Is he still alive?'
'Hang on, I'll ring the hospital…' Luke made the call 'died at 02.57 hrs,' he said as he hung up.
'Luke that's almost exactly when she first rang me that's not a coincidence.'
'Okay let's go back via the hospital, check the CCTV.'

They watched the screen. A sobbing Donna in pink leggings and pink puffer jacket walked out of the hospital at 03.03 hrs. Luke headed off to get the details of the nurse on duty when Kevin Wallace died whilst Margot watched on. At 3.29 hrs out walked Colleen with her sister Janine. She looked around then walked towards the camera and stopped and rummaged around in her handbag.
'Why are you so keen to be on camera?' said Margot to herself.
Luke came back at that moment.
'Is that Colleen and Janine?'
'Yeah, making sure they are seen.'
'She rarely gets her own hands dirty, she's making sure she has an alibi for something. I got the name of the nurse and a contact number. I've left a message for her to ring me. We need to head back, boss was wondering where we'd got to.'

Margot headed straight for the DI's office when she got back.
'Margot come in sit down. Nothing to worry about. Since the incident with Kevin at her house, have you had any further contact with Donna?'
'No but she called me three times last night. At 3.04, 3.11 and 3.16. She didn't leave a message. I didn't actually realise she'd called, I never heard the phone.'
'Okay can I see your phone?'
Margot handed it over. John checked the call log and wrote down

Donna's number.
'She was at the hospital Sir. Kevin died at 02.57, she walked out the hospital at 03.03. Colleen walked out at 03.29 with her sister.'
'Margot you can't be involved in this enquiry. I'll let the investigating officer know. That's it Margot thanks.'
Margot got up to leave. Luckily she had used her own phone for Patrick, and Donna only had her job mobile. But the fact the boss had looked at her phone had unnerved her.

Luke was waiting for her.
'The nurse rang back. She said she rang Colleen at one to say Kevin had taken a turn for the worse. But it wasn't Colleen who arrived first, it was Donna. Donna arrived about half one and sat with him until Colleen eventually arrived whereby Donna rushed out in tears. Colleen made a scene shouting "who let that slag in?" Well, you can imagine how it went. Colleen would have probably been thrown out except Kevin passed away in that very instant. Not peacefully.'
'Donna did say she and Kevin were an item before Colleen. Perhaps she still had feelings for him. Anyway the Boss doesn't want me anywhere near this.'
'How did Donna know to go?'
'Donna knew a lot of people.'
'I rang Daisy too. Shelly's house burnt down last night at exactly half three.'
'There's a surprise. I take it Shelly was at her mother's safe.'
'Yeah I'm guessing that was just a warning to the rest of the estate, her little empire.'
'Do you think that's it? I mean Donna is dead. Whether Colleen did or didn't have a hand in that, everyone will think she did. So she's upped her reputation now anyways.'
'Hopefully that's it. I know you thought she would kill Donna and Shelly but I didn't think she'd go that far. She's mostly hot air.'
'I'm not so sure. She's micey Luke. Definitely the jealous type.'
They were both lost to their own thoughts.

'Perhaps Donna saw who started the fire. If she drove quickly she would just about be getting back at half three,' said Margot breaking the silence.
'That's a possibility.'

'I don't think she'd keep her mouth shut. I wish I knew what she was trying to tell me, it can't be her who started the fire, she would've still been driving back. Her car! Was her car outside her house?'
'No it was down by the river according to Daisy.'
'I feel terrible Luke.'
'Margot you were exhausted, you didn't hear the phone.'
'Yeah but even if I had heard it I wouldn't have answered. The boss said I had to keep it professional with Donna.'
'Margot I know you, you may not have answered the first time, maybe not the second, but you would have definitely answered the third time.'

Margot realised Luke was right. So she now felt guilty for taking the sleeping pills. If she hadn't taken the pills would Donna still be alive?

'Margot, Luke, my office please,' said John.
Margot was worried from his tone. She wasn't sure how much more her nerves could take.
'Metcalfe has been allocated to investigate Donna's death. A word of warning, he seems to have the ear of the new Chief. Margot don't rise to him he's just been on the phone demanding to speak to you. Right now. I'll come with you. Is there anything I need to know because now is the time to tell me?'
Luke told him about the nurse. Margot's head was full of what ifs.
'You two have to stay well clear of this. I mean it. Metcalfe is dangerous, he's going to be more interested in finding something Margot has done wrong than finding out what happened to Donna. You're not immune either Luke. Metcalfe hated your father. Anything at all that crosses over from our enquiry to his, you bring to me immediately understood.'
'Understood Sir,' said Margot.
'Yes Boss.'

Margot and John walked down two flights of stairs to Metcalfe's office. The larger than normal sweat patches under his arms told Margot all she needed to know.
'Well I don't need to tell you any death shortly after police contact can be a tricky sea to navigate.' What a total prick thought Margot, as Metcalfe paused for effect.
'When did you last speak to Donna, Margot?'

'When Kevin had his heart attack. She called me in a panic. I called the ambulance so she could do CPR.'
'I find it odd she called you and not an ambulance in the first place.'
'It's hardly something Margot had any control over. Margot did exactly the right thing,' said John.
'And why did you go in person?'
'She sounded upset.'
'You only called the police after you got there, why?'
'Because at that point she told me he was high on coke. Up until that point I thought it was purely a medical issue.'
'So how would describe your relationship with Donna?'
'Professional. She provided useful information about Shelly Morgan which helped with the enquiry.'
'So you had a professional reason for visiting Donna that night? Did you perhaps think she was capable of suicide?'
Luckily Margot saw that trap coming.
'No because I would have reported that. Made the appropriate referrals. I did want to make sure she was okay. And I thought she was okay.'
'You could have asked local to do, that why didn't you?'
'Because I wanted to be sure myself.'
'I'm going to need your job mobile and personal mobile.'
Margot looked at John who nodded. Margot handed them over. Shit, she thought.
'We are in the middle of a murder enquiry and a missing nine-year-old. I expect those returned within the hour,' said John.
'That might not be possible. You know how busy people are.'
'Make it happen. I can't afford to have Margot offline for more than an hour. A child's life could be at stake here. Margot is in contact with key witnesses. You have an hour to download them. I'm coming to collect them in an hour, download or no download. I think under the circumstances that's more than adequate.'
'The Chief Constable put me on this personally.'
'Then you won't want to disappoint him will you? If we miss something vital because you have Margot's phones I won't hold back. You know as well as I do asking for them is a stretch on your part. Margot has nothing to hide. An hour, that's it.'

With that John walked out quickly followed by Margot. Margot felt sick. Perhaps she should have refused to hand her phones over. Was that even possible? she wondered. Too late now. That had all been a whirlwind.

'Sir what are we going to do now? About Kyle and Rory I mean?'
'I'll have to think. But you can do something for me. Go and use your charm and call forensic submissions and get the bits of bodywork that you and Luke found bumped up to urgent. I need to know what kind of vehicle that was off. It didn't escape my notice the Range Rover on the CCTV looked dark. To me it looked darker than those fragments but the quality was so poor, it could be the same.'
'Yes Sir.'
'Pull up anyone in that village that owns a Range Rover Margot.'
'Sorry Sir, how do I do that?'
'Get the postcodes for the village. Then ask the PNC bureau to print you a list of all Range Rovers registered to those postcodes.'
'Will do.'

Margot busied herself with her tasks. Once she had her list she was dispatched with Luke to visit all the Range Rover owners to check for damage or any sign of repairs. She had both her phones back in her pocket, they felt heavier than normal. She didn't have time to worry about Metcalfe right now though. Her boss's words going kept going round in her head 'see if anyone jumps out to you.'

No one did. And as far as they could tell all the Range Rovers were undamaged. There were more than Margot thought, probably more than her boss had thought there would be. He was surprised they had been gone for so long. It had taken them all day. Margot felt it had been a monumental waste of time. The car on the CCTV from the farm fitters was probably an almighty red herring anyway. Although she had to admit to herself she didn't have any better ideas as to what they should be doing. She felt the whole case was slipping away from them. Kyle's Dad had a point, they had sweet FA.

As they walked back into their office John called a meeting. They sat around Luke's desk.
'An update for you whilst you've been out the office. Tracy has found a motorcycle on the CCTV heading out of town at 6am. The downside is it's just a blur. The upside it does corroborate what Kevin told Luke. So Kevin could have taken some sort of delivery from that biker. Kevin still could have lied about the car and scream. Shelly has hit the drink according to the FLOs, they say she's behaving oddly. Although she is under a lot of stress, so I'm

reluctant to read too much into that. I do however think it's time we took a good look at Shelly. So I have Division seizing Kevin's car and Shelly's mother's car. Full forensic. I don't want to get completely hung up on Kyle and Rory being connected. So as far as things that need doing, there is a bit of a lull. Go home keep your phones close. I may need to call you back in, I'll try not to. Get some rest and back in for 7am please.'

Margot was actually glad to be going home today. Glad to get out the same building Metcalfe was in. Besides she needed to go through her call logs and messages to Patrick to see if there was anything incriminating.

She drove home. She made a cup of tea and plunged into the sofa. She opened WhatsApp. Her heart jumped against her ribs. She read and reread the conversation with Patrick about the Mercedes SLK and the bill for the missing keys. There was no way she could spin that. She would get the sack for sure. It was fairly bloody obvious how Patrick got that bill. Margot didn't know what to do.

Margot

Margot hadn't slept much, she was just too anxious. She was absolutely dreading going into work. Would they be waiting to arrest her? Conspiracy to burgle. She was actually shaking as she walked up the stairs to her office. The door on Metcalfe's floor was pushed open. Margot stifled a gasp, her heart was pounding away.
'You made me jump,' she said, feeling she needed to say something as she must look like a rabbit in the headlights.
'Sorry,' said a confused looking admin assistant.
'I was miles away that's all,' said Margot. She was sure her voice was wobbling like a Masterchef pannacotta.

She reached her desk, her phone rang it, was Daisy.
'Margot an envelope arrived in the post for you at the station this morning. It's a Jiffy bag, it's got something inside it.'
'I'll come over.'
Margot just needed a reason not to be where she was. She messaged Luke: Gone to meet Daisy.

Daisy was still in the station when Margot arrived.
'It's in my locker. Come with me.'
Margot followed Daisy along to the ladies' locker room. It had always been their office.
'Feels like a USB stick Margot.'
Margot opened it. A note fell to the floor. Margot read it.

For you Margot. Hope it comes in handy. Donna.

'Let's see what's on it Margot. Wait here, I'll get a laptop.'
Daisy came back, a laptop under her arm. She fired it up, took the USB from Margot and plugged it in.
'Is that the Chief Constable?' she said.
'Yes,' said Margot.
'Flipping heck Margot, he's taking his clothes off! That's Donna's bedroom.'
'I'm not sure we should be watching this Daisy.'
'You're kidding, this is pure Gold.'
They watched on.
'Christ!' They both said together.
'What are you going to do with it Margot?'

'I think we should destroy it. It's kinda private.'
'Are you kidding Margot, this is a get-out-of-jail-free card.'

Margot could certainly use one of those right now. They watched on. The camera was turned off. Then a second video started. Metcalfe. Margot was interested in this one.
'This one's way more perverted Margot. Who is he?'
'DI Metcalfe.'
'The one that got you suspended? Shit Margot.'
'He's also investigating Donna's death. Explains why he was so keen to get the case. Do you think they know they were filmed?'
'Bloody hell Margot, what are you going to do now?'
'I don't know.'
'I won't tell anyone. Let's see if there are anymore.'
There weren't.

'I'm going to have to tell my boss about this Daisy. Metcalfe can't investigate Donna's death,' said Margot.
'I know. Well Margot, it's been entertaining as ever. I'd best get back to work. Who knew aye.'
'I'll have to be honest about us watching it.'
'Don't worry, I quite like the idea of the Chief knowing I've seen him in pink handcuffs tied to a bed getting his bits whipped.'
Margot couldn't help laughing. She missed working with Daisy. The tension finally started to leave her body. She rushed back to the station.

She ran up the stairs and knocked on John's door.
'Sir it's urgent I need a word in private.'
'Come in shut the door.'
'Sir I think Donna may have committed suicide. She posted something to me at my old station. It came with this note.' She handed the note over.
'Watch this. By yourself Sir. I've seen it so has Daisy, we watched it together.'
Margot handed over the USB and left.

She went to find Luke.
'Did Daisy have anything useful? I take it it was about Shelly.'
'Not exactly. Donna sent me something,' Margot lowered her voice. 'Boss is watching it. It's the Chief and Metcalfe in Donna's bedroom.'

'Shit. Together?'
'No.'
'What are they doing?'
'Not here. I'll tell you later.'
'Shit.'

John came over.
'Get out of here you two. I'm sure there's something you can be doing. I take it you know, Luke?'
'Luke nodded.'
'Do not tell anyone else. I'm going to Professional Standards right now.'

Luke and Margot hurried out. They decided to go Caroline's, they had promised ages ago to stop by for a cuppa and hadn't actually done so. It was also miles away from the station. Margot filled Luke in on the finer details as he drove. Luke turned pink again.

When Margot had finished describing the video clips she started to worry about her phone download again. However the new SIO would probably just confine themselves to checking her contact with Donna. That was all on the job phone. She might have got away with it although it was too soon to celebrate.
'Luke why would she commit suicide?'
'I don't know but perhaps she realised if she started the CPR earlier she might have saved him. He was oxygen deprived for too long according to the nurse. I'm guessing she took a few minutes to decide what to do. Before even ringing you.'
'Possibility she thought he was dead. CPR didn't occur to her until I told her to do it. Was there no note in the car?'
'I don't actually know, it will all come out in the wash. It's not your fault Margot.'
'You can tell me that a hundred times Luke. I'm still going to feel bad about it. I could've - should've - done better by her.'

They were both surprised to see a For Sale sign outside Caroline's house.
Caroline was waiting for them. 'Come let's sit on the lawn it such a lovely day. I've made scones and fresh lemonade. If you'd given me more notice I could have made something nice.'
'Scones sound perfect,' said Margot. 'Are you moving?'
'Downsizing. This house is far to big. I think I only kept it so Sally, if by some miracle she was alive, could find me. If I'm honest Margot,

since Mark broke in that night I haven't been sleeping so well. You know how creaky this house is. Anyways I've booked us a month in the Caribbean, Barbados so I'll have to pay for it at some point.'
'That sounds wonderful,' said Margot, both happy for Caroline and a little jealous she wasn't going too.
'So what are you two hiding from?'
'Sorry, are we that obvious?' said Luke.
'Anything I can help with? Have you found the little boy yet?'
'Not yet. We keep thinking we are getting close then it turns out to be a wild goose chase,' said Margot.
'So why are you hiding with me?'
'Metcalfe is on the war-path Or he will be shortly,' said Margot.
'The oaf that got you suspended.'
'That's him.'
'Tea or lemonade?'

They both settled on lemonade. Margot felt guilty she was enjoying her lunch. They should be looking for Kyle. She consoled herself by admitting she was actually fresh out of ideas so it wasn't as if she could be doing anything else.

They heard a beep beep from the drive.
'Oh that will be Geoffrey he's bought himself a new car. He's very excited. We had better actually sell the bloody house soon. Come on let's go and see it. Just pretend you are interested Margot.'
They walked round the front.
'It's a lovely colour Geoffrey,' said Caroline.
Bugger thought Margot that was going to be her line.
'What is it Geoffrey?' Margot asked.
'Mercedes SLK AMG. Top of the range. Only 26000 miles on the clock. They don't make them anymore but I've wanted one for years.'
'How are you going to get your wife and a St Bernard in that?'
Every one looked at Margot.
'Doctor Richard Grant. He must have another car. To fit the dog in.'
'You've completely lost me Margot,' said Luke.
'The guy with the car keys stolen. Sorry Caroline, can I use your toilet? I really like your new car Geoffrey.'
'Yes you know where it is. Help yourself.'

Margot hurriedly rang Patrick. Luckily he picked up.
'Patrick. The house with the bill for the car keys. Were there any

other cars on the drive?'
'The SLK and a Range Rover.'
'What about the garage?'
'Empty and no freezer in there before you ask.'
'Thanks Patrick. Oh and a word of warning, Metcalfe may have your burner phone number. He downloaded my phone.'
'Ok I'll send you a new number, get rid of this one.'

Margot ran out again.
'Luke I think we need to look at this doctor. Can we see if he has a second car?'
'Sure, let's go now if you like.'
'Sorry Caroline,' said Margot.
'No you have some important work to do by the sounds of things. Come on Geoffrey take me for a ride in your new car.'

Luke and Margot jumped in the car.
'The day we did the house-to-house. The wife wasn't there just the dog. I missed it Luke. The garage door was shut I didn't see any cars. There no way the SLK is their only car. The other GP had three.'
'I'm not sure I'm totally following you, but he doesn't have a Range Rover, we pulled up every Range Rover registered to the village.'
'What if he registered it to the practice?'
'Possible I suppose. Let's go anyway, we have nothing to lose.'

The SLK was outside this time. As was Colin, sitting under a tree for shade. It was just typical, the one and only nice day in the whole month Margot was at work.
'Let's just play it low key. We are just following up on the burglaries,' said Luke.
'I can ask her if any jewellery was missing, the husband wasn't sure.'
'Okay you lead.'

They knocked on the door.
'Hello Mrs Grant. DC Margot Jacks, DS Luke Jones. We are just following up on the possible burglary. Your husband wasn't sure if you were missing any jewellery.'
'I'm sorry, you have me at a loss. We haven't been burgled. I think you are getting us mixed up with the Hills, he is also a GP. They were burgled.'

'No I spoke to your husband when we were doing house-to-house. The keys to your car went missing.'
'Oh he did mention he'd mislaid them. His car was playing up so he was using mine. He didn't mention anything about a burglary.'
'We think you might have been burgled.'
'He would have said if we had been.'
'Were you away?' asked Luke.
'Just for a week. Ladies mini break to Barcelona.'
'When were you away?'
'Saturday to Saturday.'
'And you definitely are not missing any jewellery?' asked Luke.
'No.'
'Not to worry,' said Luke.
'So were we burgled?'
'That was what we wanted to establish. To be honest we aren't sure.'

Luke said thank you and ushered Margot out. Margot wanted to ask about the other car but Luke was practically pushing her out. She knew Luke would have a reason so she kept her mouth shut.
'What are you thinking Luke?'
'That if he never told his wife about the burglary he may have something to hide. We can't spook him right now because we have nothing. I don't want him covering his tracks any more than he already has.'
'So do you think it's him?'
'Not sure yet. Let's see what car he's driving.'

They drove away from the house and parked up outside the village. Luke rang John and told him what they were up to. He asked John to look up the practice and see if any vehicles were registered there.
'Luke he's got a Range Rover registered to the practice. Eiger Grey. Go swing by the practice, see if it's there and call me back. Try not to be seen.'

The practice was in a small shopping precinct. There were only three staff parking places occupied by a Focus, Corsa and very shiny new black Range Rover. The Range Rover was still registered to the dealers. A quick google of the practice revealed he was the only doctor.

'Looks like he's got a new car. I'll let the boss know then let's head to the dealers.'

They drove to the dealers. Luke pounced on the manager.
'Did you sell a new Range Rover to a Dr Richard Grant? I have the registration number.'
Luke passed him the registration number.
'Yes, Scott dealt with the sale would you like to talk to him?'
'No. It's vitally important no one knows we are asking. Did he trade in an Eiger Grey Range Rover?'
'He did…it had damage to the offside, I am assuming that information is of use to you.'
'Yes. We need that vehicle.'
'It was in our body shop.'
'It will need to be forensically seized.'
'Unfortunately I think we've just given it a full valet this morning. The damage was minor just a replacement panel needed. It was going straight on our forecourt.'
'Is it not unusual to trade in a damaged car? Why wouldn't you go through your insurance first?'
'I guess it could be a toss up between losing your no-claims and a reduced trade-in value. Dr Grant has been a very good client over the years he usually changes his vehicle every three to four years, so I guess he was maybe not far off changing it anyway.'
'Did he say how it was damaged?'
'I don't know. I authorised the trade-in, as the manager, due to the damage. But Scott would be the one to ask.'
'I'd prefer as few people as possible knew about this right now.'
'I think the moment you come and take it away tongues will start wagging.'
'You are probably right. Okay we will speak to Scott.'

Scott was called to the office. He immediately looked worried.
'Hi Scott, DS Luke Jones, nothing to worry about but I do need your assurance that what we are about to ask you goes absolutely no further than these walls. A life could depend on it.'
'It's important Scott, you can't tell anyone,' said the manager.
'I won't.'
'Do you remember selling Dr Grant the black Range Rover?' asked Luke.
'Yeah.'
'The Range Rover he traded in. Did he say how it was damaged?'

'Said he misjudged the turn into a patient's house, knocked his drystone wall over.'
'How did he seem?'
'Dunno.'
'Scott can you fetch me both sets of keys? These officers will be taking the car away.'
'Yeah.'
Scott headed off.
'When did he trade the old car in and pick up the new one?'
'Monday afternoon, not Monday just gone the previous Monday. Completely out the blue, he just turned up.'
'That was a quick sale.'
'As I said he's been a very good client. He pointed out he needed a car as he was on call and he couldn't drive his around like it was. He saw and liked our demonstrator and we did the deal there and then. I offered a courtesy car and to repair it but I think his mind was made up.'
'Thank you,' said Luke. 'Would you excuse me whist I call my boss?'
'Use my office, I'll step out for five minutes. Tea, coffee?'
'No thank you,' said Margot and Luke.
'You don't still have the old panel do you?' added Luke.
'I doubt it but I will check for you now.'

'Luke, forensic could take a long time. I think we should bring him in.'
'It's the boss's decision Margot. It's a biggie.'

Luke called John.
'Luke I'm a little tied up, is it urgent?'
'Very.'
'Give me one minute please, I'll call you back.'

'What did he say?' asked an excited Margot.
'Nothing. I'm guessing things are a little spicy right now at the station.'

Luke's phone rang. Luke brought John up to date.
'Great work Luke.'
'It was all Margot Sir.'
'Give me another few minutes to think. I need to run this by DSI Walker. If Kyle is alive and if, and that's still a really big if, if it is Richard Grant then what we do next will have consequences. I'm

inclined to arrest. My thinking is if he's with us we know what he's doing. Put Margot on please…Margot the torches in the woods, is that more likely one or two people? I'm asking you - if it is the doctor is he working alone?'

'I think it was probably just one person in the woods but I can't be sure. The doctor's wife was on holiday. If it was a burglary gone wrong it was probably just him in.'

'The car keys were missing. If he caught him in the act he'd have the keys. So maybe he went after him. If he went after him the question is why. Put Luke back on…Luke wait for the car to be uplifted. I'll set someone away on trying to find out if he's got another property anywhere. I'll come back to you shortly.'

'Boss wants us to wait till the car is uplifted.'
'He's worried there's more than one. So if we move on the doctor we could alert whoever he's working with. Could there be more than one?'
'I don't know Margot.'

Luke's phone rang. They both nearly jumped out their skins.
'Luke the boss is thinking of putting him under surveillance. How tight are the car dealers?'
'The manager is tight. The workforce I'm not sure. I don't think they'd tell the doctor but they might gossip. It's a big dealership, lots of staff. We've caused a stir just being here.'
'Okay I'll pass that on.'

'Are we arresting him?'
'Not yet. Super is thinking about surveillance.'
'He could lead us to Kyle!'
'If they are connected. There has to be an outside chance he's still alive. Also he could still be in the process of disposing of Rory. If we catch him with a body part it's a slam dunk.'
'So that's what they will do then?'
'If they do and he's already cleaned up - let's face it he's had time - then we get nothing but a doctor going to work and walking the dog. And the chance of any decent forensic diminishes.'
'I'm glad I don't have to make that decision.'
'I thought you wanted to be a Detective Super one day Margot?'
She had said that. She hadn't really thought it through. It was a moot point it would never happen. She knew she wasn't good enough. Just suppose this was her decision here and now. What

would she do? She thought the decision was simple: save the kid. But it wasn't. You were expected to make a decision with less than half the facts and pros and cons to both. Pick wrong and a child's life could be on your conscience. She really wasn't cut out for this she decided.

The vehicle was uplifted. They still hadn't heard anything. Luke rang John.
'Sorry I was just coming back to you. Division are on route to arrest him. We will shortly be on the clock. A search team will be going through his house with a fine tooth comb soon. I need you two on finding out if he has access to another property, nothing listed to him as far as we can tell. Wait till I give you the all clear then turn over every rock he has ever sat on.'
'Yes Boss.'
'Metcalfe is suspended. Apparently he searched Donna's house himself.'
'And the Chief?'
'I have no idea Luke. I will never be privy to what was said there. Personally I think it will be hard for him to survive putting Metcalfe on the case.'

Luke told Margot everything.
'Where would you start Margot, you are closer to this than me?'
'He said he'd been friends with the other GP that was burgled for twenty years. We could try him. Dr Hill.'
'Let's do that as soon as we get the go ahead.'

Margot and Luke were soon knocking on Dr Hill's door. A lady answered.
'Hello I'm DS Luke Jones, my colleague DC Margot Jacks. Sorry to intrude but this is important. Are you Mrs Hill by any chance?'
'Yes. Come in.'
They sat down in the living room.
'How well do you know Richard Grant?'
'Richard and Sue? Sorry you threw me there. I assumed you'd come about our burglary, I was rather hoping you were going to say you had found my necklace. It was my wedding present.'
'Richard Grant?' prompted Luke.
'Richard is Adam's friend. Has been from medical school.'
'You don't like him?' asked Margot.
'I have nothing in common with him or his wife. It's not that I don't

like them, it's just I have lots of other friends I'd rather spend my time with.'
'What's he like?' asked Luke.
'Why, is it important?'
'I can't say but yes it's important.'
'Incredibly boring. I really know nothing about him and I've know him for fifteen years, so read what you like into that. You would be better talking to Adam, he always go for a pint or two with Richard every Sunday afternoon in the village pub.'
'Does Richard have access to another property?'
'They have a house in France.'
'Closer to home.'
'I don't think so. I'm sorry, Adam may know more. Shall I ring him for you?'
'Did they go to the pub the day of the burglary?'
'Yes but Adam was home by four. We think the burglar was in the house between six and seven thirty.'
'It would actually be handy to speak to Adam.'
'I'll ring him for you.'

'Adam, the police are here please can you talk to them.'
'Hi Adam it's DS Luke Jones. I need to ask you about Richard Grant.'
'Yes I've just had his receptionist on the phone to me in a panic. He was arrested in his surgery. The place is being searched.'
'Why did she ring you?'
'Richard is a one man band at the moment. So I provide cover.'
'Does Richard have access to another property nearby? Possibly north of the village?'
'No.'
'Are you sure.?'
'He never mentioned anything and I'm sure he would have told me if he'd bought a house.'
'What's he like?'
'Most people would probably say he's a little dull. But he's a very good doctor. And very kind. Nothing is ever too much trouble. I've known him a very long time.'
'You said he was a one man band at the moment why is that?'
'Nothing sinister detective. His partner died two months ago. Motorcycle crash abroad, Thailand. He has been interviewing potential candidates. How can I say this without it coming out wrong. His practice isn't in one of the most desirable areas. I kept

telling him to come and work with me but it was his baby. He said he couldn't let his patients down.'
'Did you go to the pub the Sunday you were burgled?'
'Yes we walked home together at around four I think.'
'How many pints did you have?'
'Three, is that relevant?'
'I don't know at the moment. It was properties he has access to we are really interested in. The partner, did he live alone?'
'George Morrison. Yes.'
'Do you know where?'
'Somewhere up north. Ahh I see what you're thinking. Richard was the executor of the Will. George had no children. And I wouldn't be surprised if Richard had a key to George's house. Can I ask what he's been arrested for?'
'Sorry I can't answer that right now.'
Luke thanked him for his time and hung up.

'Thank you, sorry we need to rush,' said Luke to Mrs Hill.
They headed to their car.
'I'll fill you in in a minute Margot. I just need to call the boss, get him to contact the team at the surgery, find us an address,' said Luke as he quickened his pace.

Peel cottage was remote. Margot immediately questioned what sort of person would want to live here. It was surrounded by conifers. In a damp little clearing on the edge of a forest reached by a rutted drive. The house looked cold. Margot wouldn't want to return to this house in the dark. The house itself was an old stone cottage. The stones were turning green. It had four small rotting wood framed windows and a bright red door that looked completely out of place.

A panda car slid to a stop. Margot was pleased to see Daisy and Mo get out.
'We've got the enforcer. We haven't had the course but who cares. Shall I do the honours,' said Daisy.
'Go ahead,' said Luke. 'We can't go in, we have to stand well back. We've just been to his house this morning. One of you will have to go in. Are you okay with that? You just need to clear it make sure Kyle isn't alive in the house then get out. There could be parts of a dead child in there just to warn you.'
'I'll go,' said Mo.

Daisy splintered the door open. Margot tried to peer in from a distance. A pair of wellingtons waited for George in the hall. Other than that she couldn't see anything. Mo put latex gloves on and squeezed through. 'A quick search Mo. Touch as little as possible. Watch where you step.'
'I'll be careful.'
'Forensic will be here after they have done the car and surgery. So just leave everything in situ, please.'
'I won't move anything.'

Margot wanted to be the one in the house. She crossed her fingers. Time seemed to have stopped. The house was too silent. Mo came back out after a few minutes.
'No sign of Kyle. There's a freezer. I looked inside, the lid was up. There's nothing in it. It's turned off now empty. Looks like it's been cleaned.'
'Thanks Mo.'

'If it was him why not bury them around here it's perfect. Why risk going to Scots gap?' asked Margot.

'Too close to home I'd guess. Didn't want to take the risk of anything being found near here. The first place we'd have looked is the house. He would have known this house would lead back to him very quickly,' said Luke.

John arrived disturbing Margot's thoughts.
'I've managed to negotiate some overtime. A couple of CSIs are on their way. This will still take a while to process. Do we know if there's a freezer in there?'
'Yes Boss. Empty and cleaned.'
'I want the whole freezer seized. In fact once it's sealed I think I want it straight down to the lab. How big is it?'
'A chest freezer Sir, big enough for one body if he cut it up like he did,' said Mo.
'Okay that's doable in the back of a van. A cadaver dog is also on its way. Make sure the CSIs are fully briefed on the fact we think something like an electric saw was used to sever Rory's arm. I want all electronic devices seized too. Luke, Margot, after you have briefed them back to the station, I want you two to interview. Daisy, Mo, sorry but can you stay here, your sergeant knows. He'll get you relieved when your shift ends.'
'No problem Sir,' said Daisy.
'Sir may I make an observation?'
'Of course Mo, you don't need to ask just speak up.'
'We passed a couple of properties on the road before we turned off for this one. Their wheelie bins are all at the bottom of the drives on the road. This house has no wheelie bins.'
'A good point Mo. So if the occupant had died the council could have been informed because of the council tax and the like. They possibly reclaimed the bins. Check that Luke, because we may be missing wheelie bins.'
'He also might of dumped rubbish in the other bins Sir,' said Margot remembering the feuding old couple.
'Another good point. Knock on the neighbors' on your way back get them to confirm any rubbish in the bins is theirs, obviously seize anything that isn't.'
'So do we really think it's him?' asked Daisy.
'I watched him brought into custody, that was one worried man. He lawyered straight up. If he did do it Rory wasn't planned, he's made mistakes we just have to find them. I've still to be totally convinced

Rory and Kyle are connected though. On that front I've sent a sample of the paint from the Range Rover you seized from the dealers to the lab for matching to the bits outside Five Acre house. I think that was it. Oh, one more thing; if the CSIs find anything significant I am to be informed immediately. I'll arrange a blue light run to the lab. We have twenty-three hours left to find something that connects him to the murder of Rory Elliot.'

Luke and Margot decided to divide and conquer the bins. Despite the bemused looks on the faces of the residents everyone was more than happy to empty their bins out and confirm the rubbish was theirs. Margot was regretting having this idea. She hadn't dressed for wading through rubbish. She was on her last property. She was beginning to smell.
'Mr Ritter is it? Hi, I'm DC Margot Jacks. I'm investigating a murder. Do you mind if I check your bin? I need you to help if that's okay. I need you to tell me if there's anything in your bin that you didn't put there.'
'Aye.' They walked down the drive together.
'Can you give me a hand to tip it out please.'
'Aye.'
They upended the bin between them.
'Well that shouldn't be there,' he said pointing to a black bin bag.
'Are you sure?'
'Aye. We use white bags.'
Everything else was indeed in white bags.
'Okay don't touch it. I'm just going to grab an evidence bag from the car and put some gloves on…' Margot looked round. 'I just need to call my colleague, he has the car.'

Luke arrived and handed Margot gloves and an evidence bag.'
'Recover it in the bag Margot don't open it.'
'It feels heavy Luke. I think it could be the saw wrapped in something.'

Margot placed it carefully in the evidence bag while Luke took a quick statement from Mr Ritter. She sealed it and carefully filled in the exhibit details. She gave it a squeeze whilst Luke was busy. She'd always been unable to resist squeezing presents, it drove her mother crazy. She was convinced it was a saw wrapped in something like a towel. She knew it was a key find. She knew Dr Grant had killed Rory.

Margot

Margot and Luke were about to go in and interview Richard Grant. Margot was nervous, she didn't want to screw it up.
'Margot let Luke do the talking. Remember you are still learning. Let's just see if he's going to talk for now. Just get me the suspect agenda,' said John. 'I'll be listening.'

Luke sat holding a file full of papers. She didn't know what was in them. Neither did Luke, he'd just grabbed a file off someone's desk. Luke switched the recording equipment on. It beeped a few times then buzzed. Richard practically leapt off his chair.
'The time is 14.31 hours. You are in an interview room at Newcastle police station. Please state your name and date of birth.'
'Richard Grant. Ninth of April 1977.'
He was speaking so quietly Margot could barely hear him. Margot zoned out. She watched tiny little beads of sweat appear one by one on his top lip. Then on his brow. He shuffled his hands under the table. Margot suddenly realised Luke had got to the interesting bit. She concentrated hard.
'You are under arrest for the murder of Rory Elliot. Please state your movements two Sundays ago, so the day after your wife went on holiday.'
'No reply.'
'Were you involved in the death of Rory Elliot?'
'No reply.'
'What were your movements on Friday night, just gone into Saturday morning before your wife returned?'
'No reply.'
'Interview terminated.'

Margot thought the doctor was expecting more. She was expecting more. They went to find John.
'So he's going to make us do the work. To be expected given his brief, par for course. Heads to the grindstone. We now need some actual evidence to go back in there with. CSIs have found a computer hidden at George Morrison's house. It's been dusted for prints and swabbed for DNA, so can you pick it up and get it to tech please Margot? The rest of the house looks like it has been cleared but that was left. I find that odd. I want to know what's on it.'
'What's happening with the black bag we found in the wheelie bin?' Margot asked.

'I've sent the whole thing to the lab as it is Margot. If that has his and Rory's DNA on we have him. It's being blue lighted down there as we speak. Like you I think it's the saw.'
'What shall I do Boss?'
'Luke, I need you to stay on top of forensic for me. We are running six scenes at present. The surgery. His house and garage. The wife's SLK. His old and new Range Rover. And his partner's house. Sort what needs doing now from what can wait. We interview again first thing tomorrow. By then the very least I need is enough to go for the extra twelve hours.'
'Yes Boss.'

Margot headed back to the house. Daisy and Mo were still there, she quickly brought them up to date. The CSI emerged from the house with the laptop.
'Where was it found?' asked Margot.
'Under the freezer in a plastic bag. Looks like the house was partially cleared, just the large furniture left. Seemed a really odd place to put it. We have also found what could be the proceeds of your burglaries. Hidden up the chimney in a plastic bag.'
'I'll take the laptop please.'
'I'm guessing you'll need a password. I noted some of the keys had grease on. Like someone was eating something greasy at the same time as using the keys. I wrote it down for you. Here.' The CSI gave Margot a piece of paper. Margot looked at it.

EOAGKBN the shift key and the .?123 key.

Margot looked blankly at the CSI.
'It may help you with the password - only a few keys were touched, like someone logging in.'
'I get it thanks.'

'I love a puzzle, said Daisy. Let me write them down, it will give me and Mo something to do while we are sitting here.'
Daisy wrote them down. Margot actually thought she had it already but she'd had a clue. She might not be right and she didn't want to spoil Daisy's fun.

She drove the laptop back. Trying to work out what it all meant. Richard must have put the laptop under the freezer. But if she was right the laptop belonged to George. Why would Richard hide it?

She pulled into the station that housed technical support and rushed to their office. It was as if tech needed to work in the dark. They had been allocated the dingiest office possible. The only light came from all the computer hardware. Nigel was waiting for her. Nigel was very tall, his spine had taken the shape of a question mark from having to permanently stoop. Margot had always thought he was surprisingly normal for a tech guy. Then she realised she was comparing him to TV stereotypes. Margot liked Nigel. He always squeezed her in. At first she wasn't sure why, but it had transpired Margot had done his mother's hair for years. His mother had been devastated when Margot joined the police. Margot wasn't sure why this had got her preferential treatment but she wasn't complaining.

'Let's take a look…yep password protected…do we know it?'
'No but I have an idea.'
'We only get three chances then we are locked out.'
'The CSI reckons the keys used were these,' said Margot showing him. 'So I was thinking Bangkok3.'
'Why?'
'Because he died in Thailand. The letters practically spell out Bangkok and the E is a three.'
'And usually there's a symbol in there. Why not Bangkok33. Why not Bangkok@33. A is also @. B is / . G is *you get my drift.'
'Bollocks I thought I had it.'
'You could have most of it but we need all of it and we need to be sure.'
Margot felt deflated.
'Look it's not a sophisticated password by the looks of things. Ask anyone that might know first. Ask about any other passwords he uses. He probably goes along similar lines. I'll see if there's a back-door way in while you do that.'

Margot rang the officer at the surgery and asked to speak to the receptionist.
'Hi it's Margot. Do you know what password George used for his laptop?'
'No.'
'What about the computer system at work?'
'Phuket*333. With a capital P.'
'His phone?'
'I don't think that made it back from Thailand. It was his date of birth

backwards though six digits.'
'Thanks.'

Margot relayed the message.
'He keeps things simple. We could give Bangkok*333 a chance. I'm not prepared to put anything else in if that doesn't work mind.'
'Try it.'
'Bloody hell it's worked Margot. Let's see what's on it.'
'Bloody hell,' said Margot as Nigel opened up a file. Margot and Nigel were looking at picture after picture of prepubescent naked young boys.
'This is sick,' said Margot.
'There are video files as well.'
'Stop go back…that one. Does that look like a doctor's surgery to you? Print that one off for me please.'
'You think he photographed his patients!'
'Maybe. I'll go and see if it's his surgery after. Carry on.'
'These ones could be Thai, the skin is much darker.'
Margot looked at the images of close ups of boys genitalia. She had to agree.
'I think I get the gist. Just try one of the videos,' she said.
They watched in silence. A tear rolled down Margot's cheek.
'Sorry Margot I can't watch this. I have a son that age.'
'Stop it. I actually don't want to know what happens next.'
'I can tell you that one was downloaded from the internet. I'll download everything for you. Check all the other files. Shame he's dead.'
'I was going to say I'm glad he's dead.'
'He got away with it Margot. He should have paid for this.'

Margot rang Luke and John and told them what she had found.
'I'm going to swing by the surgery and see if the picture I printed off was taken there.'
'Good Margot. If it is, are you okay to go through the files and see how many other patients are involved. Identify them and see when they were seen and by whom…are you still there Margot?'
'…Yes Sir.'
'Margot if you don't want to please say. Child abuse cases are not for everyone. Would you rather I pass it on to child protection?'
'I don't want to let you down Sir.'
'Margot you haven't, you've cracked this case wide open. I fully understand if you can't to do it and I won't force you.'

'I can't do it Sir.'
'Are you okay to go to the surgery?'
'Yes I can do that.'
'I'll get child protection to do the rest. Good job Margot.'

Margot was relieved. She rushed to the surgery. A DC Tommy Jennings was in charge.
'Hi Tommy, Margot, we spoke on the phone. I was the one who wanted to speak to the receptionist. Are the CSIs done?'
'Yeah. Place looks clean. Obviously it is regularly cleaned. I'd stake my pension there's nothing here. We've done the bins and the sharps disposal boxes. We are just waiting on the thumbs-up to clear out.'
'Hold that thought, I need to see if this was taken here. The date on the file was 1/6/2023 so not that long ago.'
'Do you want to start with Dr Morrison's consulting room?'
'Please.'
Margot immediately noticed the paint on the wall was the same colour. The consulting table was the same too. Perhaps the NHS had a job lot of paint and the tables were bound to be generic. She tried to recall the colour of her own doctor's but couldn't. Margot noticed a chip in the wall crudely painted over on the photograph. She angled the photo and saw the same chip on the wall. 'I'd say it was definitely taken here. I need to let my boss know.'
'I guess that's me stuck here now for a while. And here's me thinking I'd get to my footy match tonight. I'll be popular again.'
'Sorry.'

Margot rang John. She explained about the photo.
'Okay I'll get child protection to take over. So the biggie is whether Morrison was acting alone or whether they were both paedophiles. I'm minded to go straight back into interview now. Margot get your tech friend to send over something that really turns your stomach.'
'There's a video I'll get him to send it to you.'

An hour later and the solicitor had been summoned back. They were sitting in the interview room. John walked in with Luke. Margot was watching on a remote monitor. After the formalities had been gone through, John pressed play on the video.
'Turn it off please,' said Richard.
'What is the relevance of this?' asked the solicitor.
'Start talking Richard,' said John. Margot noticed the solicitor didn't

interject. John knew he wouldn't, realised Margot.

'It's not mine. It's George, my partner's. I only found out after he died. I was flicking through the pictures when I realised some were our patients. I was sick. I didn't know what to do.'

'I'm going to need the PINS and passwords to all your devices to make sure you haven't shared these.'

'I'll give them to you now.'

Luke wrote them all down.

'So when exactly did you discover this?'

'I cleared his house out two weeks ago. I found the laptop then. I took it for safe keeping because I knew he could access patient details on it. I logged in for no reason other than curiosity. I got the shock of my life.'

'You've done nothing for two weeks.'

'No, I logged in when I got back from the pub last Sunday because Sue was away and I knew I shouldn't be looking really.'

'Rory disturbed you didn't he?'

'Yes. It was an accident I promise you.'

'What happened?'

'I left the laptop open while I went to get a whiskey. I had to go through it. I had to identify the patients. When I came back into the study this kid was watching it. He thought it was mine, called me a nonce, said he was going to call the buzzies. He grabbed the laptop and ran. I rugby-tackled him but he hit his head on a stone at the edge of the drive. I took him in the house but he was unconscious. I could feel his skull was broken. He died. I panicked. I took him to George's house. I tried to put him in the freezer. But he didn't fit. I cut his limbs off to fit him in. It was an accident I swear. I was just trying to get the laptop back.'

'The missing car keys?'

'In his pocket, only I didn't know that for a while.'

'Where is he now?'

'I can show you.'

'So you used the Range Rover to take him to George's?'

'Yes.'

'And you crashed.'

'Yes. I'd been drinking and I was in a panic, driving far too fast. I lost control.'

'Where?'

'About five miles out of the village. I can't remember exactly where.'

'And Kyle Morgan, how does he fit in?'

'The missing boy on the TV. That wasn't me. I don't know anything about that. I'm not a paedophile and I didn't know George was either.'
'What time did Rory die?'
'Around eight, maybe a bit after. I didn't think to check the time.'
'Okay, I'm going to need you to show us where you put Rory.'
'I'd like to consult with my client for five minutes please.'
'No problem.'

Margot waited for John to come back with Luke.
'Did you believe him about Kyle?' asked Margot.
'I think he's smart. He gave up Rory because he knew if we had the video we had the laptop. If we had the laptop we had George's house and we had the freezer. He's cutting his losses, going for manslaughter. Kyle can't be dressed as anything other than murder if he did it. One thing I'm certain of, is if it was him, he's confident we can't connect him to Kyle via the cars or the house. He didn't take Kyle to the house. I don't think we got the whole truth there. Ask your tech friend to see how many times and when that laptop was assessed after George died. I think Richard put the reputation of his practice above the welfare of his patients. He was never going to come clean on what George was up to. Let's face it, in reality he would be tarnished with the same brush. Let's recover Rory before we start throwing ideas around. See if cause of death backs any of that up. You two do the honours. Put him in the car with you and his brief. Get two uniforms to follow you. I'll get the cadaver dog to join you. Rory doesn't appear to be in the woods by George's house.'

This felt just like a detective series on the telly thought Margot. The killer in cuffs in the back seat next to Luke. Margot in the front with the solicitor. A panda car, dog van and CSI van behind them.
'You are aware anything you say will be recorded and can be used in evidence against you,' said Luke.
'I am,' said Richard.
'Where too?'
'Go to Scott's Gap.'
Margot set off and promptly stalled the car. That never happened on the TV. She tried again. They were off.
'Why Scott's Gap?'
'I grew up there. I wanted somewhere nice to bury him.'
'Is he all in one place?'

'Yes. But I lost an arm. I'm sorry I tried to find it. I think an animal ran off with it.'

He directed them past the woods. Margot and Luke said nothing. John had told them not to disclose anything. They went past the farm fitters. And drove north.
'Here. In the woods over there.'
'Can you show us the exact spot please.'
They let him out the car. They climbed over a wall. Walked across a soggy moorland to a small copse.
'Under the brambles,' said Richard pointing to a hollow.
Luke nodded to the uniformed officers. Margot looked around, she suspected the spot was chosen more for the seclusion than niceness. Margot wouldn't want to be buried here. It would be very lonely. A grave in a damp hollow under prickly brambles. Sucked up slowly over decades into the fruits. Eaten by unsuspecting people in apple and blackberry crumbles.

They took Richard back to the car and drove him back to the station. John was waiting for them in custody.
'Go home you two. We are just playing a waiting game now. I need you in tomorrow for interviews. I'll hold the fort here. Great work today.'

'Come up for dinner, my Dad is coming,' said Luke as they let themselves out of custody through the two doors. Margot always worried about getting stuck in-between the two sets of doors. She inexplicably seemed to always need a pee just as the first door closed and was always glad when the second door opened.
'Meet you in the car park in ten,' said Margot already looking forward to it.
Margot hurried to the toilets then waited for Luke. She couldn't wait to catch up with Tom. She hadn't seen Mervin all week either. She was itching to get going. Luke eventually came out.
'Margot I need to tell you something. Can you keep it to yourself please? The person who murdered my mother has been released. I don't think he should have ever been released but he has. John knows, so do Tom and Dad obviously. So if Dad's a bit quiet you know why. Please don't bring it up though. Dad's funny about it.'
'I won't say anything.'

Margot was still looking forward to dinner. But a little less so. She followed Luke up to his house. Tom came running out to meet her. 'Margot, it's so good to see you. Mervin is already here. I hear you got him. We want to hear all about it.'
Tom led Margot into the house.
'Tom dinner smells incredible.'
'It's just a roast.'

Tom's 'just a roast' didn't disappoint. Margot piled her plate with everything. She let Luke tell the story of how they had caught Richard so she could concentrate on eating. Mervin was actually on good form. He slotted straight back into Detective Superintendent mode asking Luke so many questions. Most of which still needed answering. Luke kept saying 'Dad we don't know yet. We are still working on that.'

The whiskey came out after the meal. Mervin was clearly staying. Margot excused herself. It was a long drive back and a busy day tomorrow. She had enjoyed herself. She drove home with a smile firmly fixed on her face.

She parked her car up and let herself in. She pulled the curtains shut and slumped on the sofa. Her phone pinged. She looked at the message.

I know what you did. You ugly cow. You are a fraud Margot.

Her first thought went to Colleen, then to her Dad which she quickly dismissed; not because he wouldn't say those things, he'd said them all at some point. He just wouldn't use a different phone. Could it be Metcalfe?

Margot went to the window and suddenly swiped the curtains open. She wasn't entirely sure what she'd been expecting but there was no one there, she shut them again. She headed for a bath before bed, hoping it would relax her enough to sleep. She ran the bath and threw off her clothes onto the floor. She tested the water temperature with her hands, perfect, she was about to jump in when her phone pinged again. She dried her hands and reached for her phone.

Enjoy your bath it might be your last.

Margot nearly dropped her phone. She rang Patrick.
'Patrick are you anywhere near my house?'
'Twenty minutes why?'
'Someone is watching me. The back of the house, can you check.'
'Be right there.'

It couldn't be Patrick could it? How did he know where she lived, he shouldn't know. Although she had to admit she wasn't surprised he knew where she lived. No she really didn't think it could be Patrick. She put her dressing gown on. She immediately started looking for cameras. She realised she was breathing in short gasps. She forced herself to think. This felt like Colleen. So what did she mean by: I know what you did. Did she think she had something to do with Kevin's death? Fraud, didn't sound like Colleen though. She was coming round to thinking it was Metcalfe. He was vindictive enough and he was weird enough. I know what you did.

Margot started going through her phones for incriminating evidence. There was nothing apart from that's WhatsApp message to Patrick. That was enough. Had he seen it or was he just bluffing? If it came out Patrick had burgled Richard Grant's house it could screw up the case against him. She would lose her job. Margot felt sick. She forced herself to think. Metcalfe always jumped the gun. If he had that WhatsApp message he would already have used it. He was bluffing.

Her phone rang. It was Patrick.
'All clear out here now. Do you want me to come in? I can sleep on the sofa if you want.'
'No. Thank you but not necessary.'
'Any ideas who?'
'Not at the moment.'
'You sure you don't want me to stay?'
'No I'll be fine thank you.'

Margot's bath was now cold she let the water out. She headed to bed and quickly wished she'd said yes to Patrick. If it was Colleen would she burn her house down? If it was Metcalfe what was his plan?

At one in the morning she decided it was definitely Metcalfe, he'd searched her house and he knew where the bathroom was. At two she realised the bathroom was obvious as it had a frosted window.

At three she realised whoever it was had been close enough to hear the taps running. At four in the morning she made the decision to tell Luke and her boss first thing at work about the messages. At four thirty she decided not to tell anyone. She deleted the WhatsApp conversation with Patrick. At five she decided to ask Patrick to follow her home from work tomorrow to see if she was being watched. She fell asleep around six. The alarm went off at six thirty.

George Nolan

His mother had shaken him awake at half one in the morning. George was struggling to stay awake now. He was sat on the sofa fiddling with the matches his mother had given him whilst watching the clock on the wall. Finally the hands reached half past three. He ran out the door, only just remembering to take the crowbar at the last second. He ran the short distance down the street to Aunty Janine's and silently opened the side gate. He climbed over the fence using the bench and dropped down into Kyle's garden. He forced the back door like his uncles had shown him and he let himself in.

He knelt down in front of the old sofa, took a match out and struck it. He held it to the orange fabric of the sofa. A small hole melted away exposing white foam. The flames were so small, silent, fragile. Then like Aladdin emerging from his lamp they grew with a whoosh. They soon reached the ceiling, then raced along it. He felt the heat on his cheeks. Black smoke started to make him cough. He ran out the house and back to his. He looked out of his window and watched the house burn. He looked at the box of matches. One little match did all that he thought. The fire had also lit something inside of him. He felt like the flames were racing through his veins. He didn't think he'd ever sleep again.

His mother had told him Shelly murdered Kyle. It was only right her house burned down she had said. He was still awake when his mother returned.
'Good boy George. George, I have something to tell you. I'm sorry but your Dad has just died. This is all her fault. She did this, don't worry she will pay. You don't have to go to school tomorrow.'

George headed to his room and cried. His dad could be an arse at times but he usually made it up to him afterwards. He loved his Dad when he wasn't on the drink. When the tears had dried up he thought about the fire. If she murdered Kyle and somehow killed his father was it enough to burn an empty house down? His mother always said he couldn't get in trouble with the police until he was ten. That wasn't for another three weeks. He should burn down the actual house she was in. He had overheard she was staying with her mother. He knew from Kyle roughly where that was. He'd cycle out there this evening and try and find the house. He knew what

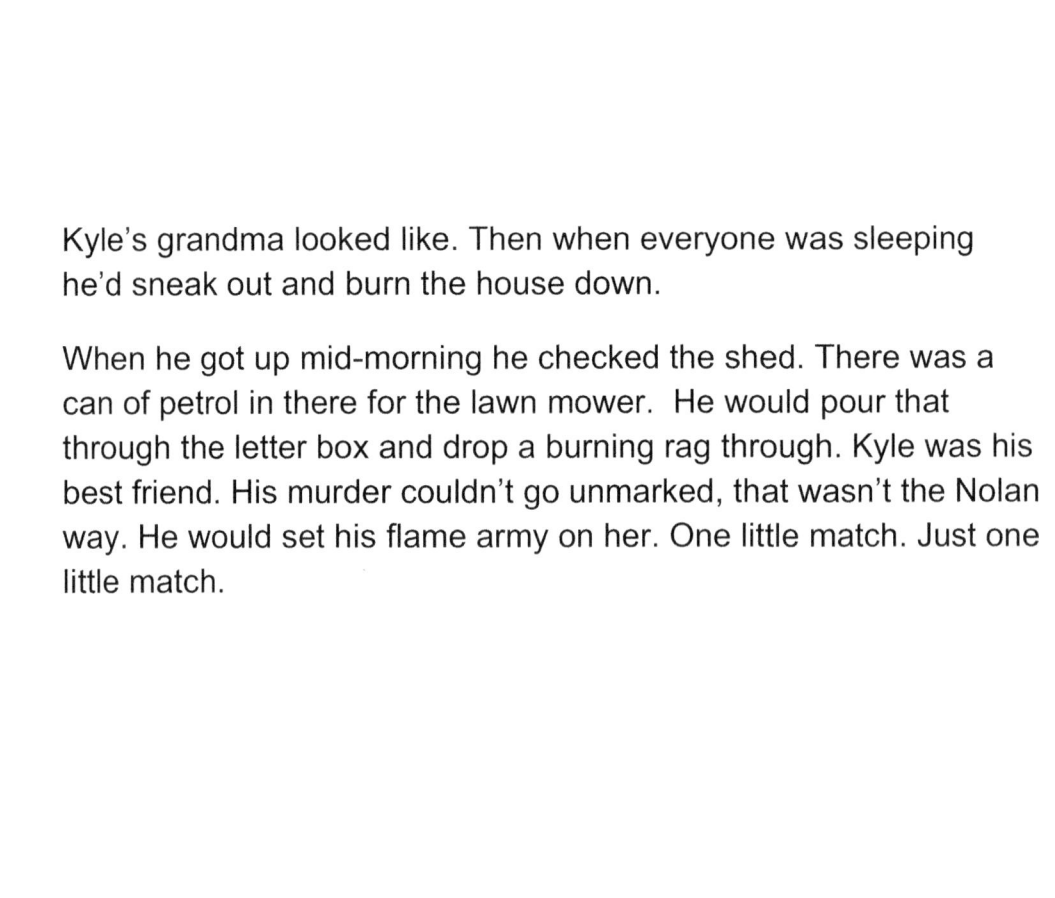

Kyle's grandma looked like. Then when everyone was sleeping he'd sneak out and burn the house down.

When he got up mid-morning he checked the shed. There was a can of petrol in there for the lawn mower. He would pour that through the letter box and drop a burning rag through. Kyle was his best friend. His murder couldn't go unmarked, that wasn't the Nolan way. He would set his flame army on her. One little match. Just one little match.

Margot

Margot's phone rang. She grabbed it and was relieved to see it was Luke.
'Margot are you up and ready?'
'Pretty much.'
'I'll pick you up in ten minutes. A body has surfaced at the water treatment works in Riding Mill. Wearing the clothes we think Kyle was wearing when he disappeared. Oh, and you should also know someone set fire to Shelly's mother's house last night. Shelly and her mother were pulled out unconscious by the fire brigade. It was arson. Both are critical in hospital. A petrol can was recovered at the scene. And Colleen has no alibi for this one she said she was at home asleep.'
'I'll be waiting outside. Come to the front.'
Margot was finding it difficult to get her head around all that happened whilst she was tossing and turning last night. She hurriedly finished her make up. Trying to cover the dark bags under her eyes.

She locked the door and double-checked it. She turned around to see Luke driving towards her. She waved and ran to the car.
'I don't think the boss actually went home. A quick update on forensic for you. Rory's DNA was recovered from Richard's original Range Rover, a single hair. His DNA from blood was found in the freezer caught in the seals. So far no trace of Kyle's DNA anywhere. Which by the sounds of it is because he went straight in the river. And of course he had time to plan Kyle.'
'So we definitely think he killed Kyle then?'
'The fragments of bodywork are from an Eiger grey Range Rover, they can't say more than that unfortunately. The saw you found in the rubbish has Rory and Grant's DNA all over it, blood and tissue and skin cells respectively. The black bag it was in is an exact match to a roll at Morrison's house that has Grants prints all over it. They matched the serrated tears. Boss is putting all that to him and then going to the CPS.'
'He's pretty much admitted all that already.'
'Yes but it shows he was trying to dispose of evidence. Less panic more planning. What we don't have is anything to connect him to Kyle.'
'Rory's body was it there, where he said?'
'I think so. They are still recovering the body. It was buried quite

deep. I guess losing the arm to a fox panicked him. So far they have recovered two legs and the other arm; they think those may be on top of the torso but it's slow going.'

They drove the rest of the way in silence. The car was making Margot yawn. They were met by a uniformed officer and shown where to go. The smell from the treatment works wasn't pleasant. Margot looked at what she assumed was human excrement being stirred around in large circular pools. They emerged on to the banks of the Tyne next to a weir. Water was rushing over the weir. On the bank was a small body. Margot was shocked. The red hair told her it was Kyle but this wasn't the sweet smiling boy in the school photo. His features had been eliminated by bloating and decomposition. Her first thought was how could she give him back like that to his parents? Margot was no expert but he looked like he'd been in the water a long time. He was also covered in abrasions. Probably from the river she concluded. Why did Donna float and Kyle sink? Why was she even thinking that?

'You okay Margot? I suggest we do the ID via DNA. Luckily because they were both arrested we already have their DNA. I've arranged for the body to be transported to the morgue. I think there's zero chance of forensic. Tracy is checking all the CCTV we have for the new Range Rover and the SLK to try and put Grant near Kyle's house. I think it's safe to assume Kyle was dumped in the river somewhere upstream of here. Probably on the morning he went missing. Probably with the idea it would look like an accident. A runaway who fell in the river.'
'So we couldn't have saved him could we?'
'No Margot. He would have been dead before we even left the station. Obviously that will need to be confirmed by the pathologist but I'm sure.'
'Kevin having a heart attack is really inconvenient isn't it?'
'Yes. I just don't get him and Donna. She had to be fifteen years older than him. He's been with Colleen since George was born. So he'd have had to still be a teenager when he was with Donna.'
'I think they were in love. Perhaps it was people saying she was too old that drove them apart. I think maybe they both had regrets.'

They waited for the body to be recovered. Margot noticed the care that was taken putting him in the body bag. Like he was being tucked up in bed. She felt sorry for the two guys as they carried him away. She imagined they'd be hugging their own kids just that little bit longer, that little bit tighter tonight.

Margot and Luke headed back to the station in silence. They found John busy in his office, he looked tired. He hadn't shaved and was wearing the same clothes Margot had last seen him in, definitely didn't go home thought Margot.
'Sit down you two. Well Rory is nearly out the ground and he does have an obvious head wound on the side of his head. The good doctor logged on that computer at 16.23 and logged off at 19.56 on the Sunday and that was actually the first time he logged on. So what he said could well be the truth. All of his own devices are completely clean. I wasn't sure Kyle and Rory were connected at first but an identical Range Rover as his crashing outside the house where Kyle was playing just can't be a coincidence. He confirmed thats where he crashed when I confronted him with the evidence.'
'He must know that's how we are connecting him,' said Margot.
'And he's smart enough to know it's meaningless on its own.'
'If Rory was an accident like he said. It's a big leap to murder. He's a doctor and a good one according to Adam Hill. Could he kill a child? What in reality could Kyle have seen in the dark? Rory went missing on Sunday, Kyle Thursday. If the police hadn't come knocking by then it probably meant Kyle had said nothing that could connect him,' said Margot.
'I take all that on board. If not him then is it's probably Shelly or Dan. Do you think either is more likely Margot?' asked John.
'Definitely not Dan. Actually I don't think she did it either Sir.'
'What do you think Luke?'
'Cutting the body up, putting it in the freezer. That was planned, cold. Panic is dumping the body somewhere in a hurry. He was thinking clearly at that point. He put it in the freezer so it didn't smell. Give himself time to dispose of the body. I think at that point his mindset switched to getting away with it. All of it.'
'The keys don't make sense,' said Margot. 'Why when I did the house-to-house did he admit losing the keys? It brought him into focus. Why would he do that?'
'He was on the spot. He didn't think it through but he knew the keys were crucial in some way; he needed to distance himself from those keys. And he said he recovered them from Rory's pocket?' said Luke
' ...Shit, Kyle had the keys. Rory didn't steal them. Grant had to move the SLK out the garage. To put his car in to get Rory in

without being seen. He must've dropped the bloody keys after he crashed. He goes back to search but they're not there so he assumes Kyle had picked them up. What if those keys had Rory's blood all over them, that's why he had to say the keys were missing.'
'It's a good theory Margot. By telling us Rory had the keys and admitting he killed Rory he knows we won't be that concerned where they are now. I'm not saying you're right Margot, but we need to find those keys.'
'I hope they weren't in Shelly's house,' said Luke.
'Check the photos taken when we searched Shelly's. Check the exhibits we seized from there, make sure we don't already have those keys in our possession.'
'Boss we should speak to George and Nathan. Kyle wouldn't have told his Dad because he promised not to go out the garden but he might have told his friends.'
'Luke you check the photos and exhibits. Margot talk to his friends. Hold off on George for an hour or two till I give you the nod. Colleen is getting arrested for attempted murder. The arson last night. The petrol can recovered had Kevin Wallace's prints all over it. Unless he came back from the dead it wasn't him.'

Margot headed to Nathan's. She should just catch him before school. Unfortunately Nathan didn't know anything about the keys. She hadn't got the all-clear from the boss to see George yet so she decided to wait it out at a cafe. She ordered a coffee. Then another. Then another. The caffeine finally seeping through into her bloodstream. Finally she could go and see George who was now at the police station along with his sister and social services.

The two ladies from social services weren't the two most helpful people she'd come across. At first they said it wasn't appropriate to speak to George at present citing child welfare. When Margot pressed how important it could be they reluctantly gave her two minutes. Margot thought Mrs Trunchball was actually timing. Although according to her ID badge she was Zara Marsh. Zara hovered behind Margot. Margot made a funny face to George who burst out laughing.
'Hi George.'
'Hi Margot.'
'George, I'm really sorry but something has happened to Kyle.'
'It's okay I know he's dead.'

'George, did Kyle mention anything about some car keys he found on Sunday night?'
'Yeah. I swapped them with him for a soccer card he needed.'
'Do you still have them?'
'Yeah. I was trying to find the car they belonged to. Couldn't get anything to open.'
George looked up, she could imagine Mrs Trunchball's face behind her. Margot pulled another face and rolled her eyes up. George struggled to keep a straight face.
'I think I know what car it opens. Can you tell me where the keys are?'
'If you tell me why they arrested my Mum.'
'Someone set fire to a house last night.'
'They think that was my Mum?'
'They need to speak to her about it.'
'Can we go in the pink car again?'
'Sorry you can't go. And I don't have the pink car today just a boring old CID car. The keys are very important so a special person has to put them in a special bag.'
'A CSI has to put them in an evidence bag?'
'Yes, how did you get so smart?'
George smiled 'under my bed, in the blue box. Why are they so important?'
'They might help me catch Kyle's killer if they open the car I think they do.'
'Shelly don't have a car.'
'Not Shelly.'
'I thought Shelly killed Kyle.'
'I don't think it was Shelly.'
'Mum said it was Shelly She lied didn't she?'
'Enough. Time up detective.'
Zara moved behind George and put her hand on his shoulder. George made a face this time. Margot smiled and thanked George.

Margot practically ran out the station and rushed up to George's house. Forensic were already searching it Watched by the whole street who stood in doorways and at windows. Margot explained to a CSI what she needed. They disappeared and came back with a set of Mercedes keys in an evidence bag. Margot grabbed the bag and rushed back to the station with her prize.

She ran across the yard. And then took the stairs as quickly as she could. She was completely out of breath by the time she staggered into the DI's office.

'I got them. Kyle traded them with George Nolan for a football card. They were in a box under George's bed.'

'Great work Margot. Complete the paperwork and I'll get authority to send them to the lab. I have authority to charge Grant with the murder of Rory Elliott. I'm not going to arrest him for Kyle just yet. We need our ducks in a line first. You've convinced me he's our man Margot, but we still have no direct evidence linking him to Kyle's death. Until we do I'm not going to arrest him. He's not going anywhere now. Would you like to go and do the honours Margot? Go and charge your first murderer. You solved the case after all.'

Perhaps she wasn't a fake after all. 'Yes please. Now?'

'Now is as good a time as any, off you go.'

Margot headed down to custody. She felt like a real detective as she cautioned Richard Grant and read out the charge wording. As Margot said the words 'murdered Rory Elliot', she finally felt Rory mattered to the world.

As she headed back up to the office she knew Rory himself was finally en route to the morgue. She knew a postmortem would happen the moment he got there. She hopped someone would reattach his arms and legs before he was buried or cremated or at least pretend they were attached - dress him in a suit perhaps. She stopped herself. Did everyone have odd thoughts like this? She was surviving on caffeine, perhaps that had something to do with it. Perhaps when your eyes see things you don't want to see, you get odd thoughts. Or was she just actually odd?

She walked into her office and looked around. She decided her Luke and John were a great team. They had worked short-handed and got the job done. Well half done, there was still Kyle. She suddenly felt guilty about withholding the threatening messages from them. She decided she needed to come clean as far as the messages went, but if she did that and they checked the download and found the picture of the bill for the car keys days before she actually found it, then they would know Patrick burgled the house. They might think she set the doctor up. That Patrick did. She couldn't come clean.

Somewhere in this station was a disc with the download of her phone on. Two discs - an evidential copy and a working copy. On those discs was the photo of the bill for the new keys and a WhatsApp of Margot and Patrick talking about it. She had to destroy the discs, there was no other way.

She knocked on the door to John's office.
'Sir, was Donna a suicide in the end?'
'Yes looks like it. No evidence of foul play. Note in the car.'
'Can I ask what it said?'
'It just said 'Sorry'. Nothing else. It wasn't your fault Margot. You look shattered, go home.'
'Is there not stuff to do?'
'Always Margot, but I'd rather have you refreshed tomorrow than tired today. Go.'

Margot rang Patrick and told him she was going home. Patrick wasn't expecting the call so early and said he'd be an hour. Margot thought it would look too odd if she hung around for an hour so she told Patrick she would go shopping in the big Tescos at Kingston park then drive home for him to watch her house for a bit when she got home.

She needed shopping there wasn't anything to eat in the house. She was out of toilet rolls and toothpaste too. She'd squeezed the last out of both this morning. She slowly wandered the isles picking up all sorts of calories she didn't need, trying to pass some time. She mused over the wines. She hadn't got a clue. Tom always had nice wine, probably not from Tescos she had to concede. She eventually headed to her car with four full bags she loaded into the boot. Bollocks, toilet rolls! She sighed under her breath and headed back into the store. She came out carrying a 24 pack of toilet rolls. Her phone pinged.

Forget the toilet rolls. Well you are full of SHIT.

A different number. Not Colleen then, she should still be in custody. It had to be Metcalfe. She hurriedly got in her car and rang Patrick.
'Patrick he's here I'm at Tesco Kingston park. I think it's Metcalfe. I'm heading home now.'
'Okay I'm nearly there. Head straight home I'll be there before you. You won't see me, will you come up the 694 from town? Do you know what he drives?'

'Yes that way. I have no idea what his own car is.'
'Call me if you're worried but go straight in and lock the doors.'

Margot drove home. She unlocked the front door and hurriedly carried her shopping in. She slammed the door closed and locked it behind her. He heart was racing. She started to put away the shopping hoping it would settle her down. She had treated herself to a nice bubble bath, it had said 'calming' on it and it smelled lovely. She carried up to the bathroom with the toilet rolls. She shivered. She was sure she'd left her nightdress on the bathroom floor. Pretty much where it had fallen. She checked under her pillow, it's usual place. It wasn't there. She checked the laundry basket it wasn't there either. She began to feel uneasy. She rushed and checked the back door and all the windows. All locked. She thought about it. Metcalfe had her keys when he searched her house. Would he have got a copy made way back then? Patrick was the bloody good burglar. Right now the only people she trusted were Luke and Tom.

She waited ten minutes and rang Patrick.
'Anything?'
'No you weren't followed.'
'Thinking about it there would be no need it was obvious with that much shopping I was going home. He knows where I live. He's done for today. He won't risk anymore.'
'Shall I hang around?'
'No need I'm heading to Luke's. I might go now if it's safe. And I might stay the night.'
'Good idea. I'll hang on till you leave then go.'
'I really appreciate this.'
'You're welcome.'

Patrick sounded sincere. At the moment she trusted him sixty percent. She packed an overnight bag and headed for Luke's, shoving in a couple of bottles of the wine with the prettiest labels.

Tom was in, Luke wasn't, she guessed he was probably still at work. Margot just burst into tears. Tiredness and worry flooding out.
'Margot's what's wrong?'
'I screwed up Tom. I really screwed up.' She told Tom everything. It was a like a tremendous weight had been lifted off her. She felt she was finally breathing air that had oxygen in it.

'Let me see these texts…Margot he's threatened you…So you think it's Metcalfe or Patrick now?'
'Yes. More Metcalfe.'
'I'd say more Patrick.'
'Can we test that out? And what the bloody hell do I do about Patrick breaking into Richard's house?'
'I can't believe I'm saying this but if you come clean on that his defence will have a field day. There's no reason that should ever come to light now. I think we need to see who this is first. Maybe now is not the time to be mentioning that to anybody else. Definitely do not tell Luke. If it does come out it will finish your career Margot. If Luke knows it could finish his.'
'I won't, it's on me. If it comes out I'll admit it.'
'First we need to find out who this is. The phones will be a dead end. Get Patrick to put hidden cameras in your house. If it's him, he won't go back in. If it's Metcalfe he should be captured. Are you sure the nightdress is missing?'
'I'm pretty sure. I haven't turned the house upside down. I'm ninety nine percent sure I left it on the bathroom floor.'
'Stay here tonight.'
'Thanks. But I can't. I don't want Luke anywhere near this. I shouldn't have even come. I was just scared.'
'I don't like that, you will be alone.'
'I'll be fine.'

She got back in her car and drove off. She couldn't stay. She pulled over and rang Patrick.
'Patrick can you put hidden cameras in my house?'
'Sure I can do it in the next hour. Do you want me to break in?'
'No I'm coming home. I can't drag Luke into this. I'll cook tea while you do it.'

How odd was this getting? Patrick rigged cameras in the bedroom, bathroom, kitchen and living room. He connected them directly to Margot's phone. He was now checking the cameras, waving at Margot who was shouting 'it's working'.

'Okay so they are on a motion sensors which records if it senses movement. It also notifies your phone, I chose cowbells. You have to press this here to make them live. So obviously you can turn it off if you need a crap.'
'Thanks. I've made chilli con carne and rice, are you hungry?'

'Yes please.'
'Five minutes. Can I see if I can spot the cameras?'
'Go for it. Tenner says you won't find any of them.'
'On.'

Margot handed over a tenner. She served the rice and put the chilli con carne on the table in the frying pan.
'Help yourself, I have wine if you want.'
'No thanks. I'm driving.'

After the meal she was as sure as possible it wasn't Patrick. Patrick she realised was complicated but straightforward all at the same time. Bad things had happened to him of that she was certain. But he had an honesty about him. He didn't talk in riddles. He made no secret of what he was. And Margot sensed he saw her as a comrade because she'd covered for him over Mark. Patrick was the sort of guy who took a bullet for a comrade. He was loyal.

'Margot I'll stay if you want. On the couch. This guy, he's a stalker. Stalkers are dangerous.'
'No I'll sleep with the cameras on. You can't see these cameras too can you?'
'Not unless you want me to. Go into the menu, go to add phone, add me if you want.'
'Thanks.'
'Goodnight Margot.'

Margot headed to bed it was only ten o'clock. She grabbed her baseball bat and slipped it under the duvet. She made sure her cameras were live and she put the phone next to her pillow. Her head sunk into the pillow and she was asleep.

She was in the Olympics, skiing down a mountain. She didn't know how to ski. So why was she skiing to the sound of cowbells? She woke herself up with a start. Her heart was beating so hard she actually thought it would shoot clean out her ribs. She was instantly alert somehow, standing by the side of her bed, bat in hand. Her skin tingled. She picked up her phone. A balaclava'd figure was creeping across her living room. Metcalfe, she knew that shape. She raised the bat above her head, gave a war-cry of Swiss yodelling and ran down the stairs just in time to see the front door close. She ran into the street. He was halfway up the street already.

She didn't follow, she had her answer. Besides, the adrenaline surge was wearing off and she was losing her courage fast.

She wasn't sure what to do. She needed to report this now. If she didn't Metcalfe would think there was a reason she hadn't, he would know she was hiding something. If she didn't report the break in, then effectively she was committing herself to Patrick dealing with it. He was more than capable of dealing with it but Margot didn't want that. She called 999. A young policewoman soon arrived, blue lights flashing.
'You reported an intruder?'
'Yes I disturbed him. I have no idea how he got in.'
'There is no sign of forced entry?'
'No.'
'Are you sure it was an intruder?'
'Yes. Look I had a camera system installed. I thought someone was in my house yesterday, my nightie disappeared. I wasn't sure though, I could have just mislaid it. I've been working flat out. I should probably tell you I'm a detective on MIT. It's a new system, let me see if I can work out how to get it up for you.'
'I've got one of these, I'll do it,' said the policewoman. Margot was always fascinated by how quickly young people moved their thumbs.
'Look you were right. He's got a balaclava on unfortunately. And gloves. Are you okay if I email this clip to myself?'
'Go ahead. Actually can you show me how to do that.'
'Sure.'

She talked Margot through it.
'Shall I get Forensic?' she asked when she was done.
'We both know there won't be any,' said Margot.
'I might be criticised if I don't.'
'I don't think there's much point but please run it by your supervisor.'
'You need to change your locks. Does anyone else have a key?'
'Ex-Detective Superintendent Mervin Jones. It's definitely not him and he's the wrong build.'
'Any ideas then?'
'The shape reminded me of someone but I'd rather not say as it's a serving officer and I could be way off base.'
'Will you be okay?'
'Yes. I'm actually going to head into work I think. I've plenty to do.

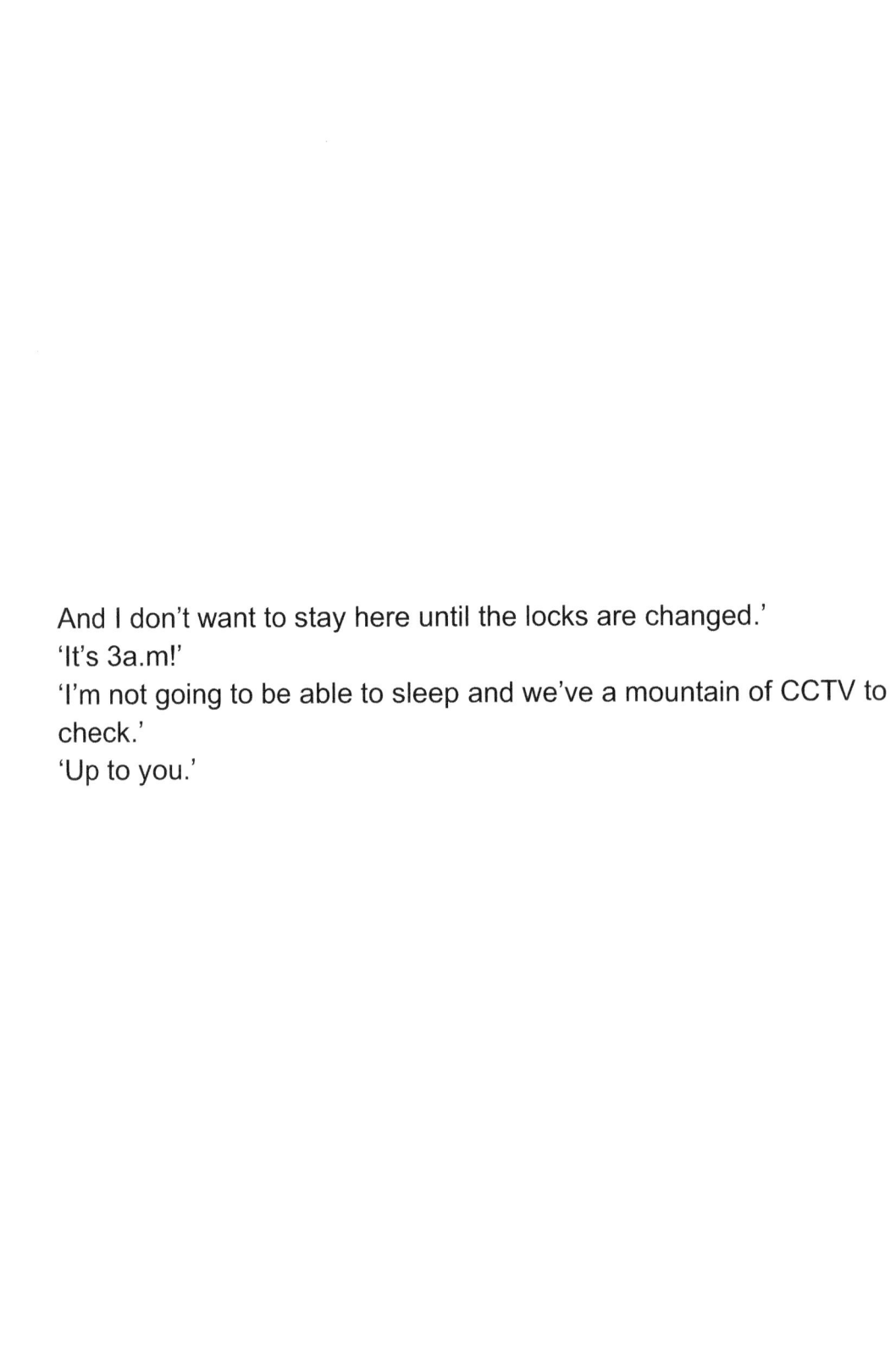

And I don't want to stay here until the locks are changed.'
'It's 3a.m!'
'I'm not going to be able to sleep and we've a mountain of CCTV to check.'
'Up to you.'

Margot

Margot needed to be at work when no one else was. She had discs to recover. She parked her car and headed to her office. She made sure no one was on her floor. She put on latex gloves and grabbed two blank discs. She crept down two flights of stairs and checked no one was around in CID. The office was in darkness, she found the office of the new SIO. It was keypad entry. She held her breath and pushed in the code used by CID. It opened. She saw the file on his desk. She opened it. She flicked through it looking for the property number and seal number for the discs. She had them. She sneaked out. The main part of her plan would have to wait. She couldn't break into the property store. She'd need a reason to be in there though. And she'd need to use the computer without being noticed. The property officer started at 8am. She hoped Luke and John would start later given the hours they had put in lately.

She needed an evidence bag with a similar number just one digit out - she knew they were delivered in sequential batches. She headed to the admin store and routed through the pile of new evidence bags. She found what she was looking for B 1017717 as opposed to the one she was replacing B 1011717. She was about to take the one bag when she realised a clever detective might pick up on the fact the number was so far from the other bags. She picked up a wad of bags and put them in the CID with the other bags so if anyone thought to check similar numbers were being used at a similar time. She was pleased with herself for thinking of that. She used the rest of the time to delete anything she didn't want on her phone.

She logged into her emails. John had sent her one. She opened it. It said he was starting at ten as was Luke. Kyle's post-mortem was at midday, John was going to attend that. He asked her to get the keys she'd seized from George Nolan's house out of property and confirm they were the keys to the SLK before they headed to the lab. He had underlined DO NOT REMOVE FROM EVIDENCE BAG. It was as if the sea was parting for Moses.

At eight she rushed down to grab the property officer before he properly woke up. He wasn't a morning person. He needed a couple of cups of coffee before grumpy wore off. And the basement was well and truly his domain. Margot knew no one else would be bothering him this early.

'Sorry I need something out of the property store - the Mercedes keys I seized yesterday.'

'Property number,' he sighed.

Margot passed the number and watched exactly what he did on his computer.

'Anything else before I fetch it, technically I don't start for another five minutes you know.'

'No, sorry it's important.'

As soon as he left Margot typed in the property number for the discs. She hurriedly wrote down their location on her arm and changed the evidence bag number to the one she had in her pocket. He came back with the keys.

'Thank you.'

'I've signed them out to you,' he shouted after Margot.

'Thanks,' she shouted back.

Margot left. She returned after ten minutes and asked to look at another exhibit.

'Tell me where they are I'll go. You finish your coffee. I just need to quickly take a photo of it, no need to sign it out,' she said.

The property officer gave her the location and key to the property store. She headed along, her heart-rate increasing with every step. She looked back as she unlocked the property store and dived in, pulling the door to behind her. Panic immediately set in when she couldn't find the discs. She fumbled through the box. She felt sick. She looked at the location again written on her arm. She realised she had remembered it incorrectly, she was looking in the wrong place. She hurriedly found the right box. She soon found the discs. She tried to control her breathing and calm herself down. It was taking far too long, he'd be suspicious. She switched them out with the blank discs, copying the writing as best she could on the discs and evidence bag. She quickly compared them, she'd done a good job considering her shaking hands. Perhaps she'd missed her vocation as a forger. Frank's words haunted her. If you make a mistake just own up to it. Only it wasn't a mistake, was it? It was a crime. So was this. She hurriedly found the bill for the new keys for the SLK and took a photo on her phone of the bill. She closed the door and hurried back down the corridor to return the property store keys.

'That's it, promise. I'm off out,' she said as naturally as she could.

'Did you find it okay?'
'Eventually,' said Margot showing him the picture.
'And you put it back in exactly the same place?'
'I did.'
'Is this to do with the murder of the kid?'
'Yeah. The keys I needed should be the original keys but I need to go and verify that. I suddenly thought I might need to prove it wasn't the replacement keys as well. I don't know much about these things but I'm guessing keys have codes. That someone will be able to tell me.'
'I think you'll find they have the same code. Let me see that photo you took,…. Look see there. That's the code there, see. You need that code to get replacement keys.'
'Oh. Thank you.'

Her plan couldn't have gone any smoother in the end, he didn't seem to notice how long she'd taken. And she had a totally legitimate reason for being there that the property officer would remember. Even if she hadn't understood a word of what he was trying to tell her. The Gods were on her side today.

She headed to the Doctor's house and knocked on the door. Margot hadn't even considered his wife. The state she might be in, the questions she would volley at her. The wife was now in tears.
'No one will tell me anything. Why has my husband been charged with murder? Richard wouldn't hurt a fly. You must have the wrong man.'
'I'm sorry I'm not allowed to discuss the case. I have just come to see if these keys open your car.'

Margot looked over her shoulder at the car.
'Of course. Try.'
Margot pressed the keys through the bag the car beeped and opened.
'What does that mean? Is that good or bad?' She burst into tears again.
'I'm sorry. Look, he's in court this morning at ten. Go down and see if you can see him,' said Margot. 'I can't stay I'm sorry.' Margot got back in her car. As she drove off she could see Mrs Grant in the rear view mirror, just standing there on her drive, wiping the tears from her face. Margot remembered only too well discovering your husband was a totally different person to who you thought. She felt

guilty leaving her standing there but she knew that's how it had to be.

When she got back to the station John was just arriving. She bumped into him on the bottom of the stairs.
'It's the right keys it opened the car. Sir, can I have word? It's personal.'
'Sure. Shall I make the coffees while you return those keys?'
'Thanks.'

Margot took the keys back to the property officer. He was now her best friend. He seemed satisfied the keys had opened the car. She headed upstairs. John was in his office, a cup of coffee waiting for her.
'Sir I was broken into last night. I didn't tell the officer who attended because I wanted to speak to you first, I'd had some texts before.'

Margot showed him the texts and the video.
'You think it's Metcalfe, don't you?'
'Do you Sir? I'm not being silly, am I? It's his shape.'
'Why didn't you come to me earlier?'
'We were busy. I thought it was Colleen. Because of Donna and Kevin. I didn't want you to think I'd done anything wrong because I hadn't. Then the text about the toilet rolls - I went home via Tesco yesterday, he had to be following me. It couldn't be Colleen, she was still in custody. I was going to tell you today. I put hidden cameras in that alerted my phone yesterday evening. I disturbed him. I didn't think he'd break in with me in the house.'
'You reported the break-in and you showed them this footage?'
'Yes.'
'How did he get in?'
'He must have a key.'
'I don't like the guy Margot. But I'm finding it hard to believe this is him.'
'I'm not Sir. Not after that video Donna gave me.'
'Okay I'm passing this on to professional standards too. Dave Caldwell the Super to be precise. He's a good cop. It's who I took the videos to. He will need to talk to you. If he had your key Margot he can only have copied it when he arrested you. That was months ago.'
'I know. My nightdress was missing when I got home yesterday. I can't say for sure I haven't mislaid it. To tell the truth I haven't been

sleeping because of this. I couldn't stay at home after last night so I came in here.'
'Margot my door is always open.'
'I know Sir.'

Margot didn't feel manipulative at all. That was heartfelt from her. And all she had done earlier was get rid of her own phone records. They weren't even evidence anymore; they were listed as unused - they were satisfied Donna tried to call her but she didn't answer. And she did what she did so a child killer didn't walk. If it wasn't for that, she had been prepared to admit what she'd done. She was really worried about Metcalfe however. She immediately rang a locksmith who agreed to come round at five. Then she rang Tom and told him what had happened. She didn't mention that she'd destroyed the evidence of the conversation on WhatsApp with Patrick. She did feel a little manipulative this time.

Margot was soon summoned to see Superintendent Caldwell. Suddenly her stomach started to churn.
'Hi Margot, I've spoken to the attending officer. I've seen the footage from last night. And the texts. I'll need your phone downloaded. She handed both phones over knowing this time the incriminating WhatsApp messages and calls were no more.
'He messaged both phones?'
'Just my personal.'
'Then I only need that. I'll make sure it's returned to you within an hour. Why do you think it's Metcalfe?'
'Mainly the shape on the video Sir.'
'That's the first time you suspected him?'
'Sort of. The first text I thought was Colleen Nolan. It wasn't till yesterday I thought of Metcalfe because Colleen was in custody and whoever it was must have been watching me shopping. I thought it might be Metcalfe then. But I wasn't sure until the video.'
'You put the cameras in because you believe your nightdress was missing?'
'Yes. I'm sure it is. I thought I'd left it on the bathroom floor.'
'Can you describe it?'
'I can show you. If you promise not to use the picture.'
He handed her phone back. Margot found the picture she'd taken of Mervin and her in the lakes.
'Is that Mervin Jones?' said Caldwell trying not laugh.
'I know there's not much material but it was bloody expensive Sir.'

'Your photo is safe with me Margot. Have you got a picture of it without you in it?'
'Why would I take a picture of my nightdress Sir?'
'What does he mean by 'I know what you've done. You are a fraud'?'
'I don't know. When I worked for him the first thing he said was he didn't want me on his team. Because I didn't have the experience. Only not quite like that. He actually asked if I was shagging Luke's Dad. I am now. But I wasn't then. Then he was really pissed off when I didn't do as I was told. I went to the scene of Frank's suicide when he told me to investigate some unsolvable burglaries. Then I went to MIT and he arrested me for the murder of my husband. Which I didn't do.'
'Perhaps it means he knows Margot gave me the video of him in Donna's bedroom,' interjected John.
Margot hadn't even thought of that. Perhaps he didn't know about Patrick after all. She couldn't think it through any further, the Super was asking another question.
'At any point has he made any sexual advances?'
'No. I think he hates me,' said Margot cringing at the thought.
'You did your shopping at Tesco Kingston park?'
'Yes Sir.'
'Where did you park?'
'Practically at the entrance. I was lucky someone was pulling out as I got there.'
'Okay. I'll check CCTV. If he's on it then he will be arrested. Change your locks. Write down the route you took from here to Tescos for me please.'
He pushed a pen and paper to Margot. She scribbled down the route. There was an awkward silence whilst she did. Margot felt under pressure, she scribbled as quickly as she could.
'A locksmith is coming at five o'clock Sir. If I can be home by then,' she said when she'd finished.
'Yes. I'll make sure an officer accompanies you home and remains with you whilst that is done.'
'I can sort that Sir,' said John.
'If he goes back my phone will make a cowbells sound Sir. The cameras are on motion sensors.'
'Okay. Cowbells means intruder.'
'Go back to our office Margot. I need a quick word with the

Superintendent,' said John.
Margot left.

'Christ John, where did you find her?'
'She is different. She bounces back and forth from genius to bonkers. Mark Rohan was all her. As was catching Richard Grant. She somehow gets there.'
'Do you think it's Metcalfe?'
'Maybe. I do think she's being stalked. We need to find out who it is. I am worried she's in danger.'
'Does Mervin know?'
'Not yet. Margot knows his wife's killer has just been released. Luke told her. I guess that's why she didn't confide in them. Sensitive time.'
'Okay I'll get officers straight on this. I don't want to tell you how to suck eggs but partner her up and brief whoever that is.'

Caldwell looked at the piece of paper where Margot had scribbled down the route: out the station turn left. Through the traffic lights. Past the garage with the posh cars. Turn right by the zebra crossing past the house with the pink curtains. Turn left by the shop that sells over sized clothes the one with the big dresses in the window that says 18 to 30 like the holidays but it's meant to be clothes sizes. Straight on until you get to the flats. I don't shop in that shop by the way. Turn right at the flats….
'Christ!'

Margot

'Margot, I want you working with Luke. You can't be on your own. Which means I'll have to tell Luke,' said John as he got back to the office.
'That's okay. I was going to tell him anyway. I kind of already mentioned it to Tom. That was before it all kicked off with the intruder.'
'I don't think Grant used his own car for Kyle. Start ringing round the hire companies please Margot.'
'Do you think he used George Morrison's car boss, then got rid of it?'
'Did Morrison have a car?'
'He must have done to get to work.'
'Find out if any vehicles are registered to him. Check the airport.'
'Yes Sir.'

Margot soon discovered he had a Skoda Octavia. It was unfortunately still parked at the airport. Margot started calling all the hire companies. By the time Luke arrived in work she had rung them all and nothing. John summoned Luke in. Margot knew why.

Luke emerged looking really concerned.
'Are you okay Margot? You should've said.'
'I wasn't that worried till last night. I was going to tell you today.'
'Stay with me and Tom if you like. Does Dad know?'
'I haven't told him. I might stay tonight if that's okay. I have to go back at five, a locksmith is coming.'
'Of course the spare room is free. Have you done all the hire car places?'
'Yes and nothing.'
'Tracy hasn't got his Range Rover or the SLK on camera. Plus there was no forensic. He has to have used a different vehicle. He was too confident we couldn't pin Kyle on him.'
'I found Morrison's car. It's still at the airport, it never left.'
'What about patients, does he visit any elderly patients? Anyone who wouldn't notice if he borrowed their car for a few hours, someone with dementia perhaps.'
'Let's pop along to child protection, they should have a list of patients.'

They walked along and explained why they were there. They were directed to a tired-looking detective in the corner. Margot couldn't

help but notice the height of the in-trays. So much pain and suffering towering precariously on desks.
'I can give you a copy of the list of people registered at the practice. I'll just run you off a copy,' she said.
'How many so far?' asked Margot her voice breaking.
'Six. Most of the pictures and videos you found are downloads from the internet…Coming off the printer for you now.'
'Thanks.'

They headed back to their office. Margot just couldn't understand how someone could have a sexual interest in children. She just could not see how that could be.
'Shall we go older ones first? You shout them out, I'll see if they have a vehicle registered at that address. Then I guess we just go and ask.' said Luke. Margot had only half heard what Luke had said. She nodded.

After sitting at their desks for over an hour they eventually had a list of twenty-one people to visit and that was just the over-eighties. They hadn't even looked at anyone younger. They tackled them in the order Margot had written them down. The first eleven were a blowout. Margot had to admit despite their age they were all more with it than she was. None had seen Dr Grant recently and none had lent him the car.
They pulled into a rundown estate heading for the next on the list. At the end, next to the playing fields, tucked in the corner was a semi detached house. It stood out because of the beautiful garden. Full of flowers. An artist's palette of colour, so different from the drab canvas of the rest of the estate. On the drive was a twenty year old Ford Fiesta. Still shiny. A few bumps and scraps hinting at the drivers reduced capacity to actually drive it. Just as they got out of their car a Lexus pulled up and out stepped the Chief Constable.
'Hello Margot. What are you doing here?'
Don't look at his crotch. Don't look at his crotch, she repeated the Mantra under her breath. Margot looked at his crotch and couldn't stop.
'We are visiting Mr Roy Harper Sir,' she said.
'My Dad?'
Luke was nudging Margot. She looked up.
'Sorry Sir, we didn't make the connection. Anyway I would have thought your Dad would live somewhere posher than this. Sorry that came out wrong Sir.'

He laughed 'I grew up in this house Margot. Can I enquire why you need to speak to my Dad? He has dementia, he gets extremely confused.'

'You are aware we arrested his doctor for murder?'

'I was. Although I was surprised. I always found him very accommodating, he went above and beyond for Dad.'

'We have linked him to the possible murder of Kyle Morgan. We think he borrowed one of his patient's cars to commit the murder. Without their knowledge of course.'

'He was definitely murdered then?'

'Postmortem is happening as we speak Sir, our boss is there. But we have evidence linking Kyle to Grant,' said Luke.

'He might have used Dad's car. I visit every Sunday, Wednesday and Friday. Last week the car was moved, between Wednesday and Friday, and Kyle I believe went missing the Thursday morning between. On the Friday when I arrived it was parked dead centre of the drive. I had put it right at the edge to make it easier to walk up and down past the car, as it is now. I asked Dad about it but it was a pointless conversation. I confiscated the keys. He's not safe to drive. I should have sold the car before he got bad really. I can't now until I get Power of Attorney, I'm still waiting for that to be granted. I guess you need me to go home and fetch the keys so you can uplift it. If you need to speak to my Dad I'll come with you if that's okay.'

'No need to speak to your Dad, Sir. We can uplift it without keys. I'll arrange a forensic recovery. But if you could get us the keys at some point that would help,' said Luke.

'Good, good, you carry on. I'll nip in and make sure he's okay.'

'Are you okay to wait here for recovery if I check the estate for CCTV? Lock yourself in the car. The Chief is just there and I'm a phone call away,' said Luke to Margot.

'Of course. He won't try anything here Luke.'

Margot waited. Her thoughts quickly turned to the Chief. Would he even know she'd seen the video? If he did, unlike her he'd played it very cool. She still couldn't believe he'd grown up here. He'd lost the Geordie accent he must have once had. Perhaps he'd gone to a boarding school, an all-boys school. They did weird things in dormitories didn't they? How do you even discover you like pink

fluffy handcuffs and whips she wondered. How did he even end up in Donna's bedroom? He was rattling on the car window. Margot screamed.
'Sorry Margot. Didn't mean to frighten you. Do you want a cup of tea?'
'Yes please Sir. Sorry I was miles away.'
'Milk, sugar?'
'Yes please. Two sugars please.'

The Chief headed to his Lexus and removed three bags of compost placing them on the drive.
'Let me give you a hand with those Sir.'
Margot had jumped out the car and grabbed a bag before she had finished the sentence.
'Back garden,' he said.
Margot carried one bag, the Chief the other two. The back garden was even more colourful. It was a generous plot on account it was stuck on the end. A neat lawn was surrounded by deep borders that were crammed with flowers. An old man was pottering in the greenhouse. He smiled at Margot. Margot waved.
'Your garden is amazing,' she said.
He smiled an even bigger smile.
'I'll bring your tea out in a second.'
Margot took that as her cue to sit back in the car. She made her way back round to the front. The car was locked. She felt her pockets for the keys. No keys. She looked on the passenger seat.
'Bollocks.'

The chief bought her tea round.
'I'll think I'll have it out here,' she said.

Luke came back looking very excited.
'We've nearly got him Margot. I've got CCTV. A black Range Rover comes into the Estate at 3.30 am. The Fiesta goes out. Then at 7.15am the opposite - the Fiesta comes in and the Range Rover goes out. You can't see the driver or registrations, but if we get forensic from the car we have him. It's enough to arrest him at least.'
'That's great Luke, but I had to move some compost and I've accidentally locked us out of our car. The keys are on the passenger seat.'

'Not to worry, I'll ring Tracy tell her to look for the Fiesta and get her to run the spare keys down. Recovery is going to be an hour and a half anyway.'

They stood awkwardly in the street for an hour before Tracy arrived with the spare keys.
'That's the Fiesta Tracy. That's what I need you to look for.'
'I'll take pictures while I'm here those dints and scratches might help with an ID. I've got some good-quality CCTV on some routes, pretty poor on others. I'll get straight on it.'
Tracey took pictures of all sides of the Fiesta and up-close pictures of the damage before leaving.

At least they could sit back in the car and wait for the recovery truck to arrive which was late. In the end they waited two hours. They eventually headed back to the station. Superintendent Caldwell was waiting for Margot. She immediately felt sick.
'Margot come with me please.' She looked back at Luke.
The Superintendent led her to his office. He picked up an evidence bag from a pile.
'Is this your nightdress?'
'Yes. What's that on it?'
'We believe there's a sexual motive.'
'Oh... I don't want that back by the way. Not now.'
'I'm going to ask you for a DNA sample to conclusively prove that's your nightdress.'
'No problem I'll do it now Sir. Are all those bags full of my stuff?'
'No Margot. This goes no further - they are full of what we believe are other people's underwear, all different sizes. Whose we don't know yet.'
'Was mine the biggest size?'
'I don't know.'
'Metcalfe?'
'Yes.'
'Is he in custody?'
'We are working on that. He wasn't at home.'
'This is like Mark all over again.'
'Margot I don't want you alone at any point.'
'Luke said I can stay with him.'
'You should take him up on that. I'd like to monitor your cameras'
'I can add your phone so you see what I see.'
'Please Margot.' He handed her her phone back. 'You should know

another message dropped in.'
Please don't be Patrick, she prayed under her breath. The Superintendent showed her the message.

This is not over yet

She added the Superintendent's number to the camera app.
'Sir if I forget you have it. The cameras cover the bathroom too. You won't look will you?'
'No Margot.'

Luke was waiting for her round the corner. He looked expectantly at her.
'It was Metcalfe but they don't have him. They have obviously searched his house. It's full of women's underwear. I don't think I'm the first. I think he's broken into other houses.'
'Or washing lines.'
'Either way it's very creepy. And I wasn't to mention any of that. Can I stay? He messaged again, he said: it's not over yet.'
'Yes I've already told Tom. I took that as read.'

She sneaked off to the ladies to call Patrick, warn him the Super was monitoring the cameras. She couldn't understand why she was so pleased it wasn't Patrick. She knew though this couldn't carry on. She told him it was over. That him burgling the doctors had nearly cost them the case. He did point out there would have been no case if he hadn't burgled it. He was right she realised. But Margot's mind was made up, she would do things by the book from now on. She was grateful Patrick just accepted that. He was in a very odd way one of the good guys. His parting words were 'I'm here if ever you need me.' Margot's words were 'likewise Patrick.' Which she instantly regretted. Then she thought about it. If he was in trouble she would go running. But she wouldn't be doing anything illegal again.

Everything was starting to come back into balance. Then the DI returned and put a slight dampener on things. 'Kyle Morgan drowned. The PM was inconclusive as to whether it was murder or accidental. Not ideal but we carry on. Where are we?'
Luke and Margot brought him up to date. Tracy ran in just as they finished.
'I can put the Fiesta conclusively within four miles of Kyle's house at 03.57 on Thursday morning. Heading in the direction of Kyle's

house. On the direct route from Roy Harper's house to Kyle's.'
'Great work everyone. So we wait for forensic on the Fiesta. Then if we can put Kyle and Richard Grant in it, we arrest him and see what he has to say for himself. Now I think would be a good time to have a couple of days off. Tidy up any loose ends and paperwork then go home.'
'How did Kyle's Dad take it Sir?' Margot asked.
'The FLOs told him yesterday a body had been recovered from the river. They confirmed it was Kyle today as soon as ID was confirmed. He then insisted on seeing Kyle right there and then. The FLOs explained the state of the body and that it wasn't advisable, that it wasn't possible right now anyway because of the post-mortem. So he flew out the house sped off in his car and the next thing he's turned up outside the mortuary trying to break the door down. He's in the cells downstairs. Took his anger out on the mortuary technician's car unfortunately. I'll pop down and see him, explain where we are at when he's released. See if I can get him back onside.'
'And Shelly?'
'Still critical but stable. Her mother, however, is expected to die. Colleen claims she's being set up, that it wasn't her.'
'Is the petrol can all they have?' asked Luke.
'Yes, so far. Fire was started by petrol poured through the letter box.
'She doesn't usually get her own hands dirty,' said Luke.
'Maybe murder was a step too far for the family. Besides by all accounts Kevin was the one that usually did her dirty work,' said John.
'Maybe,' said Luke.

They all drifted off to their own desks. After an hour Margot declared she was ready.
'I need fifteen more minutes. Leave your car here Margot. We'll go in mine. Do you need to go home, pick up some clothes? Why don't you pick up some walking stuff, we can have a nice walk tomorrow morning. Tom has to work in the morning but he'll be back in the afternoon. We've discovered a brilliant café, we'll take you there in the afternoon.'
That all sounded just what Margot really needed, as long as the walk was short. And fairly flat. And not too boggy.
'Okay.'

Margot went through everything in her head one more time. Double checking she had documented everything correctly. That she'd submitted everything to the incident room. To John. She felt like she'd done at school when she'd finished her Biology exam an hour before everyone else, that perhaps she'd missed something. The fact Luke was still beavering away made her nervous. She had failed biology. She thought Gavin needed to know. She rang him and just said 'we got him Gavin, he's been charged with Rory's murder.'

Margot checked a third time. Luke was still working. Her mind drifted. She needed Metcalfe caught. Hopefully he'd break into her house again tonight and get himself caught. He'd think she was in there. Perhaps he wouldn't if her car was here. She should take her car home, park it in its usual place. She should postpone the locksmith too.
'How long Luke?'
'Ten minutes nearly done.'
'I'm going to drive straight home. I'll add your number so you can watch on my cameras. I'll pack for yours and you pick me up from there.'
'Honestly Margot I'll be done shortly, just wait.'
'I want my car parked at home Luke. Metcalfe knows he's wanted by now he won't try anything in broad daylight. But he might tonight but if my car isn't there he won't. I'm going to close the curtains. Park where I normally do. It's the best chance of drawing him out.'
'Actually that's a good idea. Don't stop on your way back. I'll be ten minutes behind you. Oh and Margot drive a different way home not your normal route.'

Margot grabbed her coat and keys and headed to her car. She took a really strange way home to make sure she outsmarted Metcalfe, just in case he was out there waiting for her. At this rate Luke would beat her home she thought. She was driving through the Metro Centre Blue car park when she spotted the Chief Constable's Dad. He probably isn't supposed to be here, she thought, and drove over to him.
'Hello Roy, where are you off to?'
'The garden centre.'
'Why don't I give you a lift?'
'It's all changed all this, used to be fields.'

'I think the garden centre might have moved. Jump in.'
Margot jumped out and guided him into the car.
'I need tomato plants.'
'No problem. Let's get you seat-belted up first.'

Margot looked round as she got back in the car. There was Metcalfe driving into the car park. How? She jumped in and got her phone out of her pocket. She looked in her rear view mirror, he was speeding towards her. She regretted driving a pink beetle in that moment. She put her phone on the dashboard and sped off towards the exit. He was following. She spun round the corner at the edge of the car park following the exit signs and her phone slid along the dashboard. As she lunged for it it shot past her fingers and crashed to the floor at the far side of Roy's feet.
'Roy can you reach my phone.'
'Do I know you?'
'Yes I'm a friend of your son's.'
'He doesn't visit me anymore.'
'He does Sunday, Wednesday and Friday. The phone Roy, it's by your feet. Can you pass me the phone?'
Margot sped out the exit. At least Roy was looking for the phone.
'No phone. Can you stop?'
Margot looked in the mirror 'not right now.'
'Is this the way to the garden centre?'
'It's a short cut. Do you have a phone?'
'Oh yes. 0191..'
'No a mobile phone.'
He took a phone out his pocket.
'Can you press 999 while I drive?'
Margot was having to concentrate hard on her driving and rack her brains for a route that didn't involve traffic lights to the nearest police station.
Margot could hear he had dialled, she could hear ringing.
'Can you give me the phone?'
'I'm perfectly capable…hello.'
Margot could just about hear the unmistakable tones of the Chief Constable saying 'Dad is everything alright?'
'Tell him Metcalfe is following us, we need help.'
'Fine, I'm just popping to the garden centre for tomato plants.'
'Sir it's Margot,' she shouted 'I have your Dad but I'm being chased

by Metcalfe. Can you get help please? I'm just going over Scotswood bridge.'

Roy hung up. She hoped he'd heard that. Margot looked in the rear-view mirror, she couldn't see Metcalfe anymore. She wasn't sure where and when he'd disappeared. Her phone started ringing, it sounded like it was under the passenger seat. She didn't want to risk stopping just yet. Roy's phone rang again. She decided to risk Scotswood road despite the lights.
'Roy can you answer your phone it might be important.'
He got it back out of his pocket.
'Dad can you put Margot on?'
'I don't know any Margots.'
'I'm Margot. Pass me the phone please.'

He did.
'Hello,' said Margot.
'It's Paul Harper the Chief Constable, is that you Margot?'
'Yes. Sorry Sir, I found your Dad at the Metro Centre but just as I did Metcalfe found me. I think we've lost him. I'm going to drive back to the police station. My phone is under your Dad.'
'I've let Superintendent Caldwell know. We are looking for you. Where are you now?'
'Just coming past the Audi garage, Scotswood road.'
'Okay stay on the line until you reach the station.'
'Okay.' What the hell was she going to talk about to the Chief Constable for five minutes, she worried. Not mice, don't mention anymore bloody mice.
'Did you like my Whitney Houston Sir?'
'Not really. Margot, we don't need to have a conversation; just keep telling me where you are.'
'Okay.'

Margot did. She drove back into the station. John was waiting for her and Luke was just rushing in behind. She thanked the Chief and hung up.
'Are we at the garden centre?'
'The police station.'
'Oh my son is a policeman.'
'I know. He will be here shortly to take you to the garden centre.'

'Margot what happened?' said John just as Superintendent Caldwell joined them. She told them what happened.

'He's tracking her car, he must be,' said Luke.
John looked under the car. 'Yeah, I can see it.'
'I want that forensically recovered. No doubt that's one of ours. What's his game?' said Caldwell.
'I think he's just trying to scare me. And if I'm honest it's working.' Margot realised she was stood there shaking. She wondered how much of this was Mark scaring her from the grave. Because face to face she wouldn't be scared of Metcalfe.

'Why were you on your own?' asked Caldwell.
'I wasn't going to be. We just thought the best chance of catching him was if he thought I was at home alone. I was dropping my car off. Collecting some clothes and going to Luke's.'

'Margot, write a quick statement then Luke, take her back to yours. Does Metcalfe know where you live Luke?' said John.
'Probably. He's never been there but I'm guessing he knows.'
'Right now he knows his career is over. His pension is gone. And he's looking at time. He seems to be putting the blame for all that on Margot and not himself. Whilst not wanting to scare you more Margot I'm wondering if perhaps you should enjoy your days off somewhere he can't find you,' said John.
'I think we should tell my Dad,' said Luke.
'The timing couldn't be much worse Luke,' said Margot.
'I know but if we don't tell him. He's going to be really pissed we didn't anyway.'
'I worked with Mervin for twenty years. You need to tell him,' said John.

By the time Margot had finished her statement Mervin was there to pick her up. He'd booked a posh hotel Edinburgh for two nights. Margot was really looking forward to it.
'Are you okay Margot? I've packed all your clothes that you left at mine. I'm sure we can buy anything else you need in Edinburgh. You can tell me all about it on the way,' said Mervin opening the car door for her. Margot felt safe the second she stepped into the car.
'Which bit, kidnapping the Chief's Dad or Metcalfe?'
'Everything Margot. I won't let this happen twice.'
'Metcalfe is just a prick Mervin.'
'A dangerous prick Margot. If he wasn't before, he is now.'

Margot told him about the messages and the break-in and the Metro Centre. Mervin just listened. They lapsed into silence, except

for Margot constantly exclaiming childishly she had seen the sea every time she saw the sea. They were heading north on the A1.
'Shall we stop off at Bamburgh and get an ice cream from somewhere?' said Mervin.
'Yes please I've never been.'
'You've never been to Bamburgh!'
'No. Before I joined the police I'd never really been anywhere except Gateshead and Rowlands Gill.'
Mervin stared at Margot.
'You are in for a treat Margot.'

They sat on the cricket pitch looking up at the castle built on top of a rocky outcrop, licking ice cream. Margot breathed in the air. This was so nice after a child's arm hanging from a barbed wire fence. A child's unrecognisable body hauled out the river to lie there in the stench of sewerage. They finished their ice creams.
'Come on let's go for a paddle.'
Margot's mouth dropped as they emerged from the sand dunes onto the beach. She immediately threw off her shoes and raced for the sea. Reclaiming the childhood her father had stolen with his moaning and put-downs. Why hadn't he brought her here? Mervin joined her rolling up his trousers and wincing at the temperature of the North Sea. They walked hand-in-hand down the beach for a bit. Margot coming up with endless stories about the castle in her head.

As they got back in the car her phone rang. Withheld number. She took a breath and answered it.
'Margot can you speak, it's Paul Harper?'
'Yes Sir.'
'I wanted to say thank you for rescuing my father.'
'No problem Sir.'
'I've been fully updated with the Metcalfe affair. And I now know you have seen the video of me. I just wanted to say to you I had no idea those videos existed or that DI Metcalfe was also a client. I wanted you to know that's not why I appointed him to investigate Donna's death. He collared me in the corridor and I didn't know him from Adam. He told me MIT shouldn't be investigating her death because it was police contact. He intimated you had something to do with her death. And you had been acting a little strangely. I know now he was manipulating me. I wanted to tell you the matter is being properly investigated by an outside force. Thank you for taking the video to your boss and no one else.'

'Thanks for telling me that Sir. Sir you don't have mice at the station.'
'I know Margot. I promise my main priority right now is to catch Metcalfe.'
'Thanks.'
'And well done on catching Richard Grant. That was an excellent piece of police work Margot.'

'Who was that?' asked Mervin.
'The Chief. I think he's actually an okay guy. I hope he doesn't have to resign over this whole Metcalfe thing and the video. I mean it wasn't illegal was it? It wasn't really sex was it? And Donna had business cards and everything.'
'If it ever hit the press I don't think he'd have a choice. Was he trying to influence you in any way about the video?'
'No. He told me, him giving Metcalfe the case, is being investigated by an outside force. He's not in it with Metcalfe, Mervin, I'm sure of that. He gave me an explanation of why he allocated him the case and I accept that. I actually like him.'
'He's a bit kinky though.'
'Do you think we are a bit old-fashioned in bed?'
'No. Do you want to try that?'
'No. I'm just saying I bet plenty of people do.'
'Why are you laughing Margot?'
'Because you've gone pink. Luke goes exactly the same colour when he's embarrassed.'
'You never told me what was on the video of Metcalfe Margot?'
'Now that wasn't what most people do. Least I'm pretty sure it's not. Do you think we are prudes?'
'I'm happy are you?'
'Very.'

They lapsed into silence again. They arrived at the hotel and checked in. They had a room overlooking the castle, Margot was impressed. They went out for fish and chips before returning to the room. Mervin made them a hot chocolate each and they sat on the bed and watched TV. Margot fell asleep.

When she awoke Mervin was gently snoring under the covers. He'd put a blanket over her. She crept up and brushed her teeth, then crept back into bed under the covers. She fell straight back asleep.

They had a long breakfast in the hotel and then set off on a walking tour of Edinburgh led by the most enthusiastic person Margot had ever met. The deluge of facts washed over her. She was just enjoying Mervin's company and turning her brain off. Half way round they gave up when Margot spotted a really nice cafe. They sat and ate cake instead.

'Are you okay Mervin? Luke told me he'd been released.'

'Yes Margot. The cop in me thinks that's the wrong decision, that he's still dangerous. Not to me or Luke but to women in general. The husband in me thinks he got off too lightly, he served 21 years. So a year per two stab wounds. For a life he robbed of sixty years. The father in me thinks I've spent too long being angry already and Luke took the brunt of that anger when he was just a bairn.'

'Does what's happening with Metcalfe bring it all back?'

'It never went anywhere Margot. I live around it Margot. And I'm enjoying spending time with you. I don't want you to think you can't talk about Metcalfe because of what happened with my wife. She was stalked by a lunatic called Dean Sycamore and stabbed 43 times in our home whilst Luke slept upstairs. I won't let anything happen again.'

'Do you think he picked on me because I handed over the video?'

'He also probably doesn't like you because of me. He completely cocked a case up once. It was the first time Sycamore was up for parole. I was on a short fuse I admit. I really went to town on Metcalfe. I could have handled it much better than I did. As far as I was concerned it was done and dusted, but Metcalfe holds a grudge. From what you said Margot he is a sexual predator. The underwear collection Caldwell found. Who knows how a brain like that works.'

'That whole car chase was just odd. What did that achieve?'

'Perhaps he thought you were going shopping again, getting out the car?'

'So you think he was going to kill me?'

'If you'd asked me that last week I'd have said you were crazy. But now I think that was his plan. Look, he won't have many places to hide, he's using his own car. It's just a matter of time before he's caught. This isn't Mark all over again. It's completely different. I actually think that was his last shot at you in the Metro Centre and he knew it. I think he will run now. He can't find us here, shall we just agree to enjoy our break?'

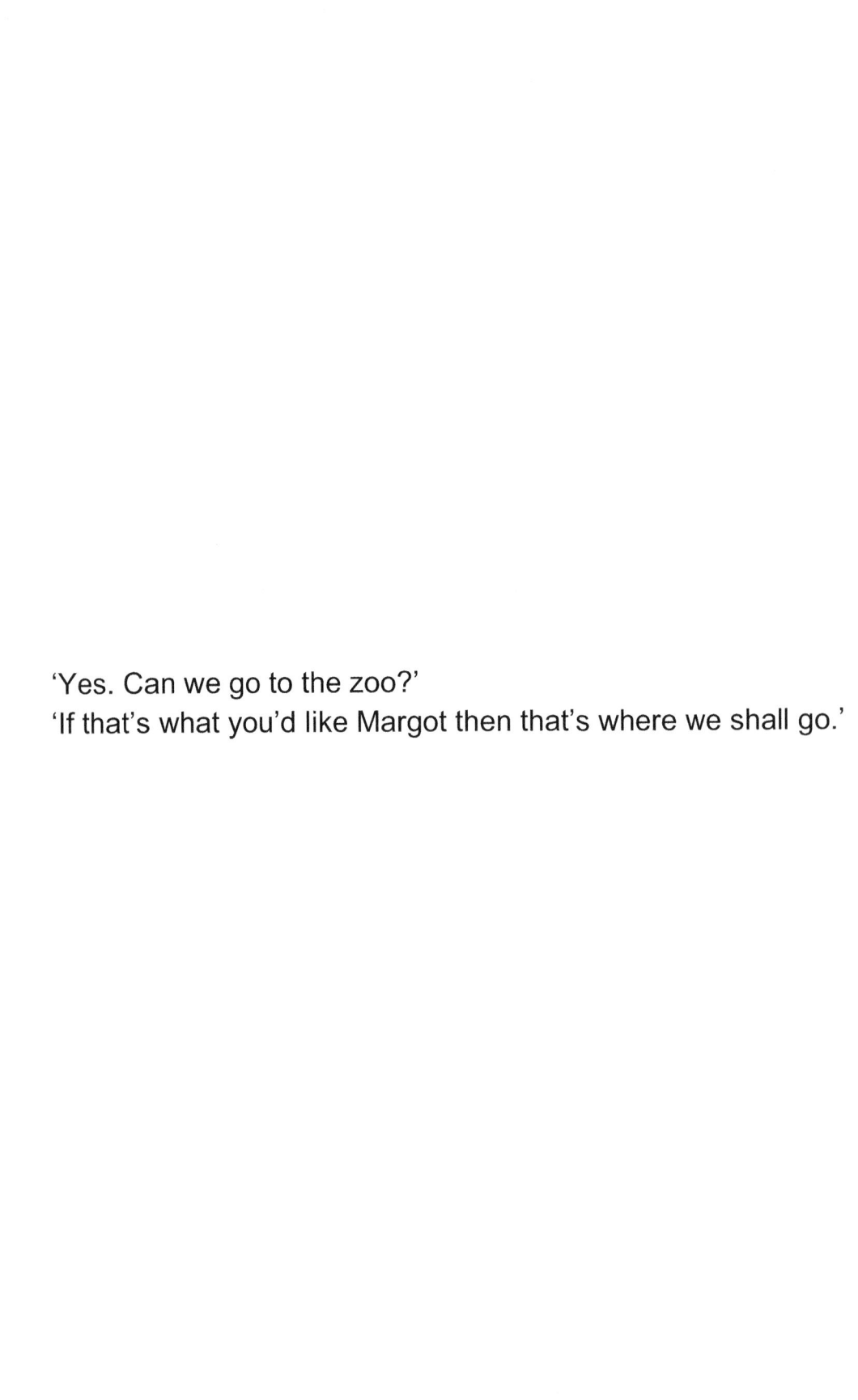

'Yes. Can we go to the zoo?'
'If that's what you'd like Margot then that's where we shall go.'

John

John Hall and Dave Caldwell were standing in the surveillance office with a worried looking sergeant in front of them.
'So it's definitely one of ours, but we don't use these anymore. And you can't tell us if anymore are missing because we can't find the inventory of how many we have or even had?' said John.
'Yes. The equipment we are currently using is all logged in and out I can show you where that's all kept.'
'Do we even know where he got it from?'
'Not really Sir. Things went missing, they got spread around stations, shoved in drawers. We've moved offices twice since they went out of use. It couldn't happen now but when I joined the job a Chief Super borrowed one because he thought his wife was having an affair.'
'Point made.'

John and Dave walked out of the office.
'Phone Mervin, get him to check under his car. Get Luke to do likewise. Anyone else likely to be a target, John?'
'No one is jumping to mind. Do we know who the underwear belonged to yet?'
'No. It's all at the lab. I don't doubt his DNA is all over it. But what's the chances of any female DNA being in the system?'
'We go public then?'
'The ACC is calling the shots on that. The Chief has stepped aside on this one given the video. I did suggest that and I was quickly shut down. "Catch him first" were his words. He is clearly only thinking about the adverse publicity that's going to come our way on this. It looks better in his mind if we are seen to be on top of this rather than asking for help right now.'
'Okay, I'll call Mervin and Luke now.'

Margot

Mervin's phone rang.
'Mervin it's John where are you?'
'The reptile house.'
'Just to put my mind at rest, check under your car for a tracker. Could be more missing, no one knows.'
'I'll do it now. Not found him yet?'
'No. Doesn't help he knows where all the bloody ANPR cameras are and every trick in the book to boot.'

'We need to check my car for a tracker, Margot.'
'Now, or can we see everything else first?'
'If you want. I think we'd have known by now if he was here.'
They saw everything. Margot insisted on buying a cuddly giraffe as she decided the giraffes were her favourite. It was the way they looked at you. Margot thought that look perfectly summed up how she felt in the job. Mervin then crawled around under the car for a good five minutes.
'We are clear. I'll just ring John and tell him.'
'Did you like the giraffes?' asked Margot. Mervin was already calling John he didn't answer.

'Luke's car was clear too. So Margot, what next? Why don't we book a nice restaurant tonight?'
'I'd like that. I could do with a nice bath first.'
'Let's head back to the hotel then. Have a few drinks in the bar before we go.'
'Don't book anything too posh I haven't got anything to wear, a nice Italian or something.'
'Okay I'll ask at reception what's good. Alrighty let's hit the road then.'

Margot enjoyed her bath. The drinks in the bar. The Italian. The hot chocolate. The sleep. The three trips to the breakfast bar. It was soon time to check out. She made sure she had her giraffe.
'Are you going to work tomorrow Margot?'
'Yes there's still a lot to do. Forensic on the Fiesta and the SLK keys should be back. I should be safe in the police station. I haven't been told not to go. Why do you ask?'
'I thought we could extend the break if you weren't.'
'Sorry Mervin.'

'No it's fine. I just wasn't sure what your plans were.'
'I'll be fine.'
'Promise me you will stay with Luke. I'll drop you off and pick you up. Do you want to stay at mine or yours?'
'Yours tonight, but tomorrow I need to go to mine please. I really need to sort clothes out for work. Get the locks changed.'
'Okay. Hopefully he'll be caught by then anyway.'

Mervin drove Margot to work in the morning. Margot threw everything in her Beetle before heading to the office. Luke was already in as was John.

'Now we are all here – meeting, my office. I have the forensic report on the Fiesta hot off the press this morning,' said John. They followed him into his office. 'So hairs recovered from the back seats belong to Kyle Morgan, he was in that car. Hairs recovered from the drivers seat and back seats belong to a St Bernard.'

'Colin,' said Margot. 'Richard Grant's dog.'

'A small plastic trophy was stuffed down the back seats that had Kyle's DNA on, I'm guessing that's the prize he wanted to get from school. I'm getting Grant produced tomorrow. I want you two to arrest and interview him for the murder of Kyle Morgan then. So you are aware, Shelly is awake in hospital. She should be fine but her mother died last night. Colleen has been rearrested on suspicion of murder.'

'Do they have more than the petrol can now?' asked Luke.

'They have a string of messages from Colleen to Shelly threatening to kill her for sleeping with Kevin.'

'Shall we get a sample of hair from Colin the dog Sir?' said Margot.

'Yes please at some point, but let's see what he says first. Make sure you're on top of the interview first. If you do need to go out of the station please stay together at all times. I need to find Jasmine, I need some authorisations. Not like her to be late.'

'You don't think Metcalfe went for Jasmine do you? He doesn't like her,' said Margot.

'No... Would he...? Perhaps we should check regardless. I'll get her address, meet me in the yard in five. Make sure you have radios and batons.'

Margot held on to the handrail in the back as John drove. Luke was doing the same in the front. Margot kept trying Jasmine's phone but it was answer message only.

'Still nothing Margot?' asked John.

'No she's not picking up.'

Margot didn't think the car could go any faster but John squeezed more out of it. Margot was now feeling car sick. She stopped looking at her phone. As they skidded to a stop they all noticed her car wasn't on the drive but the front door was open. They rushed in. The house was empty.

'Out. I want forensic in,' said John. Margot had never seen her boss look so worried before.

'Margot, tell Superintendent Caldwell for me while I sort forensic. Luke get her vehicle circulated.'
Margot found his number on the camera app and rang it.
'Sir it's Margot. We think Metcalfe may have Detective Superintendent Walker. She's not at home and her front door was open, her car is missing.'
'Is John with you, I'm trying to ring him?'
'He's on the phone to forensic.'
'Tell him the underwear. It all belongs to colleagues. Including Jasmine Walker. The lab has literally just called me.'
'So he took their door keys from their desks. Copied them all.'
'Maybe Margot, we haven't got that far yet. I'm going to get everyone traced right now.'
'So he could be in one of their houses right now?'
'I suppose he could. I'll get all the houses checked. Put John on Margot.'
'Sir we need to swap. You need to talk to the Superintendent, it's urgent. I'll sort forensic.'
They swapped phones.

Margot explained everything to Luke after she'd finished. John had moved away and was looking even more worried as he was talking. They couldn't make out what was being said. He walked back over looking shaken.
'What's happening sir?'
'Superintendent Caldwell is trying to account for everyone who's DNA flagged up but that still leaves three unidentified profiles. Not all police officers provided their DNA, it was voluntary. Possibly another three policewomen. It still amounts to three people we don't know. He is also getting the home addresses of the officers we know checked. Doors will be put in if there's no answer.'
'What should we do?' said Margot.
'As much as I hate to do nothing we need to stay here, preserve the scene until the CSIs and uniform get here. Everything that can be done is being done.'

Margot couldn't help but thinking the action was somewhere else. She really really wanted to be the one to catch him. Perhaps if instead of running away at the Metro Centre she'd confronted him then she would have been, and Jasmine would be safe. She liked the Detective Superintendent.

John's phone rang again. It must be Dave Caldwell again thought Margot. She waited anxiously for the call to end. John didn't seem to be saying much.

'Jasmine's car has been found abandoned down by the river at Newburn. No cameras.'

'How did they find that so quickly? I've only just got it circulated,' said Luke.

'Was already a job in for it. It's causing an obstruction. Switched-on radio operator made the connection.'

'That's a smoke screen Sir,' said Luke.

'You could be right there.'

'You don't think he's gone to Donna's do you?' said Margot.

'No,' said John. 'Bloody hell, you two are a bad influence on me. Get in the car.'

They sped to Donna's. As Luke shouldered the door they could hear a shout.

'Help… up here.'

'It's her,' said John.

John rushed upstairs, opened the bedroom door. Closed it again and said 'Margot you go in, we'll check the rest of the house.'

Margot looked confused until she went in. Jasmine was handcuffed naked to the bed. Margot found a blanket. Then rooted round for her handcuff keys.

'I'm glad it's you Margot. This was Metcalfe.'

'We know. Did he..'

'No…He just took a lot of photos, some up close. He said he was going to post them all over my Instagram. He has my phone. Margot can you check my Instagram?'

'Sure I'll just get you untied first. Where are your clothes?'

'I don't know…please see what he's posted.'

Margot handed Jasmine her own mobile.

'The bastards just done it…shit.'

Jasmine burst out crying.

'Sorry Ma'am, you said he's just done it?'

'Literally just.'

'He must be watching…Luke I think he's watching the house,' shouted Margot. 'I'm so sorry Ma'am.'

'I'm not going to able to look anyone in the eye ever again. Christ look at this one.'

Margot looked. The photo left nothing to the imagination. Margot

didn't know what to do or say. There was a knock at the door.
'Ma'am it's John. Can I come in?'
'Yes.'
'Luke's checking outside but looks like we missed him. What car is he using?'
'Black BMW 3 series. I'm pretty sure it's his own car.'
'We have traffic cars waiting for him. Did he give any indication of where he was going?'
'No.'
'Sorry Ma'am, I have to ask. What did he do?'
'Just photos, I think. I was out for a bit.'
'Do you want to go to the rape suite?'
'No.'
'Ma'am…'
'It's not up for discussion John.'
'At least go to hospital get checked out.'
'I'm fine.'

'Boss turn your radio on. Traffic have him but he's not stopping,' shouted Luke from the bottom of the stairs.
John got up to leave, 'excuse me Ma'am.'
'No I want to hear this,' said Jasmine.

John turned the radio on…. 'Crash. Crash. Crash. He swerved head on into a lorry….stand by…one fatality.' John turned the radio off.
'The bloody coward,' said Jasmine.
'What's the code to your phone Ma'am?' said John.
'318340'
John ran out. Margot and Jasmine looked at each other. They heard a car speed off.
'Ma'am I'm going to ring a friend, get her to bring some clothes down for you. They should fit,' said Margot. Jasmine nodded. Margot rang Daisy who luckily was at home. Daisy said she'd be half an hour. John poked his head round the door. 'Margot,' he said. Margot headed onto the landing.
'Daisy's bringing clothes down.'
'Good. Can you please take her home after that? I'll get your car brought here. Take her home, stay with her for a bit if she'll let you, then go home yourself. Are you still okay to do that interview

tomorrow?'
'Yes Sir. I really want to.'

Luke rang Margot. 'Tell the Super I've taken the photos down. There weren't many views.'
Margot passed the message on.
'Tell him thank you very much,' said Jasmine.

Daisy arrived with some clothes.
'I went for joggers and sweatshirt because I thought they were more likely to fit. Then half way here I suddenly thought she might look like a prisoner but I didn't want to go all the way back.'
'I doubt she'll even notice Daisy. Thanks. Catch up next week?'
'Defo.'

Margot took the clothes off Daisy and headed upstairs. As she gave Jasmine the clothes Margot saw Tracy pulling up in her Beetle out of the window. She ran down to grab the keys and waited. Jasmine came down.
'I feel like a bloody prisoner.'
'They look nice Ma'am,' said Margot.
'Let's go Margot.'
Jasmine jumped in the front. Margot jumped in the driver's seat. Margot reached onto the back seat.
'Here have my giraffe,' said Margot giving it to Jasmine. Who started to subconsciously strangle it. Margot set off wishing she'd not given her her giraffe.
'I'm sorry Ma'am, I think that was supposed to me in there.'
'Margot I'm glad it wasn't you. It shouldn't have been anyone. Metcalfe had it in for me ever since I got a promotion he thought was his.'
'He stole underwear from policewomen. I also think he made copies of their house keys and got into their houses. He was just a pervert ma'am. I told you the first time I met you Ma'am, he's a complete prick.'
'When did all this come out?'
'This morning.'

They got back to Jasmine's, the door was still wide open. In the rush they'd not shut it. Margot hoped she hadn't been burgled. They both checked the house a little tentatively. It was as it should be.
'I'll be fine now Margot just go. Any idea where my car is?'

'I think we have it, it was abandoned by the river. I can stay for a bit.'
'No need Margot I just want to be by myself. I just need a shower. I'll call Mum, she'll come over.'
'If that's what you want. But I don't mind staying.'
'It's what I want. Thank you Margot. How did you know I was there?'
'Just a lucky guess really. Can you return the clothes to Daisy please Ma'am? Daisy was the policewoman Mark abducted. She's really nice. And she can keep a secret.'

Margot pulled out into the street and pulled over to call Mervin so she could tell him it was over. Mervin said he'd meet her at her house. Margot drove home. She put the radio on and sang at the top of her voice to Taylor Swift. She was glad Metcalfe was dead.

She turned the radio down and drove into her street. Mervin was already there. She gave him a peck on the cheek.
'Shall we go inside or do you want to go somewhere for lunch?' he asked.
'Shall we go inside.'
Mervin kissed Margot as soon as she was through the doors. Her phone rang.
'Margot you might want to remove me from the camera app.'
'Shit sorry I forgot. Did the cowbells go off?'
'Yep.'
'Hang on I'll fix it.'
Margot and Mervin between them eventually worked out how to take Luke and the Superintendent off. And turn the cameras off.

Margot

Richard Grant was getting produced at midday. Luke and Margot were planning their interview strategy. Margot noted Jasmine wasn't in. The station was buzzing with rumours and whispered conversations about Metcalfe. Margot ignored them all. The time for the interview was soon upon them. Margot suddenly felt really nervous.

He had the same solicitor. Luke did the introductions and cautioned him. Margot thought he looked worried. The plan was to get him to tell as many lies as possible. Luke would be good at this. She'd just stay quiet.

'You understand you have been arrested on suspicion of the murder of Kyle Morgan.' Luke showed him a picture of Kyle. 'Kyle was playing in the garden of the house you crashed next to, when you have already admitted you were in the process of taking the body of Rory Elliot to George Morrison's house. Did you see Kyle? Did he see Rory's dead body?'

'I should have told the truth before. I didn't because I knew you'd think I killed Kyle and I didn't. Rory didn't steal the keys. I had to move my wife's car. I put the keys in my jacket pocket. I was panicking, I was driving too fast. Kyle - although I didn't know his name at that point - ran out into the road after a cat. I only just missed him. Of course I went back to make sure he was okay. He was crying but he begged me not to tell his Dad. Normally I'd have taken him to his Dad, but I couldn't - I'd just accidentally killed Rory. Kyle didn't see Rory. I wasn't thinking straight. I must have dropped the keys. I realised when I got to George's. I panicked because they'd be covered in Rory's blood. My hands and clothes were covered from where I'd tried to save him. I went back to look for them the next day. I couldn't find them anywhere. I thought the boy might have taken them. I walked up the drive and saw the van. I guessed that was his Dad's. I knew that was Lucinda and Conrad's house. I knew they were away and I knew their grandchildren were much older. I still didn't know what to do. In the end I followed the van Wednesday night but I lost it in the estate. I saw him drive into the estate but not where he went. I didn't have a plan so I went home but I couldn't sleep, so I went back out early figuring I'd just have to go street to street. But literally he was just there walking

down King Street. I asked him about the keys and he told me he'd given the keys to a George Nolan. He pointed out his house. I asked him what he was doing up so early, he said he was heading to his Dad's. And that was it. I just wanted to get out of there. He was a bit upset he said it was because his Mum had found a new boyfriend. I should have taken him to his Dad's but I couldn't be seen with him. I promise you he was alive and well when I left him. I was going to knock on George Nolan's door at a more reasonable time, ask for the keys back. I'd have given him fifty quid, I wasn't planning on killing anyone.'
'What car did you go in?'
'I'm sorry I'm finding this very hard. Can I have a short break, I feel sick.'
Luke temporarily suspended the interview.
'Can I go to the cell please, I think I'm going to be sick.'
Luke took him along.

Luke and Margot headed up to see John.
'That was unexpected. It's as if he knows we have the keys,' said John.
'He does. Sorry I've really screwed up Sir,' said Margot. 'The wife was there when I tried the keys. She was upset. Asking what was happening. I told her to go to court, that she might be able to see him. She must have told him we had the keys. He knows Kyle had the keys.'
'That's on me Margot, I told you to go. They wouldn't authorise forensic until we'd proved those were the right keys,' said John.
'By saying he knew George had the keys he takes away any motive and makes it look like he's telling the truth,' said Luke.
'The best lies include a lot of the truth. He hadn't thought it all the way through though, had he? He's now wondering if we know about the Fiesta. Does he stick with the Range Rover knowing it's clean? Or does he twist and risk handing us the Fiesta?'
'He could say that conversation took place in the Fiesta Boss,' said Luke.
'He could. If he's really smart he'll refuse to answer any more questions until he knows our hand. Right now he's not being sick, he's thinking. Okay, go back when he's ready. Let's not play the Fiesta card just yet. Just ask him times. Routes. Then ask him again which vehicle he was driving.'
'Would Kyle tell him all that?' asked Margot.
'He could have got some of that from social media, he's bound to

have followed the case. Or he was just nice to Kyle, got him chatting. Offered to take him to his Dad's,' said Luke.

John was right. He didn't answer any more questions. He obviously wasn't going to back himself into a corner. They suspended the interview again. And reconvened in John's office.
'So shall we hit him with the Fiesta now Boss?'
'Yes we've got no choice.'
They headed back into interview.

Luke restarted the interview. He cautioned him again.
'Have you ever driven a Fiesta owned by a Roy Harper, one of your patients?'
'Yes. I borrowed it that Thursday morning to go back to find the keys. I didn't want my car to be seen in the area. He gave me permission to borrow it.'
'Did Kyle go in that car?'
'He sat in the back while I spoke to him.'
'To be clear, did you drive anywhere with Kyle in the car?'
'No.'
'So the last time you saw him, he was in King Street?'
'Yes.'
'Where did you drive afterwards?'
'I took the Fiesta back.'
'Which way?'
'I don't remember exactly, the way my phone sent me.'
'Did you throw Kyle Morgan in the river?'
'No I did not. I promise you. I'm a doctor. I admit I accidentally killed Rory. And stupidly I tried to cover that up rather than own up to it. But I panicked. Then it was too late to go back, I'd moved the body. I made some bad decisions but I didn't kill Kyle. I wasn't thinking clearly when I tried to cover up Rory's death. The stuff on George's computer really upset me.'
Luke terminated the interview.

They reconvened in John's office.
'He killed Kyle in cold blood. He's pissing me off now. Ideally we need to put Kyle in that car out of the estate. Luke run and see Tracy, let her know what he said. Get her to check and recheck all the CCTV we have. We know Kyle was taken just before six. We know Grant didn't go back the way he came; Tracy has already

checked that. We know Kyle went in the river upstream from Riding Mill. Get rid of him for now. It's not as if he's going anywhere. Put out another appeal for dash-cam footage for me please.'
'All he had to do is get him to lie down in the back and we wouldn't see him. I read the forensic report boss, the hair was on the actual seat not the back of the seat, as if he was lying down. He was way too confident with the whole 'I left him in the street' bit,' said Luke.
'We still have a duty to check all the CCTV regardless. Besides I'd like to put him near the river if we can. Actually put a picture of the Fiesta out there. Tracy has some. Specifically ask if anyone saw it. I'll run it by the Chief out of courtesy. Obscure the plates.'
'Yes Boss.'
'Forget that, I'll do it. I need to see how much footage she still has to go through. I also need to thank her properly for helping us out. She's been a Godsend. She hasn't even come out that room for her lunch. She's done the work of three people over the last week. I'm actually going to see if we can keep her.'
'If you ask the Chief Sir I'm sure he'd authorise it.'
'Margot I'm going to pretend I didn't hear that.'

Tracy came into the office.
'Your ears must have been burning Tracy, I was just coming to see you.'
'Can I have a word with Margot for five minutes Sir?'
'Of course. Use my office.'
Margot panicked. She must have her and Patrick on the CCTV.

Margot followed Tracy into John's office.
'Margot do you know DI Metcalfe was my boss before this?'
'I didn't.'
'You know about the underwear I take it?'
'Yes, oh God was some yours? The bastard took my nightdress and ejaculated all over it.'
'Yeah, same thing. They found a copy of my front door key in his car. I think they found more than mine. The guy from professional standards came with more than one key to try in my lock this morning.'
'Yeah he must have had my key too. The horrible thing is he probably had mine for months.'
'Do you think he was in our houses?'
'I think he probably was.'

'I know it was worse for you because you knew while he was still alive. By the time I knew he was dead. So why do I feel so, so helpless? So shit, for want of a better word. Why am I worrying about what might have happened. Are you?'

'I guess I'd be feeling a lot worse without the distraction of this case. I don't actually think it's hit me full force yet.'

'I feel like the whole station is looking at me. Wondering if he had my knickers. I don't want to be called a victim of Metcalfe. I don't want people talking behind my back. You know what police are like, making jokes out of everything. I get why they had to search our houses, an officer's life was at stake. But it's stripped me of any chance of anonymity.'

'He's the pervert Tracy. Why should we feel embarrassed? If anyone asks me, I shall just say the pervert wanked all over my nightdress.'

'Thanks Margot.'

'Look, don't tell anyone I told you this but the boss wants to keep you on MIT. John is one of the good guys. If you want to join us I'm sure there is a way. That way we can stick together.'

'I'd like that.'

'Also you should tell the boss. He wants to see you. Shall I send him in or do you want five?'

'No I'm good. What did he want?'

'Just to see what CCTV options we have. Grant admitted Kyle sat in the Fiesta but said he left the estate alone.'

'Well that will be bollocks.'

'Yeah that's pretty much what we said.'

'I'll go and see him. I had an idea you know - Luke got dash-cam from a taxi; I checked it again it doesn't help. But no other taxis sent in their dash-,cams as a result of the appeal. Might be worth a go, I mean their office isn't far from the scene.'

'I'll have a run out with Luke, see what we can turn up.'

'Thanks again Margot.'

Luke and Margot headed to the taxi office. The owner's wife was in. Margot could see she was the organiser of the business. She was talking away to herself when they walked in. 'Who inputed that…another double booking…' she shook her head. She suddenly seemed to realise someone was there. Luke explained what they needed and why. She told them to come back in two hours by which time she would have the dash cam footage for any of her drivers that were on duty at the relevant time. Margot and

Luke took the opportunity to visit Caroline again.
'I don't see you for months, now I can't get rid of you. Come in.'
'We aren't intruding are we?'
'Never. So I saw on the news you'd made an arrest.'
'Yes. We aren't quite there yet. My Dad always said he hated leaving it to a jury to read between the lines,' said Luke. 'We need a tiny bit more.'
'If anyone can find it you two can. So are you hiding again?'
'Not this time.'
'Do you have time for a cup of tea?'
'Yes please. Where's Geoffrey?'
'Golf course. We may have bought a house too. Not far away so you can still visit. Still need to sell this of course. I'm starting to sort through everything. All my things simply won't fit. All the stuff I'm getting rid of is in the dining room. Why don't you two go and have a rummage, see if there's anything you want? I shall be disappointed if you don't find something.'

It was like visiting an antique shop. Margot didn't think there would be anything she would like at first glance. But the more she looked the more she saw that interested her. She ended up with a globe, an antique sword and a hat. Luke chose a chess board and pieces. Caroline wasn't satisfied and thrust a decanter and glasses at Luke. And a picture of a horse at Margot.
'Take care of that picture Margot,' she whispered.
Margot wondered if it was Caroline's horse.

They loaded up the boot of the CID car. Caroline wrapped up the painting in cardboard and then mummified it with sellotape. They then headed into the kitchen for tea and a slice of homemade fruit cake. It was soon time to head back to collect the dash cam footage. They said their goodbyes.

The lady was on the phone when they arrived back at the taxi office. 'Mr Wells I'm sorry but if you don't settle your account then I can't dispatch a taxi. As I've just explained you owe us £176…And I am running a business not a charity; you can get your prescription delivered for free…You are not going to starve, you can get your shopping delivered too…'
She handed a memory stick to Luke without stopping her conversation. Luke nodded a thank you. Margot was being seduced by the smell of chips from the chippy next door. She wasn't even

hungry after the extra slice of fruit cake she had eaten, but chip stotties were on special.

'Let's head to the station and watch it. I need to catch up with Daisy,' said Margot quickly before she caved.

'May as well.'

Luke loaded up the footage. Margot and Luke watched. Daisy joined them.

'Did Jasmine return your clothes Daisy?'

'Yes. We put the world to rights over a bottle of wine. What are you watching?'

'More taxi dash cam footage. It would be really nice if we could get the Fiesta on camera.'

'Not the Range Rover?'

'No, he borrowed a patient's car.'

'The sly bastard.'

'This one's miles away too, shall we even bother watching it?' Just as Luke said that the taxi drove around a bend and a Fiesta turned left in front of it down a small lane. The driver unmistakably Richard Grant.

'That lane leads to the river,' said Daisy.

'You can't see anyone else in the car unfortunately. We think Kyle might have been lying on the back seats. But it does rather contradict his account of driving straight back to Harper's. This is completely the opposite direction. This will swing it as far as getting him charged. Let's just hope a jury can see right through the doctors charm. I think this is as close as we are going to get on this one.'

Luke updated John while Margot took the opportunity to have a chat with Daisy.

'I see Colleen got charged with Murder. I don't like her Margot, no one does, but she's not going to leave incriminating evidence at the scene.'

'Do you think she was set up then?'

'The family certainly do. Joe and Al her brothers have been asking around. There's a lot of frightened people on that estate now.'

'What happened to her kids in the end?'

'The lovely Janine is looking after them.'

Luke was back.
'Sorry Daisy. We need to head off. Boss wants us to head down that lane and do house-to-house. See if we can get anymore CCTV and check the access to the river.'
'Okay catch you later. I can answer that for you now though. There's no CCTV or houses. It's just a short track to the river. Only fishermen really use it.'

Luke and Margot took a drive down anyway. Both Luke and Margot were convinced this was where Kyle was thrown into the river. They both watched the river flowing past. Margot wondered what Luke was thinking. She was thinking she'd wished she'd gone for the decanter now. Luke probably wouldn't want to swap.

They drove back to their station, parking in the compound. Margot put her hat on her head and carried the globe and antique sword to her car.
'Why on earth did you choose that hat Margot?' asked Luke.
'Because I don't have a hat.'
At that very moment the Chief Constable emerged. He looked at Margot and didn't so much as bat an eyelid.
'Hello Margot.'
'Hello Sir.'
Margot put the globe, sword and hat in the boot of her Beetle and returned to fetch her painting. She put it carefully in the boot and closed the boot lid gently.'

They headed up to their office. Margot told John what they had found.
'That's excellent work. I think that takes us close enough. Let's seek authority to charge.'
'It was Tracy's idea Sir,' said Margot.

Margot's phone buzzed. It was a message from Daisy: girls' night out tomorrow night? Jasmine, you and me.
Margot texted back: Yes.

Margot sat at her desk and thought about the doctor. She didn't think he would have been a killer if he hadn't found that computer belonging to George Morrison. She vowed again to do things by the book herself in the future. She didn't want to end up like Richard Grant. Besides she couldn't cope with her heart permanently in her mouth. She wasn't the type of person who would enjoy parachute jumping she concluded.

She also decided as soon as she got home she was putting all her underwear on a hot wash. She thought she'd leave the cameras in. And she had a place to find for the globe sword and picture too. She'd mount the sword above the bed. The picture could go above the mantelpiece in the living room. The globe could spin in the living room too, so she could cheat at the geography questions on Pointless.

'Margot, Margot.'
'Sorry miles away, I was thinking of Pointless countries Sir.'
'Margot can you go and see Shelly Morgan, update her with what's happened. She won't speak to the FLOs but she might speak to you. She's still in hospital. I'm sending Luke to see Dan Morgan. Come to my office, I'll brief you with what you can and can't say.'

Joe and Al Nolan

Joe and Al Nolan were sitting on Colleen's sofa in her front garden. They had just returned from a prison visit. Janine walked up the street with George and his sister in tow.
'Go play in the house yous two. We are having a family meeting,' she said. She watched the kids disappear inside. 'Well?' she said after they had disappeared.
'Colleen reckons it was the fat little detective, the one who used to work here in uniform. Margot she's called,' said Joe.
'And what did she say to do about it?' asked Janine.
'She said teach her a lesson she won't forget. But get her to admit she set her up first.'
'And did she provide any details as to how we were to do this?'
'She's on remand, it's not as if she could give us a step-by-step guide, Jan,' said Joe.
'Well I say no. I'm not getting involved. If we all go down - which we will if you two are making the plans - then who's going to look after the kids? You do realise you are talking about kidnapping a police officer don't you?'
'We can't let this lie Jan,' said Joe.
'I think you should at least be sure of who it was first.'
'She has a point there Joe,' said Al.
'Who else? If you got other ideas then we'll sort them at the same time,' said Joe.
'Listen to yourself will you Joe. What you are going to do, kidnap and torture anyone whose name gets banded about?'
'If I 'ave to.'
'How did it go with the new supplier?'
'He's thinking about it. He's worried there's too much police interest in us at the moment.',
'And he'd be right. You shouting your mouths off in the pub saying you will kill whoever set up Colleen is hardly the idiots they want to get involved with right now. So on top of everything else we are now drug dealers with no drugs to sell.'
'We can use Kev's old contact in Carlisle he can get us some.'
'He cuts it with all type of crap. Only if we are desperate. I'm heading back to cook the kids tea.'

Janine fetched the kids and headed back down the street to her house.
'So we aren't going to do anything then?' asked Al.

'We aren't going to tell Jan what we are doing. No one ain't going to take us seriously if we do nothing. Our Dad would turn over in his grave.'
'So what's our plan?'
'Give us time. I seen her today you know. She was at the taxi office. With all this going on she'll be out here again. Why don't we keep it simple, just grab her.'
'I don't like Jan not being involved, it should be a family decision.'
'No. Jan doesn't have balls like our Colleen. And she's right, someone needs to look after the bairns. I don't want our George and his sister brought up by the social. No, it's just you and me on this one bro. Colleen told us to get that detective. Time to step up.'

Margot

Margot headed up to the ward. At first she couldn't see Shelly, and she got a shock when the nurse pointed her out. Margot hadn't recognised her. She had aged ten years since Margot had last seen her. An oxygen tube was plastered below her nose, her eyes were closed.

'Hi Shelly, do you remember me, I'm Margot.' Shelly opened her eyes and looked at Margot. Margot wasn't sure if she recognised her or not. 'I came to see you that first morning Kyle disappeared, at your house. I've come to tell you we are seeking authority from the CPS to charge someone with Kyle's murder.'

'Who,' said Shelly in a croaky voice. She reached for some water. Margot passed it to her.

'You won't know him. Richard Grant. Kyle was in the wrong place at the wrong time. He crossed paths with this Richard Grant unfortunately. I'm not allowed to disclose too much at present I'm sorry. I really want to tell you everything but I can't. It will all come out later. I can tell you Richard Grant has been charged with the killing of another boy.'

'Could I have stopped what happened?'

'No. Richard Grant would have found Kyle one way or the other. We believe Kyle unbeknown to himself came across a piece of evidence that connected Richard Grant to the killing of the other boy.'

'But Kyle ran away. They found his school bag in the shed. Why did he run away?'

Margot knew if she told her the reason it would hurt Shelly. Before she'd taken the lift up to the ward she'd wanted to let her know what a terrible mother she'd been. However now Margot felt sorry for her. She could see she loved Kyle, she could see she was suffering. Margot didn't tell her so she would be haunted forever by her mistakes, she told her because she owed her the truth.

'Kyle thought you'd found someone else. He was running away to his Dad's.'

Margot looked at Shelly. The haunting had begun.

'Thank you for being honest Margot.'

Margot walked down the hospital stairs slowly. She was close to bursting into tears. Not for herself but for Shelly. She made her way to the car and just sat there for ten minutes. Her phone buzzed, she checked it. It was Daisy confirming the arrangements for tomorrow night. Margot didn't feel like going anymore. It seemed wrong when the world had stopped for Rory, Kyle, Shelly and Dan that it should keep on spinning for everyone else.

Margot nearly replied she couldn't make it. Then she remembered something Mervin had told her "our place in all this is to catch them Margot. We can't take on more than that."
She hadn't really understood his meaning at the time. She thought now she was starting to understand. She had to have a life too. Besides this was about Jasmine not her. She messaged a thumbs up back.

As Margot drove home she decided to swing by Eldon Square and treat herself to a new top for tomorrow. She thought about ringing her sister, trying to rebuild some bridges. They had never been close close. There were four years between them, Margot was the younger annoying sister. They were very different in pretty much every way. Shopping had always been their thing though. Since the incident with Margot's nephew and husband, Margot and her sister hadn't spoken. Margot rang her now. She didn't answer. She set off on her own. Margot's heart wasn't in it. She left the shopping centre with nothing.

She headed home. She immediately set about collecting all her underwear and piled it into the washing machine. She added an extra pod and set it away on a hot wash. When it had finished she set it away again. She hung it out to dry. It did look like a knicker tree had sprouted in the garden. Margot didn't care. She put out some clothes for tomorrow night knowing she would be going straight from work. They were meeting at Daisy's parents' farm first for wine, then planning on hitting the pubs. Margot was going to stay the night with Daisy as it was closer and they would be getting a taxi back. The part Margot was looking forward to the most oddly was seeing the farm. Margot hadn't actually seen Daisy's farm yet. Daisy had given up her flat and moved back home. Margot knew this was partly for financial reasons, rents were sky high. Partly because her younger brother was at agricultural college and her parents needed more help on the farm as a result. And partly because of Mark.

Margot added her wellies and jeans to her overnight bag. She looked at her hat. Even Margot couldn't quite imagine an occasion she could actually wear that hat. She sat on the sofa and flicked on the TV. Some antiques program was on. She'd normally flick straight past but there was a picture that looked awfully similar to hers. She turned the volume up. The camera panned in on the signature.

'I'd say at the right auction this could comfortably make between ten and fifteen thousand pounds.'

The lady on the telly had a dumbfounded look of complete surprise on her face. Margot had the exact same look, sitting on her sofa. She ran and checked the signature on her painting. She immediately rang Caroline.

'Caroline I think that painting you gave me is very valuable. I'll bring it back tomorrow.'

'Margot I want you to have it, for everything you did.'

'Caroline I can't accept it and I think there are probably rules about police officers taking things.'

'It's got nothing to do with you being a police officer. I gave it to you friend to friend Margot. I'm old. I simply don't need it or the money. I've accepted an offer on the house - two and quarter million. I'll never spend that before I go. I want you to have it.'

'Thank you but it doesn't feel right.'

'Well it's made me very happy knowing you have it.'

Margot rang Luke and told him.

'We should declare it to the boss tomorrow, keep it above board. We met her through the job, so the gift to a friend doesn't really cut it. I thought it was just tat. I only took something to not hurt her feelings,' said Luke.

'I should have twigged on. She wrapped it up and everything. I thought it was her horse.'

'Don't worry about it Margot. We'll sort it tomorrow.'

Margot headed to bed. She couldn't sleep knowing she had a very valuable painting hanging in her living room. She got back up and took the painting down. She wrapped it carefully in sheets and a towel and placed it under her bed. Then she worried mice might eat it. She didn't know whether she had mice or not but she got up once again and looked for a mouse-resistant place to keep it. She settled on a drawer in the bedroom. After another hour of tossing and turning she got back up and wrapped it in clingfilm as well for good measure using the whole roll. She finally dropped off to sleep wondering if she needed a cat.

Margot headed into work.
'Stabbing overnight,' said Luke as soon as she walked in. 'Victim was Gavin Mason. Happened outside his flat. It's obviously part of this ongoing feud. Boss has asked us to give the team dealing a hand with the house-to-house.'
'Rory's cousin?'
'Yes. The working theory is he was killed by someone working for the Donahues because he was dealing for the Carrs, and the Carrs took baseball bats to two of their dealers earlier in the evening. They already have a name in the frame.'
'Did you mention the painting?'
'Yeah, to the boss, he's going to speak to Caroline and professional standards. Are you ready to head straight out? We have to work in pairs.'

Margot and Luke headed out. They had been allocated the area around The Three Stars, as Gavin had started his walk home from a friend's house near the pub. They were tailed by a group of young boys on bikes. Most doors weren't being answered. Margot remembered Gavin's warning to her, she was starting to feel a little uneasy. The streets felt different today hostile. The constant drizzle wasn't helping, it was as if even the weather was giving them a warning to stay inside. A car cruised past, the driver wound his window down and stared at them, before wheel-spinning off. Ten minutes later the car drove past slowly again. The passenger taking a long purposeful drag from a spliff. Margot could smell the cannabis as the car was driven past. The passenger then fired an imaginary handgun at her. Margot thought the passenger must be all of fourteen. Rory's age. Margot wasn't scared, she was frustrated. She just wanted to shake him and say 'can't you see you're wasting your life? That this is wrong?' She wondered if that's what his mother told him. Margot wondered why people made the same mistakes over and over.
'This is pointless Luke.'
'It needs to be done Margot.'
They trudged on. The car came back for another circuit. The kids on the bikes cheered. Was that the limit of their ambition, to move up from bikes to car passengers, wondered Margot. The car stopped and the bikes swarmed over. Music blasted from the car.
'Ignore them Margot.'
'No one is going to answer the door in front of them Luke.'
'I know, but it is telling us which doors they don't want us to knock

on in particular. They haven't realised they are actually helping us.' Margot hadn't realised that either. Sure enough the car disappeared when they'd finished the street they were on. Margot remembered another of Luke's sayings - if they had brains they'd be dangerous. She'd actually thought the less brains the more dangerous, but she understood now what he was hinting at.

The house-to-house had taken them all day. They handed over their findings to the incident room and clocked off. Margot drove straight to Daisy's. Daisy had promised her a tour of the farm but they'd got no further than the piglets. Margot had watched Babe about twenty times. Daisy couldn't pull Margot away. Margot really wanted one, until Daisy had pointed out they would quickly reach the size of their mother. And Babe had been filmed using several piglets as they grew so quickly.

Jasmine arrived. Margot couldn't help but notice she looked a million dollars. Next to Daisy and Jasmine she was going to be the prudish chaperone again. Margot almost suggested she'd stay and play with the piglets but she hit the red wine hard instead. By the time they had actually gone out Margot was already very tipsy. They headed for Corbridge. The pubs were all very civilised, all five stars. Log fires and upholstered seats. They giggled their way into the first, putting the world to rights and Metcalfe to his grave. Margot wished she'd paced herself a little more.
'I'm just heading to the ladies,' she said. Margot looked at herself in the mirror. Why couldn't she have been tall thin and pretty like Jasmine, like Daisy, like her sister? She patched up her make up. A teenager in huge heels came in. Margot wondered at first if she had her dress on back to front. She realised it was supposed to be like that. Margot suddenly felt old. That she didn't belong. She wanted to go home. She went and found Daisy and Jasmine and told them she was feeling under the weather, that she'd just take a taxi home.

Margot walked to the market square and sat on a bench in front of the church. She was trying to find the number for the taxi firm behind the chippy on her phone when someone sat beside her. She didn't bother looking up as she concentrated hard on trying to remember what the taxi firm was actually called. She put what she thought it was in Google but an insurance company popped up. She was vaguely aware of a van pulling up right in front of her but didn't pay it any attention. She fumbled with her phone and it dropped onto the floor. She heard a van door slide open. She bent down to pick her phone up. She felt both her arms grabbed, she was hauled up and thrown into the back of the van.

Daisy and Jasmine headed to the next pub.
'I'll just call Margot, make sure she got a cab,' said Daisy.
'I can hear a phone ringing,' said Jasmine as they headed through the market place.
'Sounds like it's coming from the churchyard. Margot's not picking up.'
'It's stopped ringing too…just try Margot again.'
The ringtones on Daisy's phone were echoed by ringing from the churchyard. They kept ringing Margot's phone and following the rings. They headed into the churchyard; in the grass the ghostly light of a phone could be seen. They rushed over, the screen was cracked.
'Is Margot here, she was quite drunk?' said Jasmine.
Daisy shone the light of her phone round. 'I don't see her.'
'Do you think something has happened? Perhaps we should call it in.'
'Perhaps we should check to see if she made it home yet. Margot put cameras in her house. I can get into her phone I know the code, it's just her collar number. If she'd got a taxi straightaway she should just about be home.'
'Check if she called a taxi too. We can ring the taxi company.'
'Good idea. That's odd, she didn't call anyone. Let me get in this camera app.'
Margot's house was eerily empty.
'Keep checking the camera Daisy, I'm going to call John. I don't see any CCTV that would cover this. Where is she?'

Margot was being bumped along on the cold floor of the van. She felt sick, more from too much wine and the motion than from her situation, which she was still trying to work out. There was a strong smell of cheap aftershave. It was dark but she knew someone else was in the back of the van with her. She reckoned they had been driving for at least fifteen minutes. All off a sudden the van slowed, turned and started bumping along a very uneven track. Margot was bounced up in the air and came down hard on her nose on something solid. She let out a yelp. The van stopped. She could feel blood pouring out of her nose.

The van door slid open. Whoever was in the van with her jumped out and the door was immediately shut. There was no light outside, wherever they were was very dark. Margot listened.
'Light a fire.'

A man's voice. Why did they need a fire? Were they cannibals, she wondered. Margot tried to think more clearly. No one would miss her till tomorrow morning when she didn't show for work. Again she wished she'd not hit the wine so hard. She was getting very cold now. Perhaps a fire would be nice after all.

George Nolan

George spotted Nathan walking to school, he ran to catch him up.
'Mum says I can't walk with you.'
'I had an idea. I think we should do something for Kyle. I thinks we should do a giant art project like a memory wall of him. Kyle's favourite lesson was art. Like a monument in the school.'
'I don't want to walk with you. You smell.'

George walked to school on his own. He waited outside the school gates until the bell rang. Mr Graham was talking to Nathan when he walked into class. Mr Graham took registration, everyone held their nose when George's name was called out. George knew who had started that.
'Okay class. We all know how sad it is that Kyle can no longer be with us. Nathan has had a wonderful idea. A memory wall for Kyle. Of all the memories we have of him. So this week we will all work to produce a short story and a piece of art that is a memory we have of Kyle. As Kyle's best friend Nathan has asked if he can put them all together in one big artwork that we will hang on the main wall in the hall. I think it's an absolutely wonderful idea.'

That break time George punched Nathan and was promptly hauled before the headmistress.
'George Nolan, striking a fellow pupil is not acceptable. I have called your Auntie in. You will be suspended. You can wait with Mr Graham until she gets here.'

'Why did you do it George?' asked Mr Graham.
'I was Kyle's best friend,' sobbed George. 'Does that mean I can't do my memory?'
'Why don't you do it and I'll collect it when I drop off your schoolwork? I'll sneak it on for you.'
'Thanks.'

Janine fetched him from school. They walked home together.
'Do I smell, Auntie Jan?'
'No...is that why you punched Nathan? I hope you hit him really hard.'
'I made his nose bleed.'
'Well done George. It's important you don't let people get away with crap like that.'

George headed to his room. He wanted to write his memory for Kyle.

My memory is when everyone was playing football at break. I wanted to play but I didn't really know anyone. You came over and asked me if I wanted to play. We walked home together that day. That was the day we became friends. I liked you because you never left me out.

He started drawing a picture of them playing football together. When he'd finished it he didn't really think it was that good. Kyle was the one who could draw. He screwed it up. He'd have another go later. Nathan would probably not put it on anyway, or rip it off. George's mind festered with thoughts of Nathan. Kyle was the one who stuck up for him. Kyle wouldn't have ever let Nathan call him smelly. Nathan didn't know how powerful he had become. What he could do with a single match. Tonight he would find out. He shouldn't have stolen his idea. He needed more petrol. He'd already stolen everyone's lawnmowers alongside his uncle's, so he'd have to go faraway and burgle a shed to get some. The allotments would be a good place. He'd do exactly the same as he did at Shelly's Mum's house.

He should tell Auntie Jan that was him at some point. But his mother deserved to be taught a lesson. That's what she was always saying herself. She shouldn't have lied about Shelly killing Kyle when it wasn't true. George was also really worried what his mother would do to him when she found out he was the reason she was in prison. Perhaps he should just say nothing, he preferred living at Auntie Jan's anyway.

He crept out as soon as it was dark and headed for the allotments. He soon found what he was looking for. The petrol can felt heavy, it must be full. He undid it and smelled the fuel. He returned home, hiding the petrol can in Kyle's old garden.

He waited till midnight and crept back out. Making sure he had the matches and an old T-shirt. He made his way to Nathan's. He poured the petrol onto the rag. Then through the letter box. It spilled all over his shoes and trousers as he did it. His hands were slippery with petrol. He lit the match and lit the rag. There was a sudden roar. He screamed. He was on fire. His whole body. He ran but the flames ran with him. The pain was unbearable, the world disappeared.

A neighbour immediately jumped up and looked out the window on hearing the screams. Screams that cut right through you. He saw a child on fire. He rushed out with a blanket and managed to extinguish the flames. He hammered on other people's doors whilst calling for an ambulance. Other neighbours bravely smashed the back door and ran in and dragged out Nathan and his mother. A nurse took over the care of George. His body unrecognizable, no one knew it was George Nolan. The nurse called for clean wet towels. She swathed his body in them. An ambulance arrived and immediately incubated him. From the look on the faces of the nurse and ambulance crew everyone knew it was bad. Everyone looked on in silence as if the funeral had already started.

Margot

Margot heard a phone ring. She'd been in the van ages now. She couldn't make out what was said. She heard a muffled almost panicked conversation in the distance. She heard the van doors open. Two figures in balaclavas manhandled her out, threw her on the floor next to the fire. Jumped in the van and disappeared. The taillights tracing out the bumpy track. Margot got up and stood there by the fire that was blazing away. What the bloody hell was that all about she wondered? She had no idea who it was or why she was here. No idea where they had gone. She wasn't tied up. Wasn't hurt, bar a few bruises and bloodied nose. It then dawned on her it was pitch black, she had no phone, was in a ridiculous pair of heels and she didn't know where she was.

Margot sat down by the fire. She'd just have to wait till it got light and walk. She couldn't hear a thing either she realised. She wasn't near civilisation. The fire was attracting moths. They dived for the flames. Margot thought about Rory and Gavin.

Luke

John and Luke arrived shortly after the Divisional Sergeant. Daisy and Jasmine had to explain all over again what had happened.
'So was she unwell?' asked John.
'Possibly with the wine. She disappeared to the toilet and when she came back she said she wasn't feeling well. I feel terrible, it's the first rule of going out - stay together,' said Daisy.
'Any ideas anyone? Check the camera again Daisy please,' said John.
'Not home. Something has happened but I don't know what,' said Daisy.
Jasmine shook her head.
'Let's just start with an immediate search of the area. Perhaps she's just fallen over somewhere. Have you checked in the church?'
'Locked,' said Jasmine.

They commenced a search. They had been looking for fifteen or so minutes when the sergeant shouted 'I have to go. House fire, persons reported.'

They continued looking. Until John's phone rang. Luke and Jasmine stopped in their tracks as soon as John said 'I'll be right there give me the details.' They rushed over.
'Arson Ma'am. If I'm not mistaken at the house of our young witness, Kyle's friend who booked the taxi. Luke come with me. A young child has been rushed to hospital with life threatening injuries.'
'Nathan?'
'No. He's going to hospital with his mother but they are okay.
'So what happened?'
'Let's go and find out. The sergeant who was with us has requested we attend.'

It didn't take Luke and John long to piece together what had happened.
'This is the same MO Boss as Shelly's mother's house. I think I can guess who the child might be.'

They knocked on Janine's door. The smoke from the fire could still be seen against the night sky. Janine looked at it. Before she could say anything Luke jumped in.
'Janine it's important. Where is George?'
'In bed.'
'Please go and check.'
She came back looking worried.
'He's not there.'
'Janine somebody just set fire to a house..'
'That won't be him.'
'Please just let me finish. It's a young boy. They have been seriously hurt.'
'Everyone knows George, can't you tell if it's him?'
Luke shook his head.
'Oh God. I have to go to the hospital. I need to ring Al to look after Maisie, George's sister. She's asleep.'
'We can take you to the hospital if it helps.'
'No, Joe can run me down. Will…will he be okay?'
'I honestly don't know but I think you should go quickly. We didn't see him, he'd already gone by the time we got here.'
'Thank you. Thank you for telling me.'

Luke and John walked back to the car.
'You know it could be George who set fire to Shelly's mother's.

Colleen could actually be innocent Boss.'
'I know one thing Luke, that bloody woman is not innocent. Maybe in the eyes of the law but she's far from innocent. I'll organise forensic to attend the house in the morning alongside fire investigation. For now let's head to the hospital and talk to Nathan and his mother.'
'Actually Boss, their teacher. With a bit of luck he'll be staying at his girlfriend's which isn't far. Let's swing by there first, see if he knows why George would want to burn Nathan's house down.'
'Good idea.'

The teacher and his girlfriend took some waking up.
'Sorry to bother you at this time. It's very important. Did something happen between Nathan and George at school today by any chance?' asked Luke.
'Yes, do you want to come in?'
'Please.'
Mr Graham was wearing his girlfriend's dressing gown. He tried to sit himself down and keep everything covered. In the end he grabbed a cushion.
'George punched Nathan at break time and got himself suspended.'
'Do you know why?'
'I asked him and he said because Kyle was his best friend. Nathan had an idea to do a memory wall for Kyle. I suspect that was perhaps George's idea and Nathan stole it. Nathan can be a little selfish, he's an only child not used to sharing. Since Kyle went missing Nathan has been quite mean to George, I've had to pull him up a couple of times. George struggles to make friends on account that most of the other kids' parents have told their kids to stay away from him. George really misses Kyle. Kyle was incredibly considerate, he always included George. Am I allowed to ask what's happened?'
'It appears George might have tried to burn Nathan's house down but he has seriously injured himself in the process. Please keep that to yourself for now,' said John.
'Is he going to be okay?'
'We don't know.'

Luke and John left for the hospital. They spoke to Nathan and his mother. It was clear they had no idea what had happened. All they could say were that neighbours had woken them up and dragged them out of a burning house.

They spotted Janine and Joe in reception on their way out.
'Have you had any news?' asked Luke.
'No. We just have to wait here for now. Someone will be out to see us as soon as they can,' said Janine.
'We should be allowed in. It's not right,' said Joe.
'Don't be a dick, Joe. They are trying to save his life. Burns can get infected really easily. They said wait here and that's exactly what we are going to do.'
'I hope he's okay,' said Luke.
'Spare us the sympathy, you were only here to arrest him,' said Joe.
'For fuck's sake Joe. If you're going to have a go at everybody just piss off home. I don't need this,' said Janine.
Joe opened his mouth then closed it again.

Luke and John walked over to the reception.
'Any chance of a condition update on George Nolan?' John asked the nurse in reception showing his warrant card.
'He's still in resus, call in an hour.'
'Please can you give me some information?'
'Wait here.'
She disappeared and came back.
'Ninety percent burns.'

Luke and John walked to the car in silence.
'Boss there's nothing more we can do on this now. I'm really worried about Margot can I go back and look for her?'
'We'll go together. I'll drop you back for your car. You take Daisy I'll take Jasmine, let's keep looking. The girls are still walking around Corbridge somewhere.'
'Perhaps we should check where Donna was found. She took that pretty badly.'
'You do that. I'll start checking her route home in case she lost her phone and decided to walk.'

Margot

It seemed to be taking forever for the light to reach where she was. Margot could make out the tops of tall conifers first. Then water as the sky lightened. The fire had died down but it had kept her company and warm. She was at the edge of a small lake in a forest. A track headed off into the trees. She took off her heels and set off bare foot. Luckily the track had just about enough grass growing down the middle not to be too uncomfortable to walk on. She did a strange dance every time she stood on a stone.

She had half thought perhaps the van would come back. She was on high alert for the sound of an engine. Constantly working out where she could dive for cover if they came back. She walked on and on. It started to rain. Margot was soon shivering. She saw a deer, she froze. How magical was that she thought. It saw her and she watched it's white tail bobbing away into the distance. Eventually she broke out onto a bigger track. This one was made of countless small stones. She had to put her heels back on. The heels sunk into the stones. At this rate she'd starve to death, perhaps that was their plan all along. One thing that wasn't starving to death were the midges. Margot was truly miserable. She took her shoes off and tried to snap the heels off. Quality, always go for quality Margot if you can afford it. Her mother's words now haunting her. Margot sat down. What was she waiting for she asked herself - a bus? She pushed herself back up onto her feet. She set off again. Everything hurt now. She was also really thirsty. She had red wine mouth and head, on top of everything else.

At least the rain had now stopped. She guessed a couple of hours had passed since she set off. Suddenly Margot saw the trees stopped ahead. She could see open moorland and sheep. She quickened her pace. She emerged onto tarmac. She still couldn't see any houses. At least a road would have traffic on it. Even a single track road like this. Margot sat down and waited. And waited.

'Where the bloody hell am I?' she said out loud. Left or Right? It was Rory's right arm on the fence so she decided to turn right. She kept walking. Finally Margot heard a car. She flagged it down. In that instant she didn't care who it was. Although the thought had crossed her mind, only serial killers and crazy people drove to

places like this. She was pleasantly surprised to see it was a middle-aged lady. The car stopped but the windows stayed up.
'Can you help me please? Someone dumped me in the middle of the forest last night, I've no idea where I am.'
The lady looked worried it hadn't occurred to Margot the lady was probably thinking the same thing. - only serial killers and crazy people would be out here.
'I'm a police officer,' said Margot.
'I don't believe you,' said the lady speeding off.

'Just bloody brilliant,' said Margot. As she sat back down again she hoped the lady would at least call the police. She waited for what felt like ages, not a soul to be seen. She stood back up and tried to walk. Her body had completely seized. She sat back down again. She saw another car coming along. She levered herself up and stood firm in the middle of the road. She held her hand up to stop the car. She closed her eyes. She heard the car stop. She opened her eyes and saw it was Luke and Daisy.
'Some lady called in to say there was a mad woman in the woods. We thought it might be you,' said Daisy. 'We've been looking for you all night. How did you end up here?'
'It was all very odd. I was kidnapped but then absolutely nothing happened.'
'You're covered in blood, are you okay?'
'I had a nosebleed. Then I couldn't snap my heels off.'

Luke gave her a hug.
'You had me worried there Margot. Who kidnapped you?'
'I don't know. Two men in a van.'
'George Nolan is in hospital. He tried to set Nathan's house on fire last night. He accidentally set himself alight. He's critical but stable now, but he has ninety percent burns. He's in an induced coma. We think he might be responsible for killing Shelly's Mum too although it's two early to change our mind on that one just yet.'
'How many more lives are going to be wasted because of Richard Grant? Why didn't he just tell the truth?'
As she said it Margot felt hypocritical. She knew how one lie led to another, then another. Still she wasn't a Richard Grant. She also wondered if the ripples would stop rippling now. She doubted if Colleen would take what had happened to George lying down in her cell.

Two weeks later

Margot had been called in to see the Detective Inspector allocated to investigate her kidnapping. A DI Helen Kerr.
'Sit down Margot. I just wanted a quick chat now things have settled down. As you know we found where you were left, and I'm afraid we drew a blank with forensics. As with your phone. Do you really have no idea who it was?'
'I'm sorry Ma'am I don't. It doesn't make any sense. I admit I had had far too much wine, and I wasn't as observant as perhaps I should have been. The only thing I really remember is the cheap aftershave.'
'I'm sorry Margot but we've drawn a complete blank.'
'It's okay Ma'am, I didn't exactly give you anything to go on.'
'And you still can't think why?'
'I honestly can't Ma'am.'
'For now, without anything further I'm afraid that's it Margot.'
'I completely understand.'

Margot was a little disappointed, she had wanted to know what it was all about. It wasn't so much frightening her as niggling her. She thought perhaps she should be more concerned by what had happened. Luke was far more concerned than she was. Margot couldn't quite make sense of her own lack of worry. She could after all have been raped and murdered.

Anyway there were bigger worries now. George's mobile phone data put him at the location of the fire at Shelly's mother's house. Colleen was a free woman as of ten minutes ago. The prison service had informed the police she was threatening to make someone pay for what happened to George. Margot was now en route to another meeting with Luke and John to discuss who that someone might be. Margot tried to work out in the warped logic of Colleen Nolan's brain who or whom did she think was responsible for George setting fire to himself.

The meeting was being chaired by the Divisional Superintendent.
'I think that's everybody, let's begin. The prison service have concerns over Colleen Nolan. She's told other inmates she is going to avenge what happened to her son, meet like with like. And yes I can see the irony. So who do we need to consider safeguarding?'
'I think the officers that arrested her for the arson. Her logic being that if she was at home it wouldn't have happened.' said a

uniformed Inspector.
'Noted,' said the Superintendent.
'Shelly Morgan, maybe,' said Luke.
'She was the victim,' said the Superintendent looking sceptical.
'Yes but Colleen told us once if she hadn't killed Kyle she might as well have done. She may see her as the catalyst. Plus I doubt she's forgiven her for Kevin yet either,' said Luke. The Super wrote it down.
'Janine her sister, she was supposed to be looking after him,' said John.
'I thought the family were tight?'
'They were, but right now who knows.'
The Superintendent wrote it down.
'Richard Grant,' said Margot.
'He's in prison. Although that probably isn't enough to stop Colleen Nolan. It's certainly worth letting the prison know,' said the Superintendent.
'I think you have to include Nathan and his mother too,' said John.
'Is that likely?'
'No more or less than the names so far Sir.'
The Superintendent wrote their names down too. Margot was still waiting for him to write Richard Grant down.
'Any more for any more?'
The room was silent. The Superintendent got up to leave thanking everyone.

Margot and Luke sat there finishing their coffees. Last in last out.
'Margot could the Nolan brothers have kidnapped you?'
'I really can't identify them Luke. I don't know is the honest answer. I have only really had dealings with Joe before. It's not a definite no that's for sure. Anyway if they did, what was the point of it? Nothing happened.'
'Perhaps because they called off whatever they were going to do because of George. Janine phoned them.'
'I heard a phone call Luke. They sounded a bit panicked but I couldn't actually hear a word they said.'
'It must be them Margot.'
'But why in the first place?'
'Maybe Colleen thought you'd set her up for the fire.'
'She didn't like me. I suppose she might have thought that.'
'You should tell the DI investigating.'
'It's too late now, any forensic will be gone. And I still can't identify

them. Perhaps given what's going on it might be a useful card to keep up our sleeves for now.'
'Margot you do realise how serious this is don't you? Kidnapping you is a big deal.'
'It doesn't feel that big to me.'
'Maybe because you were drunk. Didn't you feel frightened at all?'
'I felt sick from the wine. I was having weird thoughts about being eaten. I suppose I must have been a bit scared.'
'Please tell that DI.'
'That I thought I was going to be eaten?'
'No Margot, that the Nolans are a possibility.'
'Okay but won't it make things worse if the brothers are arrested for kidnapping me practically the second she's released?'
'Margot they need arresting. If they are prepared to kidnap a police officer. And - I was trying not to say this - probably kill you on Colleen's say so, then what else are they capable of? If they had their phones with them it will be easy to prove if they were there or not. If she's planning something it's probably a good time. We might be able to reduce their numbers.'
'Okay I'll tell the DI.'
'Make sure you tell her about this meeting too so she knows what's she's walking into.'

Margot rang her straightaway. Afterwards Margot thought about it again. Why didn't it feel like a big deal? It was a big deal she could see that. What was wrong with her? She drove back to the station with Luke and John. On the way she told John as well.
'Are you okay Margot? If you want some time off please ask.'
'No I'm fine Sir. Honestly I am. Do you think I shouldn't be okay?'
'You feel what you feel Margot. But perhaps it hasn't hit you yet. So if we were betting people who's Colleen going after?'
'My money's on Shelly mainly because of Kevin,' said Luke.
'I'm not sure,' said Margot. 'She can't blame Shelly for George's injuries. Shelly's mother is dead. Her and her mother's houses have been burned down. Don't you think she's done with Shelly.'
'Nathan maybe?' said John.
'Yeah but George can't talk he's still heavily sedated. She can't know what went on at the school. Is she really going to go like for like on a nine year old?' said Luke.
'No you're probably right. That leaves us with Janine or one of us,' said John.
'I'd say police over family,' said Luke.

'I agree but let's not get blinkered on this.'
'Are we on this then Sir?' asked Margot.
'We are on the consequences.'
'So we have to wait for her to do something. That seems wrong,' said Margot.
'Before she does anything is the Superintendent's problem not ours Margot. That said, let's take extra precautions.'

Margot looked at all the in-trays in the office. They all had plenty of work. Gavin Mason's killers were in the cells. Not her case but Margot had kept abreast of developments none the less. Eavesdropping on conversations. Gavin was visiting a friend. He was stabbed just once on his way home in a reprisal hit. Left to die on the pavement. He was twenty, his killers fifteen, fourteen and thirteen. They had boasted about it on social media. Margot wondered how far the ripples from Gavin Mason would travel.

Luke asked Margot to stay the night. She had Tom's cooking in mind when she said yes. She also wanted to ask them about bathroom fittings. She had finally secured a plumber. He had rung her up and asked her what shower she wanted putting in. She didn't know. One like Luke's, but was even possible given they had a walk-in shower and she had to stand in the bath?

They were also both on call tonight which would dampen proceedings further. None of Tom's wine collection. They decided to go in one car, or to be totally accurate Luke insisted on it. It made sense Margot had to concede. She always enjoyed the drive to Luke's it was like taking the scenic route. Tom warmly welcomed her as always. They chatted for a while before Tom declared everything was ready, Thai green curry. The first meal Tom ever cooked for Margot, also probably Margot's favourite. They had just sat down when Luke's phone rang. Margot could tell by his face they were about to head back to work. She shovelled in as much of the curry and rice as she could.

'Sorry we're back on Margot. Janine has disappeared.'
'Who called that in?'
'Daisy. Janine made a 999 call, there was no speech. Mobile is registered to her. Daisy attended. Her house was open but she wasn't in it. Given she's on the list we have to attend straightaway.'
'Can you finish your tea?' asked Tom.

'Sorry we'd better go.'

They headed to Janine's house. Daisy was guarding the door with Mo.
'Margot they arrested Al and Joe for kidnapping you. I'm not sure if I should be telling you that or not.'
'It's okay I knew about it.'
'They must have literally just finished searching their houses and left when this came in. I reckon Colleen came round to ask what was going on. There's no sign of a struggle. Janine's car is missing. Colleen isn't in and her daughter is at her grandma's; has been all evening and was sleeping over. She might have been planning this.'
'If she did isn't it a bit obvious it's her? Did you find Janine's phone?'
'No and she isn't answering on ring back. Control room tried several times.'

Just at that moment Janine's car drove into the street with Janine driving and Colleen in the passenger seat. Colleen jumped out carrying a Tesco's carrier bag full of shopping.
'You got a warrant to be in there?'
'We had a 999 call from your phone Janine,' said Daisy,
'Sorry must've sat on it,' said Janine looking at the ground.
'So you got no reason to be in there now. Go on, piss off the lot of you,' said Colleen.

They pulled out and parked a few streets away pulling up alongside each other. Mo and Daisy in the panda car. Margot and Luke in his car.
'Was it me or did Janine look scared,' said Margot.
'Terrified I'd say,' said Daisy.
'Colleen's toying with her. I think she did dial 999,' said Luke.
'So do you think she will actually do something?' asked Margot.
'I don't know. Make sure you two stay together don't get separated. We are on call, Margot's staying at mine. Call if you're unsure of anything. I honestly have no idea what she's planning on doing,' said Luke to Mo and Daisy.

Luke rang Tom and told him they were coming straight back. Margot had that deja vu feeling as they drove back along the road.

'I think she'll bide her time for a bit,' said Luke breaking the silence. 'She's messing with Janine's head isn't she?'
'Yes.'

They managed to finish their dinner this time. Then pretty much headed straight to bed afterwards. Margot couldn't sleep she wasn't sure if it was the full stomach or being on call. She must have dropped off eventually as the alarm woke her. For a minute she was totally confused as to where she was. She looked around. Showers, she hadn't asked about showers. She decided she'd just take a picture of it and send that to the plumber along with a picture of what she already had. They had a quick breakfast and headed into work. John was waiting for her.
'Margot just to let you know Joe and Al Nolan were interviewed. They no-replied everything. Their phones have been seized. No sign of the van anywhere. They have been released under investigation. I don't doubt their phones will put them in the area. The problem being there's only the one mast because it's so remote so no chance of an exact location. I can tell you now that by itself won't be enough.'
'I'm sorry Sir I just couldn't say it was them.'
'There's nothing to be sorry for Margot. I'm telling you because you need to know. If you see any of the Nolans off duty you call it in immediately, even if you just let me or Luke know. I also don't want you to have anymore dealings with them unless absolutely necessary for now. Not until a decision has been made on what to do with them. Certainly not on your own.'
'So what are we doing today Sir?'
'I have a job for you. Shelly has been discharged from hospital. She's being housed in Carlisle well away from the Nolans. Can you pick her up and drop her off at her house?'
'Sure.'

Shelly didn't have clothes to wear. Why had no one even thought of that wondered Margot, realising she hadn't thought of it either. She could nip home and get some but they wouldn't fit. She nipped into town and bought her a T-shirt, fleece and jeans and returned. Shelly was now sitting on a chair in the ward waiting, her bed already taken.
'Sorry for the wait. I was here ages ago but the nurse said you had no clothes. So I bought you these to wear.'

'Thanks.'
Margot couldn't help but notice her face didn't echo her words. Her face was blank, emotionless. It was odd. She walked to the toilets and changed out of the hospital gown.
'Okay let's go shall we?'
Shelly just looked blankly at Margot. They walked to her car in silence. Margot had to prompt Shelly to put her seat belt on. Margot thought it was as if someone had turned her off. Her body still worked but her personality was gone.
'Could Dan not pick you up Shelly?'
'We aren't speaking. I doubt we will ever speak again. Some pretty harsh things have been said. Do you think I was a terrible mother. Is it all my fault?'
'Do you want an honest answer?'
She nodded.
'I think you shouldn't have left Kyle like you did when you met those men. I think he was too young. I'm not sure I understand why you went out for sex with all those men. Kyle's death is on one person only though, and that's Richard Grant. Kyle was a really good kid, he looked out for people. He was kind and considerate. You must have done a lot of things right.'
Shelly was silent. Margot wondered if she'd been too honest.
'Are you going to be alright Shelly?' added Margot.
'Kyle was everything to me.'

Margot pulled out of the hospital car park and drove in silence. The sat nav took Margot to a small flat. Margot didn't want to say anything but it didn't look very nice. A lady was waiting impatiently.
'I was expecting you an hour ago,' she said. 'I have the keys, shall we?'
Margot went in with Shelly. It was clean and furnished at least. It was very much a one-person flat though, as if to rub salt into the wounds. Shelly was just one person now. She sat on the sofa.
'Thank you,' she said.
The lady spouted on about the boiler, the hot water, the bills. Neither Margot nor Shelly heard a word.

Margot left. She wondered how long Shelly would sit on that sofa before she found the energy to get up and carry on with life. Margot turned the car around. She headed for the supermarket and brought lots of fruit and vegetables, some milk, she found some chicken breasts on special offer. She drove back to Shelly's. As

Margot suspected she was still sitting on the sofa.
'Shelly, make sure you eat. I've bought you some food, I'll stick it in the fridge.'
'What's the point Margot?'
'You have to find a point Shelly. You know I got to this very place where you are now.'
'What did you do Margot?'
'I got really drunk and applied to join the police.'
Shelly almost smiled.
'I don't think I'll be doing that Margot.'
'Promise me you won't just sit there on your own.'
'Okay I'll promise. I'll be okay. Thank you Margot.'

Margot drove back to the station. As she drove into the compound looking for a parking space, Dan Morgan was being marched into custody in handcuffs. She rushed upstairs.
'Sir, did you know Dan Morgan has been arrested again?'
'A second before you told me Margot. He turned up at the Grants' house drunk. Forced his way in. Assaulted the wife.'
'Why?'
'Because he's grieving for his son, Margot.'

John's phone rang. Margot started to walk away but John held up his hand. She waited.
'Where?…Do we know how…No, we will deal Ma'am. I'll attend straightaway with Margot…Colleen Nolan has been murdered. I wasn't expecting that. Let's go Margot, you are with me.'

John drove along the military road, Margot was enjoying the views. He slowed to turn off for Cawfields. The road was closed at the crossroads. John held up his warrant card and an officer removed a cone to let them through. After about a quarter of a mile John drove into the car park. Margot saw police tape tied between two police cars, cordoning off the toilets. They suited up, Margot taking ages again. They walked in over steel square stepping-stones, making their way to the far cubicle. As Margot got closer the smell became very unpleasant. Colleen was sitting on the toilet, fully clothed with her throat cut. Faeces smeared around her face.
'Well that's a statement. Doesn't look like she was killed here, there's no blood splatter. Whoever it was wanted her found that's for sure. I guess we start with the family,' said John.
They headed outside. Margot breathed the fresh air in. She took in

the view. An old quarry, now filled with water, right on Hadrians wall. A triangular outcrop of rock reflected perfectly back to itself in the water on the far side. Margot's first thought was that this was far too nice for Colleen, toilets aside.

'Why here though Sir? There's perfectly good public toilets where she lives.'

'It's quiet here, no chance of getting caught, would be my guess.'

'I'm not sure Sir. It's like this place is important to whoever did this.'

'Possibly. Let's start by reverse engineering our list. It can't be Shelly, she was in hospital. That leaves Nathan's Mum and Janine.'

'Nathan's Mum doesn't look that strong to me Sir. And cutting someone's throat especially Colleen's wouldn't be that easy. Then putting her in a car and dragging her here. Colleen was alive and well at half eight last night, me and Luke both saw her. We got called out because Janine made a 999, only she said it was in error. She looked scared though.'

'Tell me all about it in the car. Let's see if we can totally rule out Nathan's Mum. Then we'll go and see Janine.'

Nathan's Mum didn't have an alibi as such – she was home alone with Nathan all night who was asleep. Neither John nor Margot really thought it could be her. Janine was their next port of call. She was just heading out.

'I'm going to the hospital to see George. I can't talk to you.'

'It's important Janine,' said John.

'Not here, Colleen will be watching.'

'Janine, Colleen was murdered last night.'

Janine's jaw dropped. She froze for a second.

'Are you sure?'

'Yes.'

Margot didn't think Janine had killed her sister.

'Do you know who?'

'Not yet. We need to ask you some questions.'

'Come in. Sorry, I smoked weed last night.'

Margot saw the leftovers of several spliffs on the coffee table.

'When did you last see her?' John asked.

'When you did,' she said looking at Margot.

'Where did she go after we left?' asked Margot.

'Home with her shopping.'

'Have you any ideas who could have done this?'

'None. It won't be Al or Joe either before you ask.'

'Had she fallen out with anyone?' asked John.

'Colleen fell out with everyone she didn't care.'
'Where were you all night?'
'Smoking those,' said Janine pointing to the spliffs.
'Can we take a quick around?'
'If it will convince you it wasn't me. Then go for it.'
They checked the house.
'Can we just check the car too please?'
Janine handed them the keys. John and Margot headed outside.

'Which house is Colleen's, Margot?'
Margot pointed out the house a few doors up.
'Why hasn't that been secured yet? Margot check the car whilst I make a phone call. This simply isn't good enough.'

At that moment Al Nolan came out of Colleen's, looked at Margot who looked at him, then took off running up the street.
'Sir,' shouted Margot as she gave chase. As Margot entered his slipstream, the smell of cheap aftershave hit her nostrils. She soon lost him as he effortlessly hurdled garden fences.
'Margot let's secure the house before we worry about him. That could be our crime scene.'
They suited up again. Margot had always wondered what Colleen Nolan's house would be like. It wasn't what she expected. It was clean and tidy and tasteful. A huge TV dominated the living room. Margot started to look closely. The carpets were expensive. The furniture expensive. The curtains expensive. Farrow and Ball on the walls no doubt, Margot's brain started coming up with appropriate colour names: hepatitis yellow, cocaine line white. She forced herself to stop. The kitchen had a huge fridge freezer. Bottles of champagne where most people kept their milk. A coffee maker. Granite work surfaces. Upstairs the bathroom was small but amazing; she sneaked a picture for the plumber. She looked in George's room; another huge TV surrounded by towers of computer games. Colleen's bedroom was nice too. She loved the black and gold wallpaper. She sneaked another picture. Perhaps if she was allowed to keep her painting. She screamed.
John came rushing in. A bald cat had jumped up on the bed.
'Is that a cat? Where's its fur?' asked Margot.
'It doesn't have any, it's a Sphinx cat.'
'Bloody hell, I didn't know what it was.'
'House is clear, no blood. I don't think this was our crime scene

either. I'll run forensic through regardless. Let's try and start a timeline for her movements. Her car is still outside; have you come across any keys?'
'No.'

Just at that moment Colleen's BMW was driven off. They both watched the roof of it disappear down the street from the bedroom window.
'My guess that was Al Nolan. I guess he came for the keys,' said John.
'Do you think it was him?'

They heard a loud crash. They both ran from the house. The BMW was nose-to-nose with a panda car at the bottom of the street. Both front ends creased into each other. The airbags had deployed, filling the cars with a fine smoke-like dust. Al Nolan had crashed into the police car coming to secure the house. He was now fighting with the officers who were trying to arrest him. By the time John and Margot had run down the street the situation was under control
'DI John Hall. Are you two okay?' John asked the two officers.
'Yes Sir.'
'He's disqualified from driving, take him in for that. I need a quick word first,' said John. Al Nolan spat at John.
'Fuck off,' said Al.
At that moment Janine stormed down the street 'did you and Joe kill Colleen?' said Janine.
'What you on about?'
'Colleen is dead. Did you have anything to do with that?'
'Dead how?'
'Murdered.'
'No I didn't, I swear Jan I didn't.'
'Then why did you run?' asked John.
'I wasn't, I just didn't want to speak to you.'
'Why were you in Colleen's house?'
'To fetch the car keys. She told me to pick up something.'
'When did she tell you that?'
'Last night about eleven.'
'Was the door open when you got here this morning?'
'Back was. I hopped the fence like I always do, grabbed the car keys. Let myself out the front and I saw yous so I legged it. I seen you go in her house so I tried to ring her but she didn't answer. I

figured she'd been arrested. So I took the car so I could pick up the…shopping.'

'Okay take him away, thank you,' said John to the officers. 'Sorry - when you get transport obviously.'
'The carrier is on the way, Sir.'
'Look I'm heading to the hospital if you need me. George shouldn't be on his own,' said Janine.
'Was Colleen not going to go with you this morning?' asked Margot.
'Colleen said she couldn't bear to look at him. That she would rather he died. What mother says that?' Janine walked back up the street.

Margot and John walked back up to Colleen's house.
'Al looked genuinely surprised too didn't you think Sir?'
'He did. So that leaves Joe to trace. I'll get a replacement crew to secure the house I still want forensic in there. She could have been taken from the house. And we need to find her phone. It didn't ring in the house.'

That question was answered quick enough, a CSI rang John. Her phone was in her back pocket. It had rung at the crime scene.

'I guess we need to consider if this is a dealer she's pissed off too,' said John.
Margot thought about the lovely spot she was left. It just didn't scream drug dealers to her. 'I think Cawfields is too nice for drug dealers Sir.'

Margot liked John but this was now becoming awkward. They had been waiting over an hour for someone to show up and relieve them. She'd run out of topics of conversation ages ago. They had tried Joe's house whilst they waited but it didn't look like he was in. He certainly wasn't answering the door. Margot was surprised when Daisy and Mo turned up. She knew they should be on lates.
'What are you doing here?' she asked.
'Called in early. Sorry, we got here as quick as we could.'
'Can you watch the house until forensic are done? They should be on their way shortly, a busy morning all round by the looks of things. Oh and we need a word with Joe Nolan if he turns up,' said John.

'So she really has been murdered.' said Daisy to Margot as John headed back down the road to their car.
'Yeah found at Cawfields.'
'Odd place.'
'I thought that,' said Margot.
'I doubt many people will be upset Colleen has gone. I guess the idiot brothers will be taking over. You know we attended three overdoses whilst Colleen was inside. Obviously a dodgy batch of heroin. Crazy as it seems Colleen would have never let that happen. She ran a tight ship. Who'd have thought there could of been an upside to Colleen getting out?'
'Come on Margot,' shouted John from the car.

'Where are we off to Sir?'
'I need to head back to the station? You can team up with Luke and find Joe for me please.'
'Okay Sir but can you drop me at my old station. Get Luke to pick me up from there, I want to check out a few things.'
'Sure. Wait for Luke before you do anything, he's running down Colleen's phone records for me at the moment.'

Margot settled herself at the computer. She searched for the overdoses Daisy had mentioned. One stood out: an eighteen-year-old boy Harrison Thompson, originally from Haltwhistle, found in the flat he'd only just moved into by his father, Jamie Thompson. The flat was in Colleen's estate. Margot looked at her watch, Luke had said he would be a while. She was stuck anyway, she didn't have a car. She rang Caroline. She waited, looking out the window as Geoffrey pulled up in his new car.
'This is all very exciting Margot. Are you sure this is allowed?'
'Probably not. Can you take me to Haltwhistle please Geoffrey?'
'Of course,' Geoffrey opened the door for her.

She gave him the address. He drove to a nice house perched high on a hill above the town. How do you go from this to heroin, Margot wondered. She knocked on the door. It was opened by a lady who looked around Margot's age. She'd been crying, Margot could tell. Margot guessed it was Harrison's mother.
'Hello I'm DC Margot Jacks. I wanted to talk to you about your son Harrison if that's okay.'
'It was his funeral yesterday. Please come in.'

Margot was shown into the living room. She immediately noticed a photo on the wall. A young boy holding a man's hand at Cawfields quarry. She walked over for a closer look.
'That's Harrison, he was five when that was taken, that's his Dad. That was always his favourite place. Their place they called it.'
Bollocks thought Margot.
'How did Harrison get involved with drugs?'
'He was smart, was going to university and everything, then he met this girl and got in with completely the wrong crowd. We knew he was on drugs, he changed so much. We didn't think it would be heroin though. The coroner said he had a reaction to something they'd mixed in it. Fentanyl I think he said. He and his girlfriend took some. She made it but only just, but Harrison was already dead when my husband found them.'

Margot could fill in the gaps herself.

'I need to speak to your husband, do you know where I can find him?'
'He's in bed. He works nights.'
Double bollocks thought Margot.
'Not to worry I'll come back.'
'No I can wake him now, he wanted waking up around now anyway.'
Triple bollocks. What was she going to do - arrest him, then sit on his lap and transport him to custody in Geoffrey's new car? She didn't want to lie to his lovely wife either.
'I'll wait outside. Tell him I'm here. Take as long as you need.'
'Is something wrong?'
'I'll be outside.'

Margot headed out.
'Geoffrey, it's probably better if you leave me here. I'm going to call Daisy for a ride.'
'If you are sure.'
'I'm really sure thank you.'
Margot hurriedly rang Daisy.
'Daisy are the CSI's there yet?'
'Yeah.'
'Can you leave Mo there with them? I need digging out of a hole, I've found Colleen's murderer. I've got no car and no handcuffs. I

was supposed to wait for Luke in the station.'
'Bloody hell Margot where are you?'
Margot gave her the address.

Margot sat on the wall outside and waited. A man came out. The man in the photo. Jamie Thompson.
'Thanks for doing this low key. I expected loads of police cars. I thought you might come with guns and everything. Shall we do this?'
'I have to arrest you.'
'I know.'
'I am arresting you for the murder of Colleen Nolan. You do not have to say anything but it may harm your defence if you do not mention something when questioned that you later rely on in court. Anything you do say may be used in evidence. Don't say anything and get a lawyer.'
'Okay. Where is your car?'
'It's on its way.'
Jamie sat on the wall next to her. 'I'm not sorry you know. Maybe now other Mums or Dads won't find their kids dead in their own shit and vomit, like I found Harrison. I didn't go there to kill her. I just wanted to let her know what her drugs did. Only she told me to piss off. So I took her to Harrison's grave. You know what she said, she said "there's no refunds in this game, your son was a fucking junkie get over it." And then I can't explain, I just killed her. I couldn't control my anger. I want you to know that.'

Daisy slid to a stop. They placed Jamie Thompson in the back of the police car. Margot hoped the ripples had finally stopped. Margot was just about call John when she saw a car heading towards them. Margot wasn't sure why but the hairs on her arms all rushed to stand up. Time slowed down. She saw Joe Nolan at the wheel. She saw the passenger side window go down. She saw his left arm raise. She saw the gun in his hand. She shouted 'Guuuuuuuunnnnnn.' She saw three flashes at the muzzle as she dived on top of Daisy. She felt her shoulder explode in pain. She heard every cylinder fire in the engine of the car as it sped off.

She heard Mrs Thompson's door open. She heard every footstep. She heard the scream. She heard Daisy shouting into the radio. 'Shoooooottttsss fired, Shooooottttsss fired, assistance required.'

Everything sped up back to normal time. Daisy was pushing Margot off her.
'Margot you're hit.'
'I think I'm okay, it hurts like hell though. What about Jamie, is he okay?'
Margot couldn't get up. Daisy looked in the back of the panda car.
'Is he okay Daisy. Is he okay?'
Margot looked at Mrs Thompson's face. Margot knew he wasn't okay. Why hadn't she just done as she'd been told and waited in the station for Luke?

'We have to get inside, he might come back. Did you see who it was Margot?'
'Joe Nolan. It was Joe Nolan.'
'Mrs Thompson we have to get inside. Mrs Thompson help me get Margot inside.'

Margot was hauled to her feet and dragged into the house. All three of them were shaking uncontrollably. Margot's phone rang, she hadn't even known it was still in her hand. It went unanswered, she just stared at it. Daisy looked out the window. She updated on the radio that the shooter was Joe Nolan. She asked for an ambulance. She said there had been a fatality. Fatality was the last word Margot was aware of. It echoed around her head.

Margot

Margot woke up in hospital with Luke and Tom at her side.
'Dad will be pissed off. He's never left your side Margot, he's literally just gone to stretch his legs.'
'How long have I been out?'
'You've just come out of surgery. You were very lucky. The bullet nicked the bone and an artery but it basically passed straight through.'
'It's my fault Jamie Thompson is dead.'
'How can it be your fault Margot? Joe Nolan was on his way to kill him. Janine rang to warn us just before you were shot. There wasn't enough time to do anything. You still should have told us where you were going though.'
'I'm sorry.'
'Some plumber keeps ringing your phone.'
'I know. I wanted a shower like yours.'
'Rest up. I have to go back to work. Joe Nolan has been arrested. Tom and Dad will stay with you. They might even let you out later.'
'Thanks.'

John.

John was in Jasmine's office. His phone rang. He couldn't stop a tear rolling down his cheek. The relief was overwhelming.
'That was Luke. She's going to be fine, she's conscious. It was all my fault Ma'am. She kept trying to tell me it was too nice, too personal. I don't know, maybe it's time I retired. I think I'm too jaded. I've seen everything nothing surprises me anymore and on this occasion that clouded my judgment.'
'You're being too hard on yourself John. You are by far the best DI I have. I hold you in the highest regard. Please don't rush into anything John. On a personal note I really need you. Margot does too. Look, everything is in hand for now, why don't you pop and see her?'
'I might do that.'
'Did you find out how Joe Nolan knew that Thompson killed Colleen?'
'Apparently Gemma Watkins, Harrison's girlfriend, spilled the beans in exchange for more drugs. Jamie Thompson had confronted her and got her to give up Colleen Nolan. She heard a whisper that Colleen was dead and went to Joe and told him she'd tell him who it was for heroin. She named Jamie Thompson.'
'The stupid cow. Okay, go and see Margot. I'm off to see Jamie's wife. The Chief wants her onside.'

John headed to the hospital. He stopped at the garage and bought some flowers. Mervin and Tom were at her bedside.
'How are you Margot?' asked John.
'I'm so sorry I went off on my own without telling you.'
'It's okay Margot. I'm just glad you're okay. You are okay aren't you?'
'I'm absolutely fine. I might even get out today.'
'That's great news. Sorry I didn't listen to you.'
'About what?'
'About the place he left Colleen.'
'I wasn't sure. Anyway you did listen, you always listen to me. I know what some people say - that I'm odd. But I always feel I can tell you what I'm thinking even if it's weird.'
'I bought you flowers.'
'Thank you.'

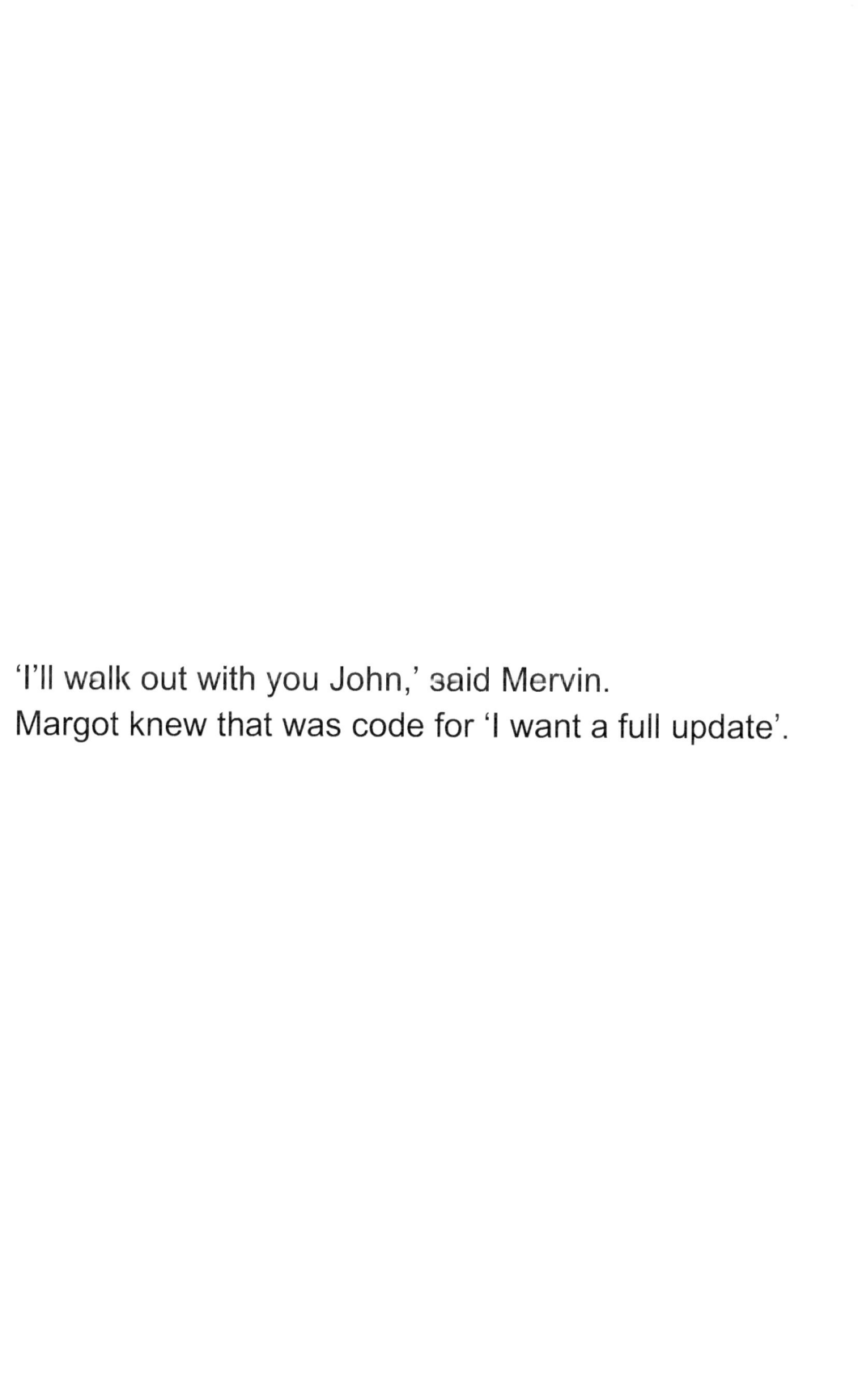

'I'll walk out with you John,' said Mervin.
Margot knew that was code for 'I want a full update'.

Margot

Margot's next visitor was a surprise. It was Janine.
'I heard Joe shot you. I just wanted to make sure you were okay. I tried to warn you but Joe was practically there when he told me what he was doing and who killed Colleen.'
'I'm fine. How's George?'
'I feel so helpless. He's so brave. He's not out of the woods yet. Infection is still a real danger.'
'I hope he's okay.'
'It's Kyle's funeral next week. Do you think I'd be welcome - if I went on behalf of George, I mean? I found something George wrote about Kyle.'
'That will be for the memory wall at school. Give it to his teacher Mr Graham. I think Shelly could really use a friend right now though. Janine why didn't you have kids?'
'Because of my family. I might have kids now. Do you have kids?'
'No. I wanted to more than anything, I just couldn't.'
'Margot this may seem odd but you don't want a cat do you? It was Colleen's. Al can't be trusted with a brush and I have George to worry about for the foreseeable. It's not the prettiest of cats.'
'I met the cat. If there's no one else I can give it a home. What's it called?'
'Harry.'
'If you haven't found a home by the time I'm well enough to come and get it I'll take him.'
'Okay, I'm going back to George.'

Christ, why did she agree to the cat? No-one in their right minds would want that. Which is precisely why she should have him, she decided.

The doctor came to see her. Margot had it in her mind she was going home. She was disappointed when he insisted she stay the night. Margot also had to insist Mervin went home. Tom too.

Daisy and Mo were next in to visit her. Daisy rushed over.
'Thanks for saving my life Margot,' said Daisy handing her a punnet of grapes. 'Not sure why you're supposed to bring grapes, but everyone does don't they.'
'I'm so sorry Daisy. I put you in danger. I'd never have forgiven myself if something had happened to you. I feel bad enough about Jamie.'

'Margot you were doing your job. You couldn't have known that was going to happen. Anyway, how does it feel to be a hero?'
Hero! She felt like a complete fraud.
'I'm not a hero. I wasn't supposed to be there. I was supposed to wait for Luke. If I'd waited it wouldn't have happened.'
'If you'd waited Joe Nolan might have killed Mrs Thompson too. He was hell-bent on revenge. I think you are a hero Margot.'

The Chief Constable knocked on the door. Daisy winked at Margot.
'We were just leaving Sir,' said Daisy.
'How is she?'
Don't say it Daisy. Don't say it, said Margot under her breath.
'Sharp as a whip..pet Sir.'
Daisy dragged Mo off.
'She's from Ashington Sir,' said Margot. 'Everyone has a whippet in Ashington.'
'Oh. I just came to check you were alright Margot.'
'I'm fine Sir. I should be going home tomorrow.'
'Take as long as you need, you've had a rough week. Getting kidnapped then shot. Sometimes it's the psychological wounds that take longer to heal. The force will support you in anyway it can Margot.'
'Sir would it be weird if I wanted to come straight back to work?'
'Do you want to come straight back?'
'Yes. Not today obviously.'
'Come back whenever you are ready Margot. I'm sorry I can't stay longer, I just wanted to see you personally. I have a press conference to attend.'
'What about Sir?'
'About you being shot Margot.'

Bloody hell, she was now a press conference. Perhaps she should call her Mum and Dad and warn them. She rang, her Dad picked up as usual.
'Dad I've been shot. But please don't panic I'm fine. It's just it might be on the news that all.'
'How the bloody hell did they miss you?'
'Dad I've been shot. Put Mum on please…Hi Mum, don't worry but I was shot at work. I'm fine but you might see it on the news.'
'What with?'
'A gun Mum.'
'Where are you darling?'

'In hospital Mum.'
'She's in hospital can we go…?'
Margot heard her father saying 'She's just told me she's fine, the football is starting soon.'
'Which hospital Margot?' her Mum whispered.
'The RVI Mum.'

Three hours later. She heard her mother's voice talking to the nurse along the corridor. She had to wait for a trolley to be pushed past before she could make out what was said.
'But I've walked all the way.'
'I'm sorry, visitors' hours are over.'
'But she's my daughter.'
'Okay, but a really quick visit that's all.'

Margot heard her mother's footsteps coming down the corridor.
'Margot are you alright?'
'I'm fine Mum.'
Her mother started to cry.
'Are you sure?'
'I'm sure. I'm probably getting out tomorrow.'
'Okay, I have to go. The nurse said I had to be quick.'
'You can stay a little while Mum. I don't have any money on me for a taxi. I'll call Mervin he'll run you home.'
'Whose Mervin?'
'My boyfriend.'
'How come I've not met him?'
'Because of Dad, Mum. Mum, why don't you leave Dad?'
'Where would I go?'
'You can stay at mine if you like.'
'He wouldn't like that Margot.'
'I know he wouldn't. Because he'd have to do his own cooking and cleaning. Has he ever taken you out anywhere Mum?'
'That's not his way Margot.'
'I know it's not, that's the point I'm making Mum.'
'I'd better go.'
'Wait for Mervin Mum.'
'Do you like being a policewoman Margot?'
'I really like it Mum. I didn't think I could do it because Dad told me I was useless my whole life. He does the same to you. So you don't think you can make it without him. It's abuse Mum, that's what it is. We call it coercive control.'

'He's never hit me.'
'The abuse is psychological Mum. It's why right now you are terrified to be with your daughter who's just been shot.'

The nurse came back in just as Margot said that Margot was grateful the nurse nodded at Margot and walked out again.

'Tell me what you do in your job?'
Margot told her all about how they'd caught Richard Grant. To her surprise her Mum almost followed what she was saying. And even asked some questions. Mervin arrived.
'Mervin this is my Mum. She's going to be staying at mine for a bit. Can you take her home, make up the spare room? Maybe stay the night.'
'Of course. I've been looking forward to meeting you.'

Margot's phone rang at midnight.
'Have you seen your mother?'
'Yes she's left you.'
'She can't.'
'She has. Goodnight Dad.'

Margot turned her phone off. Well that was an unexpected ripple she thought. Perhaps the ripples were turning positive.

One week later

'Christ Margot, what the hell is that?' said Mervin.
'That's Harry, he was homeless.'
'I'm not surprised. Are you ready?'
'Yes. Mum are you ready?'
'Nearly.'

Mervin drove them up to Luke and Tom's. Tom was soon charming her mother.
'What a wonderful view Tom. I've never seen so much green. Isn't it wonderful Margot?'
'Yes Mum.'
'Would you like wine?' asked Tom.
'I'm not allowed wine.'
'Mum if you want wine have wine.'
'I'll try a drop then.'

Margot looked out the window. She loved this view too. Luke joined her.
'Are you really coming back to work next week Margot?' asked Luke.
'Yes I'm fine. Light duties though, I'll be stuck in the office.'
'What about your Mum?'
'She's doing fine. We took her to Bamburgh yesterday, she had the time of her life. We went to Seahouses and on a boat to see the seals and everything. She will be happy pottering about the house if I'm not there. Besides she has Harry for company now. He's better looking than my Dad.'
'You aren't worried he'll turn up again but when you're not there?'
'I took out a restraining order out. And Adaeze next door is very switched on. She knows what the situation is. Your dad is going to pop in too.'
'I'm sorry, I didn't know things were that bad.'
'I didn't either Luke. It was so normal to me. It took this job for me to see it for what it was.'
'Shelly was asking after you at the funeral.'
'I probably should have gone to that.'
'Margot you couldn't, the doctor hadn't cleared you to be at work. With the ongoing case you had to be there in an official capacity.

Shelly understood. She said to tell you she got off the sofa.'
'Good on her.'
'I wonder if that's it. If all the ripples have stopped now.'
'What ripples Margot?'
'Richard killed Rory. That led to Kyle being killed. That led to George killing Shelly's Mum. Then Colleen got the blame and her being inside which meant Joe and Al used a different dealer. Harrison overdosed. His Dad killed Colleen. Joe killed Jamie. George got burned. Dan is in court for assault. All because George Morrison was a paedophile and Richard looked at his computer.'
'I see what you're saying. I suppose there's Donna, Kevin and Metcalfe too. Because it probably wouldn't have come out about Shelly and Kevin if it hadn't been for the fact Kyle was missing.'
'Exactly.'
'Luke can I ask you something. Do you think I'm odd?'
'Yes Margot, but in the best way possible.'

Margot

Margot hadn't driven since she had been shot. For some reason she was really nervous about driving her little car now. She was taking her Mum for a drive and walk in the countryside. She had put on weight again. Last night at Luke's and Tom's hadn't helped. Tom's cooking was always too good to refuse and the sticky toffee pudding had just sung to her.

She looked at her hands, they were actually shaking. If it wasn't for the fact her mother was already excitedly sitting in the passenger seat, she would have run back into the house. She drove off like a learner driver. Fifty penceing every corner. Stalling at every junction. If was as if she'd forgotten how to drive.

Her mother wanted to see all the places Margot had told her about in the case of Kyle and Rory. Which Margot found a little odd. It was nice her mother was finally showing some genuine interest in what she did after a lifetime of 'that's nice dear' - her standard response to anything Margot said or did.

Margot decided to start in Stamfordham. She pointed out the foster parents' home. Holly cottage, Margot couldn't help noticing the For Sale sign at the end of the drive, the closed curtains. More ripples, thought Margot. She went to Five Acre House next. The gardener was back, mowing the grass on his sit-on lawn mower.

At least thought Margot she seemed to have finally remembered how to drive. She drove to the woods where Rory's arm was found.
'Are you sure this is what you want to do Mum? It's a bit morbid isn't it?'
'I think it was very clever how you solved it Margot.'

Margot drove to the water treatment works. As soon as she got out of the car the smell hit her nostrils. Margot just burst into tears.
'Are you alright Margot? What a terrible smell. Shall we go and get an ice cream instead?'

Margot looked at Kyle's bloated body lying in front of her car.
'Yes let's go to Wheelbirks and get ice cream Mum.'
She helped her Mum back in the car and tentatively looked back Kyle had gone. What the hell is wrong with me thought Margot. First

I couldn't drive, then I spontaneously burst into tears and now I'm seeing things.

Despite the diet she was supposed to be on again and the walk they were supposed to be having, Margot tucked into a banana split. She decided to head to Caroline's new house next. She hadn't been yet.

A large modern bungalow with a huge conservatory and garden was tucked away in the Shire. Margot loved it. Caroline was sitting on the patio soaking up the sun reading a book. On seeing Margot's car she rushed up to greet them.
'Margot what a lovely surprise are you okay? Luke told me you had been shot.'
'I'm fine. This is my mother.'
'I'm so pleased to meet you. Sit down, sit down. So what do you think? It's a big change but isn't it just perfect? Tea, coffee, lemonade, homemade.'

They settled on lemonade. Margot settled down in a big comfy wicker chair. Birdsong echoed round the garden.
'This is nice isn't Margot,' said her mother.
'Yes,' said Margot really wishing all this was hers.

Caroline brought the lemonade out with a fruit cake and cut everyone a large slice.
'I think moving here was the best thing we could have done. That house had too many ghosts Margot. I will never forget my Sally, but having so many reminders of her wasn't healthy.'
'I understand what you mean. I think I might move out to the country too. I love Luke's house. I love your house. I love Daisy's piglets. I would have to sell the painting.'
'That's exactly why I gave it to you Margot.'
'What do you think Mum. Should we move to the countryside?'
'You do what makes you happy Margot.'
'I'll give you the tour later Margot. It has the most magnificent kitchen.'

Margot felt grounded again by the time she left Caroline's. As soon as she got home she immediately started to Google properties for sale. She immediately hit upon one she really liked. She just knew it was the one. She dragged her mother straight back out to see it. As soon as Margot walked in she felt at home. It had all the things she really wanted, a view, a walk in shower, a log burner, a nice garden - not too big not too small. Margot tried to do the maths in her head to see if she could afford it. Her house, the painting, a small mortgage now she had a steady income.

She should slow down. Get a second opinion. Her mother had reverted to 'that's nice.' She rang Mervin and booked a second viewing for the following day. She called an estate agent and asked them to come out and value her house. She rang Caroline and got the details of an auctioneer she knew to sell the painting. Regardless, she decided to sell the painting. It was after all wrapped in three rolls of clingfilm in a drawer under a mouse trap.

Margot would miss Emma and Adaeze but they could visit. Her mind was made up. She was moving. Her house had on the whole been an unhappy house. Time to leave her old life completely behind.

By the time Margot had gone to bed she was having all sorts of doubts. It was too expensive, too much of a stretch. What if she sold her house but then someone else bought the house she really wanted? Would her mother be happy in the countryside? Would Harry be cold? Would he get lost? Would there be mice? There were no immediate neighbours, the closest would be the farm along the lane. What if there was another Metcalfe?

Margot was back at work. She walked into the office, everyone looked very serious almost scared. Everyone was looking at her. No, not at her, behind her. She turned round, Metcalfe was standing there wearing her nightdress. He had a gun. He shot her. She felt the searing pain. Margot woke with a scream. Harry shot off her bed.

'Jesus!' she said. And then laughed. The image that stayed with her was Metcalfe in her nightdress. The chief had warned her about this. Perhaps she wasn't ready to go back to work next week. She hoped it wasn't like driving the car, that she'd have forgotten what to do. Perhaps she should ask for help. What should she say, that she was seeing dead children and men wearing her skimpy nightdress? Perhaps not. Perhaps that was best kept to herself. She wasn't sure why, but she rang Patrick. PTSD he said. They chatted for ages.

Margot hadn't had a lot of sleep when Mervin called to pick her up. They drove back up to the house. Mervin had his practical head on. Margot wasn't hearing anything he said. She just loved the house even more. By the end of the day Margot's offer had been accepted and her own house was on the market.
'Bloody hell,' said Margot as she got into bed that night. She flicked the small TV in the bedroom on. She fell asleep smiling. That night she dreamt of piglets and Chief Constables.

"….in other news. Paul Harper the Chief Constable of Northumbria Police has resigned this evening citing personal reasons. He was only in post for just over a month. Previously Mr Harper had said this was his dream job. The job he'd always wanted…"

Glossary

Explanation of terms in the text marked with a *

FIO – Field Intelligence Officer

FLO – Family Liaison Officer

MISPER – Missing Person

MIT – Murder Investigation Team

OSMAN NOTICE - issued if police have intelligence of a real and immediate threat to the life of an individual

PolSA – Police Search Advisor

RVI – Royal Victoria Infirmary, Newcastle

TOD – Time of Death

TWOC – Taking (usually a vehicle) without consent (but without intention to steal permanently)

Printed in Great Britain
by Amazon